Fishing for Feathers

By

Annie K Urquhart

COPYRIGHT

Cataloguing-in-publication data
Creator: Urquhart, Annie K, author

Cataloguing-in-Publication details are available from the National Library of Australia
www.trove.nla.gov.au

ISBN: 978-0-9953533-4-3 (paperback)

CONTENTS

ACKNOWLEDGMENTS

So many have provided advice and support, they are too numerous to mention, but some deserve special mention.

Thanks to Denise, mentor and friend, for the shared conversations and support over many coffee breaks. Kayla and Neive, I am delighted to have met such noteworthy women.

My undying gratitude goes to my husband and family, especially Brodie, born too soon but never forgotten.

My special thanks to that important group of people who provided the impetus for this story: Riley, Keely, Georgie, Hayden, Monique, Ben, Brodie, Ella, Abby Luciena and Edison.

Thanks to each and every one who has helped in any way to make this work happen.

CHAPTER 1

"Would you just look at the lawn down at the edge of the yard," said Jeremy in disgust. "The salt has dried the grass into frizzled chips this summer. You can't walk down there without wearing shoes. It's a blasted nuisance. Who wants to bother with all that shit just to go down to the beach?"

"Yeah, it's bloody hot," his exasperated twin agreed. "But I thought we were supposed to be on the lookout for new arrivals on the horizon, not watching grass growing beneath it."

Vessels of all shapes and sizes were always turning up in Hallies Bay. There was nothing new about the lights on the water after dark but this particular evening, the boys were hoping the bay would be empty. They didn't really want any extra company tonight, not when fishing with Dom was on the agenda.

Ever since the family came to live here five years ago, it had been standard practice – always – to check to see if there were any dinghies or other vessels anchored out front. In fact, Josh used to reckon 'that lot out there are just Peeping Toms'. Well, that was what he used to say, when he was an impressionable *t*welve year-old happily gripped in the middle of his mystery-story phase. The regular turn-up of sticky-beaks deliberately invading the bay annoyed him at the time, because his parents, Isabel and Jock, had just bought the place, and the boys both thought of the beach, and the ocean out front, as their own private domain.

Boats continually came and went, but it wasn't really rocket science to work out the reason for that phenomenon. Now that they were a bit older and less inclined towards the overly-dramatic, the boys knew the answer to that one. It could all be put down to the most common pastime which kept this region alive and hopping: fishing. When the locals, or even the tourists holidaying at the two local caravan parks, weren't catching anything much, they'd pull up their anchors and move from bay to bay, from one fished-out area to the next promising hot-spot.

This particular afternoon, Isabel, Jock and the twins were in the middle of a comfortable chill-out session on the front lawn after a very pleasant seafood barbeque. The boys were leaning against the low cement block garden wall, an empty Coke-can beside each of them. Their father was slouched in the squatter's chair with a half empty stubby of light, pale ale balanced on the wooden armrest, while their mum enjoyed a chilled glass of white wine. This sleepy, relaxed mode was brought on by good food and an enjoyable afternoon of watching the fishing craft scurry around the bay like maggots in a fly-blown tomato.

That hypnotic view of a glassed-out ocean in the middle of a hot November day is surely the best excuse there ever could be for an after-lunch siesta, thought Isabel Somerville as she stretched lethargically. Surely there won't be any stray beachcombers wandering around to interrupt our much-needed rest. There's enough distraction just watching those hopeful fishermen scooting all around our bay. She yawned as she looked over the same hundred metres of lawn which her sons had discussed earlier. Her eyes moved further seaward, scanning the horizon and following the shallow descent of the yard. Her attention skipped onto the shaly beachfront before she strained to see out beyond towards the saltwater.

This virtually private strip of sand and shell grit the handful successive owners have always adopted as part of the property's front garden. In reality, they didn't own the small beach but, because it is enclosed by a combination of mangroves, problematic beach debris and oyster-encrusted rocks, this tricky and uncomfortable route is rarely attempted by casual beach ramblers. As such, it had become Jock and Isabel's private oasis.

Fences running along both sides as well as across the back boundary discouraged itinerant visitors. Only the front of the allotment is defenceless and open to the shoreline – and the general public. The property's entrance is accessed by a narrow country lane edged by a steep, almost vertical slope of heavily timbered paperbark scrub. As a result, there isn't a safe parking area along the entire length of gravelled roadway, and provides hardly enough room anywhere along that perilous edge to bend over to tie your shoelaces, let alone turn a car around when the property gate is closed.

The afternoon was half over. It must be close to two o'clock now, thought Isabel, but being in an extremely lazy mood, she was reluctant to make a move. Jock glanced up from reading the novel he'd found a few days ago in the local Op-shop, grinned at his wife and they both looked over towards their boys who had drifted off to sleep. The sound of quarrelling seagulls, the distant drone of outboard motors and the twins' gentle snoring were the only intrusions into this peaceful afternoon.

Later, Isabel eventually shook herself out of her drowsy reverie, looked over the top of her new sunglasses. Unaccustomed to napping in the daytime and waiting for sensibility to assert itself, she glanced towards the ocean and told Jock, "It really does make me smile just to lie and watch the antics of everyone out there on the water." Her husband looked up from his reading, smiled and nodded in agreement. It was that sort of sluggish time. A day that allowed contented glances and smiles to communicate as readily as any words would ever do.

She lay there for a few more precious minutes of staring out over the ocean before sliding her legs over the edge of the striped hammock she had climbed into after finishing her wine. Isabel yawned and stretched. "Oh dear," she muttered to anyone who chose to listen to her, "I don't feel like it but I suppose I'd better think about getting up and clearing away after lunch."

"Leave it for another half an hour, Love, and we'll all do it together. It won't take long with four pairs of willing hands."

"Willing…" Jeremy groaned in response to his father's cheerful suggestion.

"Well, look at who's awake. I thought you'd be snoring for the next two hours."

"I don't snore," grumbled his grouchy son, "And I hate washing up."

"C'mon boy, fair go! Your mum's got a life too you know. If you want to go fishing with Dom tonight, then the least you can do is give her a hand. Better still, Isabel, you stay right where you are. The boys and I will see to tidying up all this food debris."

Before he pulled himself up out of his chair, Jock turned his gaze seawards and looked at a new boat coming in from the north-east. "It looks like we'll have company at the rocks this evening."

He stood up, tousled Jeremy's hair as he walked past him towards his other son and vigorously wiggled Josh's toe.

"What… Wazz-zat? …What's up? …What's happening?" mumbled Josh in a muddle-headed daze. In his dream, he'd been lying, stretched across the width of the boat-seat, his straw hat shielding him from the hot sun, and a fishing line trailing loosely through his toes as he lethargically waited for a bite. "I think I've hooked one," he said, sitting up with a start and grabbing for an imaginary fishing line. Everyone chuckled as they watched the confusion, then comprehension, dawn on Josh's face.

"I was just saying, Josh, that I reckon we three blokes are talented enough to clean up what's left on the table without your mum's help." Turning towards his other son, he continued. "Seeing how you hate washing up, Jeremy, you can wipe up. Done deal?"

"Hi ho, hi ho, it's off to work we go." Jeremy, the sometimes clown of the family, jumped up and cheerfully began chanting what the family referred to as the 'salt mine song.' The painful-sounding, jovial tone and the stilted walk with the imaginary mattock slung over the shoulder produced a glare from his still-sleepy twin.

Josh usually enjoyed the 'shuffling, I love work' performance his brother produced; even to the point at times, of egging his twin on with gusto. However, it was a different matter when he wasn't even half awake. The whole routine was doing nothing for him at all. "Don't call us, we'll call you," he muttered. With a stormy look fixed on Jeremy, he roused himself from the grass.

"Why bother?" Jeremy cheerfully replied; "I couldn't stand to work for a grumble-guts like you anyway."

"Thanks everybody. Your offer is much appreciated," Isabel grinned broadly. Then, ignoring Josh's grumbles, she winked at her husband, wiggled back into her hammock, and set her sights on the newest arrival out on the water. Those boys of ours are good value at times she thought contentedly as she burrowed into her pillow and watched the large boat rocking gently in the calm water as someone one board secured the anchor rope.

Much later, as he lightly brushed away a stray lock of hair lying across Isabel's eyes, Jock said, "C'mon lazy bones. You won't sleep tonight if you stay there any longer."

She gave Jock a drowsy smile and said, "Thanks for doing the cleaning up. I must have needed that sleep. I feel a lot better now."

*****

Late that afternoon, as they waited for Dom, the father and sons watched the last dinghy pull up anchor and head for home. "There doesn't seem to be any other boats left out on the bay except for the classy-looking cabin cruiser trailing its equally expensive-looking dinghy," remarked Jock. "That's good. We'll have hardly anyone to disturb us tonight."

They were looking forward to fishing out there later with Dom and they certainly didn't want to share the space with any interlopers. At such times, they considered the rocks to be their territory. Gate-crashers were particularly annoying, especially the half-drunken yobbos who thought that the "drinking and driving" rule was only aimed at car owners. There weren't any 'no littering' signs out on the ocean to deter them, so those idiots carelessly pelted empty stubby bottles into the water on a far too-regular basis.

The sunset was building towards its finale, an intense blood-orange-red with a bleached glare spreading low and wide across the horizon. This hallucinogenic blaze at the end of the day usually created jewel-like shimmers that danced over the ocean and left the sky so burnished that it was almost impossible to see any craft remaining on the water.

The twins were becoming quite fidgety. They hardly ever ventured out on a night-fishing expedition and had been clock-watchers all afternoon, except for that brief siesta time.

"Here he is. Finally…!" said Josh. He and his brother squinted irritably as they watched their old mate, Dom Bellini, slowly manoeuvre the old ute into his favourite parking spot in the Somerville's side yard. The elderly Mingleton fisherman, who had been born in the neighbouring beachside village, had become a firm family friend. The twins met him on the beach one day about five years ago and, after a lengthy period of 'sussing one another out,' they became the best of mates despite the massive difference in their ages.

"Come on Dom," they called out to him. "Liven up. Let's get moving."

"Where the hell have you been? We thought you'd never get here." Between the two of them, the staccato bouts of nagging never seemed to let up.

"Hey, hang on you pair. Give over, why don't you. Can't I even take the time to say hello to your mother?"

"Well hurry up, we've been waiting for you for hours."

"That's your problem, Mates, not mine," chuckled Dom. "If you were so impatient you should have arranged for me to get here earlier. You'll just have to wait another ten minutes." With that he disappeared into the house and called out to their mother, Isabel.

Jock, glanced back briefly at his sons and, with a huge grin splitting his face, caught up with the elderly fisherman and followed hot on his heels.

5

Mumbling and grumbling, the twins wandered up and down the patio and waited even more impatiently. "Here they come at last... 'Bout time, you pair of old fogeys. Let's get going."

Jock was highly amused at their irritation, but they were still teenagers and not the adults they imagined themselves to be. So, he sternly warned them to mind their manners. It wasn't the first time he noticed the old-fashioned expressions his sons sometimes used. He knew it was from spending so much time with their ageing friend but even so, he and Isabel always thought it sounded better than a lot of the expressions the twins' generation often used.

As they rounded the corner to start on the final leg towards their fishing spot, Josh said, "That nifty cabin cruiser isn't there now. Did anyone hear it leave?"

"I thought I heard a boat start up about half an hour ago while we were waiting for Dad and Dom, but didn't take a lot of notice. Besides, it was too glary out there to see much," answered Jeremy. "It'll be long gone, that's for sure. It's nearly 'happy hour' at the pub."

"That's where they'll be headed, nothing surer" added Josh.

As they walked along, Jock was highly amused by what he heard. Although the twins always baited Dom about his use of old-fashioned words and expressions, it was quite apparent to their father that a lot of their elderly mate's speech mannerisms were rubbing off on them. *I wonder if they have one set of expressions to use when they're with us and another whole teenage-type language when they're with their mates. Long gone* and *happy hour at the pub...?'* Were these common words for 16 year-old lads to use he wondered. Probably not, he decided. He chuckled at his thoughts as he followed behind the group. His grin grew wider as he thought about the reactions he'd get from all three if he made any comment about his conclusions. Better hold my tongue methinks, he told himself.

After their arrival at their favourite fishing spot, the dark descended quickly. Each had selected an individual rocky perch and now sat quietly with handlines dangling loosely in the water. At one stage, Dom leant to the side so that he could take a quick look around the rocks on the eastern side of his position and said, "You boys are right, that boat has gone from the bay. I can't see any navigation or any other lights on the water where it anchored earlier."

It was a calm, quiet night: The sort of weather when you can hear every little murmur in the area. The moon, a huge spherical ball, was in its fullest phase. Its soft diffused glow was perfect for anyone crazy enough to find enjoyment in sitting on hard, uncomfortable rocks, waiting for a big fish, or any fish for that matter, to bite.

"Well, who would have believed it, my little mates?" Dom said, at his sarcastic best. "We actually got here an hour and a half before the top of the tide after all, so there's still plenty of time to fish for an hour either side of it."

Jeremy felt cranky about the dig at him and his brother because of their earlier complaints. "That bloody Dom. He tries it on with us all the time."

"He loves to wind us up," Josh mumbled out of the side of his mouth so that only his brother, Jeremy, could hear him.

The twins constantly tagged Dom as being an old-timer, still wedged in his distant past. They revelled in telling him that his ideas, not to mention the jargon he used, were a bit crappy and out-of-date. It irritated the hell out of them when a sneaky taunt hit its mark. To make matters worse, it was more than annoying, when Dom's snipe was spot-on. The elderly man's speech patterns might be from a vintage era but there was nothing wrong with his mind. He was always more than a match for them, as they'd acknowledged on more than one occasion in the past.

Dom was well aware the twins also thought he lacked a few skills in the 'proper-talking' department. How many times had they told him his way of speaking was old-fashioned? Quite frankly, he had never been over-concerned about his personal choice of words, and that wasn't going to change on the whim of a couple of half-smart whippersnappers. His usual comeback was 'you little bastards need to accept me as I am'.

His life had been a solitary one all those years ago. Even when customers arrived at the house, in those old days, it was his mother and little sister, Rafaela, who dealt with the sea-food sales and the public. Because of his separation from the masses, his manner of speaking wasn't a serious problem, and for that matter, it still wasn't. Fishing was the thing that counted; not all that toffee-nosed rubbish.

Now, in his retirement, Dom considered his perfect fishing conditions were, to use a favourite expression 'by the light of the silvery moon', and as far away from the bloody straw-hat crowds as he could get.

'Silvery moon'…, every time he used that little gem, Josh snorted loudly in disgust and Dom chuckled with pleasure.

Over the five years the twins had known their elderly chum, some serious traditions had evolved. The most common of these adopted behaviours was Dom's deliberate use of outmoded sayings and expressions. Unknown to the twins, Dom frequently honed his skills to the best of his ability. He loved reading and there was plenty of material out there on the subject. In fact, the more hackneyed the jargon he could produce, the better he liked it. I may have lived a simple life, but I can match it with those two young blokes any day, he thought. It was a great game and the three of them thrived on it.

The fish weren't very plentiful that night. The waves hit the rocks with gentle slaps and whooshes and the curlews up on the headland were becoming serious about their eerie calls. On occasion, the thump of a wallaby's tail on the beach, a howling dingo in the far-off hills or cries of other night-birds and animals in the local scrub, could be heard.

They fished for couple of hours and only caught four reasonably sized grass Sweetlip between them when Dom commented, "Beautiful night isn't it?" The silence continued for another half hour or so until Dom spoke again. "The tide's been going out for an hour now. We should give it another thirty minutes before heading off, I reckon. What do the rest of you think? The tide will be full-low in a couple of hours and it's a waste of effort fishing for much longer; too shallow, even for the tiddlers."

The twins couldn't resist it. "Hey Dom, you'd better be careful. You're beginning to talk too much."

"Yeah …right. … Hey …Shh …be quiet. …Listen. What's that noise? It sounds like someone rowing a dinghy."

"You must be mistaken, Dom. I can't hear anything; only the water slapping against the rocks." The four of them sat silently; listening. An owl screeched and something hit the water with a loud splash.

"Wonder what jumped," said Jock. "You reckon it was mackerel chopping at some bait?"

"Probably …Shh… there it is again, listen," Dom said in his usual quiet tone.

In the midst of the natural bush sounds, a different sound, the unquestionable splash of oars followed by the scraping and splashing noises of a dinghy's hull in shallow pebbly water.

Then the four of them heard the aluminium underside grating as it neared the beach behind them: an unmistakable sound to their practiced ears; and quite loud into the bargain. "So I did hear oars before." Dom was puzzled. "Strange…," he murmured almost to himself. "It's odd that the dinghy's not using an outboard motor. As they are rowing, whoever is in it can't have come too far."

8

"It must be the dinghy that was tied to that cabin cruiser. The parent boat must still be around here someplace. So, they didn't move very far after all. They must be moored close in around the back of us, out from Boaties Beach." No-one really knew the official name of the small beach behind them and enclosed within the next bay south of Hallies Bay. Some local person coined the name and it's been used for decades. "They mustn't have left after all, just moved over here earlier this afternoon. I would have thought the water would be far too shallow. It's a wonder the skipper didn't come to grief. There's a lot of mangrove mud around here for a boat to wallow in; if you aren't familiar with the territory," Dom mused.

The fish still weren't biting and, because the group had been listening for the paddling noises that had caught Dom's attention, the boys had become more attuned to their surroundings. The gate crashers had almost reached the shore now. They were behind the big patch of mangroves and rocks and only about two hundred metres away from Jock, Dom and the twins. The voices were unexpected. The boys were rendered speechless long enough to realise they should shut up and just listen.

"Have you seen Harry yet?" A croaky voice cut through the night air.

"Nup! C-ca-can't even see the h-h-headlights yet." This second voice was higher pitched than the first one.

"Bloody Hell, He's late. He might think he's all-important because he's the ruddy supplier but he was supposed to be here to keep an eye out. We don't want things to go wrong at this stage. Bloody Idiot; hope the cops haven't caught him," continued the rusty voice.

"D-d-do ya want the other a-an-anchor out the b-b-ack?" This again from the squeaky sounding voice.

"Can't you think for yourself, you idiot? You'd better throw it out, but you'll have to watch the depth of the water. The tide's been going out for half an hour or so, now. Where the hell is that stupid, bloody Harry? I'll have his guts for garters one of these days. He thinks he can do what he likes; too bloody bad about our security and our welfare. What does he care? He doesn't seem to be too worried about that." The ranting continued. "We're the ones stuck out here in the open. He's got tree cover where he parks."

"Shit! What is going on?" Jeremy was apprehensive.

"Shh," whispered Dom. "This doesn't sound real good to me. I think we should keep our voices down."

Easily seen in the moonlight, the horrified expressions all round, weren't reassuring. The soft splashing of oars, usually as heartening to them as an outboard starting up, now sounded threatening.

"Who the hell are those blokes and what are they up to?" Josh asked.

"Nothing good by the sound of it," answered Dom. "We don't need this crap right now when we're ready to pack up and go home."

"Anyway, if they are up to no good, why have those blokes come ashore when we're sitting here? Surely they saw us arriving earlier," hissed Josh.

"Maybe not," suggested Jock. When nothing changed in the next ten minutes, it seemed certain the blokes in the dinghy didn't have a clue they had company so close.

"I agree with Josh. Why the hell didn't they see us walking over here?" Dom asked.

Jock responded with a nod towards his house. He silently indicated the edges and curves of the geographical features to emphasise the solid bulk of the landscape between where they stood and the distant home beach. It began to make more sense. Their trek tonight had taken them through the buffer of gum trees which screened the southern end of the house allotment and then along a track across the top of the beach. The scraggly undergrowth below the main tree-line stretching down to the high-tide mark provided extra cover. A parallel thicket of mangrove forest growing along the low-water tide line also complemented this. The combined result was a camouflaged, green tunnel through which their route to their fishing spot meandered.

"Acres of bloody trees," said Dom, who always glared fiercely at the jungle and grouched every time they made the trek.

The final leg of their walk took them and closer to the Point to where an outcrop of huge rocks emerged from beyond the mangrove forest and kept the group safely hidden from anyone out on the ocean. In an effort to make sense of the crazy situation they found themselves in, Jock suggested that, when they took a shortcut along the top of the beach and across the acres of spongy, rotting logs to reach their fishing spot, it was still daylight. They hadn't needed torch lights which might have given their presence away. "That's how we managed to arrive without being detected." With the mystery solved, they were just thankful no one saw them heading towards their fishing spot this afternoon.

Thanks to their customary habits, no one would have heard them after they settled on their rock seats either, as no one spoke much, except to ask quietly from time to time if anyone had a bite. Fishing is a silent pastime, particularly in Dom's company.

"He's a man of few words," their mother, Isabel, often said.

"No one, and I mean *no one*, is allowed to talk much while fishing with him," someone invariably answered. "He seriously believes noise of any kind frightens the fish away."

Jock became a bit antsy as the pair from the dinghy grew increasingly restless. This 'Harry' bloke they were speaking about now appeared to be over half an hour late. The poor little bloke with the stutter was throwing out and hauling in the anchor every five minutes. The bossy bloke continually rabbited on about Harry's possibly coming to grief with the police. The bloke reached a point where he had to decide whether to wait a bit longer or to go. He began yelling even more abuse and his hapless mate bore the brunt of it.

"If these blokes are worrying about the police, they must be up to no good. I hope they don't have rifles in the boat," Jock said. With their eyes almost popping out of their heads, Jeremy and Josh looked at their father. This was a new thought they could well do without. Now they felt like there were drums pounding in their chests like you wouldn't believe. Their heartbeats sounded so loud, they expected at any minute the blokes behind the rocks would race around to investigate the commotion.

Jock looked worried. He signalled for the twins to slide quietly down from their perches out in the open and to shelter at the base of some large rocks about three metres away. Although three metres isn't a great distance, it seems like a million miles when you can't afford to make even the slightest noise. They moved cautiously. Instinct warned each twin not to move his back foot until the front one was securely placed, and that they should hold their arms out straight in front of them to feel their way through the gloom. Loose pebbles lying everywhere could create a problem they could well do without.

It took a while, but they all made it safely with only a few scraping sounds that weren't loud enough to be heard above the other night noises. Josh almost giggled as he imagined the sight they made. He whispered to Jeremy, "We must look like one of those blokes from the silent talkies era... You know, acting like old drunks, shoes in their hands and tiptoeing in that slow and exaggerated way they did in those movies."

The tide was almost half-out. As there wasn't much variation between high and low water tonight, they would be all right for a few hours yet.

"It's pointless trying to get any closer," Dom whispered. "By the time we reach a position where we can see what is going on, they might have spotted us or heard us. We'll just have to wait it out."

With nowhere to sit down, they had crouched against the sheltering rocks for about fifteen minutes when Jeremy moved, creating a scraping noise as his shoes slipped on some slippery marine growth.

"What's that?" yelled the bloke with the harsh voice. Dom, Jock and the twins froze.

"T-t--there are l-l-lights along the track n-n-now!"

"About Bloody time too. C'mon! Quick! Up to the top of the beach and get behind the rocks. The usual ones where we can watch who comes down from the car park. If it's not Harry, we'll walk real casual-like back to the dinghy and I'll throw the cast net around a bit after some baitfish. And, for Christ's sake, don't stuff-up if that happens."

Collective breaths were shakily exhaled. That's all right for them, out in the open, thought Josh. At least they know what's happening. We don't. Even if Dom, Jock and the boys couldn't see it, they could hear an engine becoming louder as it came closer to the beach. Soon, in the distance, a car door shut gently followed a few minutes later by a curlew's mournful cry and then another one. Then, voices started again.

"Where the hell have you been?"

When Harry answered, Josh thought it would be hard to recognise this one in a crowd. It was just an ordinary voice."

"We had to drive into old Emil's yard and park out of sight behind his shed. There were a lot of cars on the Mingleton Road tonight. Don't know why. There shouldn't have been." Harry continued in a clipped voice. "By the time we'd almost reached the turn-off to this beach, there was a virtual bloody convoy of the things. If anything goes wrong, I didn't want some helpful local to be prattling on about a strange vehicle turning onto a track that never gets used after dark, not on delivery night. I waited until the traffic quietened down before continuing."

"What about this old Emil? Can you trust him?" The tone of voice suggested that the bloke doing the asking, might never trust anyone.

"I don't have to worry about him. He died last week and the family from down south haven't arrived yet. A bit of good luck, that was."

Even though Dom and crew couldn't see Harry, when he made this comment, the satisfaction in his tone was obvious. "It's the perfect spot for a lookout, now that no one's home." Emil's house was on a small hill and allowed traffic along the Mingleton Road to be seen for about two kilometres either way. "I had to park behind the house for about ten minutes until the coast was clear because everyone around here knows that the place is empty and a strange car driving out of there would have raised suspicions as well."

"Enough talk; let's move," said Croaky. "The tide's only an hour or so from dead low and the boat's high and dry now because you're late. Give us a hand to drag it out into the water before we start loading up."

Harry sounded annoyed with the other two. He raised his voice and demanded, "While we're doing that, don't forget the regular routine. Be ready to move quickly if my mobile rings. As usual, my mate's watching at the gully washout. Any sign of trouble and we'll have to hop it."

While the three blokes on the beach were preoccupied with their squabble, Dom and Josh figured that 'now' would be as good a time as any, to move. Their nerves were in tatters. They all needed to sit down. Dom moved across to long flat rock tucked in behind another larger rock and called the others to join him. "Quickly, move over here. …Quiet as you can, now."

After that, Dom, Jock, and the twins felt safer. With their feet dangling above the ground, no loose pebbles were likely to become dislodged and no-one seemed to be heading in their direction. They guessed the blokes on the beach still had no idea that there was company a few hundred metres away or the four of them would be earmarked as crab-pot bait by now.

For the next half an hour or so, there were some weird, muffled noises; crunching footsteps up and down the beach across the shell grit and small pebbles; things being loaded into the dinghy, and the noise of the waves of the out-going tide slapping and pushing the vessel which continued grinding over the small rocks. All predictable sounds that might accompany the suspicious activity that Dom, Jock and the boys suspected was happening.

At last, the visitors appeared ready to leave. The only sound now was of an anchor chain being pulled in, probably by the hapless young stutterer. After bit more splashing, thumping and verbal abuse, the croaky voice announced, "See ya next month." This was followed by the unmistakable sound of oars pulling through the water; the sweetest sound the fishermen had heard for the last hour or so.

Not too long after, from the top of the beach came the sound of a car starting up and moving away. When the engine noise disappeared from the night air, all four stood up, stretched and looked around. Visibility was still okay, although a bit of cloud cover had moved across the moon, making the night darker than it had been a few minutes ago. Not that anyone was worried. This was a bit of a bonus. For the fainthearted though, the slightly deeper gloom created more of a sinister feel than was needed.

Jock whispered, "I think the coast is clear but wait here for a while. Don't move a muscle. If you need to talk, just whisper … and I mean 'whisper' as in 'be extremely quiet'. We need to be sure they're gone; can't take any chances at this stage."

"Dad, be careful," Jeremy said, almost to himself though, because his father was to moving stealthily along the Hallies Bay side of the rocky point. Jock picked his way between the rocks exposed at low water until he could sneak a look out to the open sea.

In next to no time, it seemed, he was back. "The dinghy has tied up to the larger boat and someone is leaning over the side helping them off-load small oblong containers from the dinghy. They haven't bothered to look back towards the shore," he said. "Now the skinny little bloke is on board helping the other person grab those boxes from the bully boy who's still in the dinghy.

"Cocky bastards, aren't they?" Dom said. "It's my turn now. I'll go and check out the beach. It'll be a cinch. I know that area like the back of my hand." He pointed to the mangroves on their right. "I'll go that way, through there," he said, gesturing in the direction of his intended path. "If I merge into the scrub past the high-water mark and sneak back along the track beside what's left of my old shack on the other side, they won't be able to see me at all. I did think about doing that earlier. It would've been handy to check out Harry's number plate. What really stopped me though were the heaps of loose, dry driftwood on the high water mark. If that rubbish wasn't there, I might have given it a go," said the proud, elderly Italian. "I couldn't risk letting any rolling logs betray us at that stage, and at my age, I knew I would be a bit out-numbered if they saw me and a fight was on the cards." Dom shrugged with regret at what might have been and gave them a wry grin.

After about fifteen minutes, he reported all was clear. "Takes longer when silence is important," he said with a grin.

CHAPTER 2

"We'll be fine. We can't be seen from the vessel anchored in Boaties Bay," Dom said as they began the walk around the edge of the Hallies Bay mangroves, the most direct path to Jock and Isabel's place. This could be dangerous if the boat came around the point at the wrong time as it was the most open sector of the trip home. It consisted of 30 metres of muddy sand between where they'd been fishing and the start of the mangrove forest. They were sure the so-called crooks still had a lot of work to do in securing the little boxes for travel, so the four fishermen were confident they would have time to cover that short distance safely. Anyway, those blokes on the boat might grab a quick snooze before leaving. It was possible their departure could be some hours away yet.

Everyone agreed Dom's suggestion was the best option open to them. They usually walked along the bush track after a night's fishing. This time the logistics had changed. They knew that even if the boat left soon, Harry and the spotter remained an unknown quantity. Dom, Jock and the boys weren't quite game enough to take the usual track tonight. It was too risky... And, it was a foregone conclusion they wouldn't walk home along the same track they had arrived by.

For the same reasons that beach ramblers rarely walked along the beach in front of Jock and Isabel's home, tonight they weren't prepared to go that way either. It was too dangerous and shadowy after dark, even for those who knew it well. The sand on the beach wasn't continuous. The environment was changeable with every tide so that areas of sandy beach were broken here and there by thin, linear intrusions of mangroves, growing up towards the high water mark. These always caught and held a lot of loose driftwood, and the volcanic rocks around the tree bases also were loose and unstable because of the action of the waves.

Earlier this afternoon, they had decided to walk back along the higher vehicle track as it was much safer and they could use their torches along those stretches where the moonlight didn't penetrate. Now things had changed. Harry could be parked along the car track.

The path they'd taken this afternoon required the use of torches most of the way, which could be seen kilometres away. They were forced to rule out both the best options. After spending ages trying to stay out of sight, it would be ridiculous to be discovered when they were within a stone's throw of safety.

After a quick group conference, it was decided that there was nothing for it but to struggle across the mud flats, keeping close in the shadows of the mangroves where the moonlight still gave them some light. No doubt about it, this was going to be a difficult trip. Apart from dealing with the handicaps that the sticky sludge presented, they had to carry the fishing gear and the few fish they had caught. The tide had started to come in, so in some places, they had to walk inside the edge of the salt-water trees to avoid the rising water. This added extra challenges. The mud in there always seemed thicker, heavier and even more inflexible than it was outside.

From experience, the group knew that, as you moved along, increasing amounts of the glutinous sludge kept attaching itself to your feet. Walking became an effort and the journey developed into a struggle. The clay gunk, about four centimetres worth of it, ended up layered over your shoes. There was no escaping it. Then, bending forward to scrape the mud off your boots, often resulted in a wallop from your backpack as it slammed into the back of your head, somewhere behind your ears. Then the removal of the mud against a rock or tree trunk gave a great feeling of release until you realised it was a temporary measure. The next few steps you took began the build-up again.

So, with some trepidation, they started the long trek home. Now there was no choice but to walk through the dreaded goo, Jock said, "This must be how it would feel to be walking in cement boots." He shuddered as he wondered how close to that they could have come if things had worked out differently.

In some places where the moonlight couldn't penetrate the leaf canopy, it was hard to see the tangled roots. They all stumbled at some point. The hazards were everywhere. Sharp oyster shells were lethal on their exposed ankles. None of them had come dressed for these conditions. The walk was proving as difficult as imagined. Dom grinned through the gloom at Jeremy and Josh. "You'll sleep well tonight when we finally get home."

The incoming tide kept them pinned well inside the vegetation and it soon became necessary to create some light. "We can risk using only one torch between us," Jock cautioned them. "I'll use mine and cover the top of the lens with my hand, letting the light trickle through my fingers. We'll have to do the conga-line thing. Grab hold of the coat tails in front of you and follow the leader. If Harry is still out there somewhere, our cover will be blown if we're not careful with the torch. The light is pretty distinctive. There's no chance of an unbroken beam being mistaken for fire-flies."

"Yes," agreed Dom. "In that case, being cautious for the last few hours will have been wasted time. It really would be too bad to get caught at this stage."

By then, they were halfway across the bay and were beginning to feel safer until they heard the inboard motor start. "Bloody Hell...! Quick you lot. I'm going to turn this torch off. Hang onto a branch to help keep your balance and stand still until the boat has gone," warned Jock. They watched as the lights and the dim outline of the cabin cruiser appeared around the end of the point and headed off in a North-Easterly direction. They spent an uncomfortable ten minutes waiting for the boat to become a dot on the horizon, before continuing. "That's one dangerous moment behind us. Now there is only Harry left to worry about," Jock reminded them.

The sandfly bites were burning like little blowtorches, and every time they came upon an open area amongst the mangroves, the problem of coming face-to-face with a big 'saltie' became a bit of a worry. There were recent reports of occasional sightings. These crocs aren't very friendly and no one wanted to try to talk one out of a fight tonight. "It's highly unlikely we will stumble across one in here. They usually keep to the creeks on the other side of Mingleton, but you never know – especially after the night we've had already," said Dom.

Josh wasn't going to admit it to anyone but his heart was racing like mad. A small creature brushed past his ankle and his heart almost stopped. "Yee -ow-ch" he yelled.

"What's the matter? Are you okay?" squeaked his father in panic as he shone the thin thread of torchlight towards his son.

"Yeah," he mumbled in embarrassment. "I think a mudskipper just grazed my shin." His heart seemed as if it was going to jump out of his body. He gingerly lifted his foot and felt along his leg. Everything seemed to be still there. "I just got a fright. I was thinking about things that go bump in the night and the tips of crocodile tails."

At the the top edge of the mangroves, the mud became less of a problem as it mixed with shell grit, pebbles and sand. "Stop...! Wait just inside here for a while," said Jock as he bent and scraped every skerrick of mud from his sneakers. "I want to check the road just to make sure we're safe. Clean the mud off your shoes while I'm gone. That'll keep you occupied"

At last, Jock reached the edge of the lawn. He sat and dangled his feet onto the sand of the front beach. The other three, relieved and exhausted, trekked across the last five hundred metres and sprawled beside him. "Before we go any further, let's get our breath back before talking this through." He gave the twins a piercingly look and continued. "Your Mum expects us to be late. We're almost travelling on overtime already,but we do need to sort this thing out in our minds before we go inside."

No sooner had he said that, than the back patio light flicked on. Jock waved at Isabel standing in the doorway and called out, "Hello, Love, we're just recuperating after the walk home. We'll be in as soon as we call up our reserves of energy." Isabel waved her acknowledgment and disappeared inside the house. "I don't know if we should tell her about tonight just yet," Jock suggested

"No we shouldn't. Not straight away at any rate." said Dom.

"I'm not happy about keeping things from her, but I wouldn't want her scared when she's alone at home during the day." Looking at Dom, Jock said, "I know you just said you agree with me, but seriously, is that what you really think? My confidence has taken a hit and I'm a bit shaky, I must admit." Jock felt a reaction setting in. He hated the fact that his sons had been in danger. In addition, he didn't want to place any undue stress on Isabel. His gut feeling was that it would be time enough to tell her in a few days when he and Dom were sure that nothing unexpected had come back at them. "If I thought there was any possibility of a visit from those clowns, then I'd tell Isabel so she would be on her guard, but I'm really positive we weren't spotted."

Dom hadn't changed his mind. "I wouldn't tell her just yet; she'll only worry. To be on the safe-side, I think I'll come and fish on your front beach for a few days while you're at work. I haven't done that for a long while now. I'm well and truly overdue. Isabel won't see anything strange about it. She always comes down and has smoko and

18

lunch with me when I'm fishing around here. I'll be able to look after her, and catch some nice fish for your freezer while I'm about it."

Jock thought to himself, we've had one helluva worrying night but, on the surface, Dom acts as if he's not fazed at all. He shook his head in amazement as he thought about it. His elderly friend always tried to shield the boys from unpleasantness and to protect them as if they were his own, he thought with an affectionate smile. When the going gets tough, Dom just works around it to stabilise things; making everything seem as normal as he can.

Jock looked at Josh and Jeremy for a while without speaking and finally said, with a catch in his voice, "Unfortunately, tonight, the situation was way out of our control. We were in danger but, luckily, we seem to have gotten away relatively unscathed. I am very proud of the way you acted. If anyone had panicked, we would have been goners. Right now, it would help me a lot if you could give me your opinion, each of you, man to man, on whether you agree with Dom and me. Do you think we should tell your mother about what happened?"

Shell-shocked as he was, when his father asked for their opinion, Josh felt great. "Yeah, I don't want to worry Mum either, but if there is any sign of something wrong, no matter what, she needs to know." Then he stunned his father with his next comment and his new-found confidence, "I also think that we should try to find out just what is going on."

Then it was Jeremy's turn to have his say. He looked at the other three in turn. "I agree with Josh. Basically, Dom, you're our adopted grandfather. We trust you with our lives. Dad, we love you and Mum very much and don't want to put the family in danger, but Josh and I think alike, and it does sound as if Josh feels the same as I do. We both want to try and find out why those blokes are using our beach. What if someone else walks in on their little scam by accident and aren't as lucky as we were?"

Now that Jeremy was on a roll with his ideas there was no stopping him. He raced on with his opinions, almost as if he couldn't stop talking and seemingly stuck in top gear. He could hear himself nattering on and on but he couldn't shut it down. "And it is going to happen again. Remember, someone said 'see ya next month'. One bloke knew which rocks to hide behind for the best view of the top of the beach. Didn't someone say 'the usual ones'? So it has happened before, right under our noses."

"I agree with Jeremy. I don't want to worry Mum just yet either, but as you said, that stuff over at the Point earlier tonight, was forced on us,and it was definitely an 'under the radar' job. We didn't ask those idiots to use the boat ramp illegally. Do you honestly believe that we can just forget it? When you come right down to it, have we the right to let someone else walk unsuspectingly into that? I'm scared as hell thinking about this, but I don't believe that we can sit at home and do absolutely nothing." Josh paused for breath. He had become angry with Croaky and Harry for thinking they could come into his community and do what they liked. "Can we sleep on this a few days and talk about it again later?"

"Bloody hell," said Dom. "When you young blokes work up a head of steam, there's no shutting you up, is there?" He was so proud of them but couldn't let on because they were talking about doing something risky. He couldn't be seen to agree with them. All he could think was that, if he were their age and this thing happened to him, he would be using all the same words. A chip off the old block, and they weren't even his kids – but they thought like he did. They could be his own kids, and as far as he was concerned, they were. He loved them in the same way as Jock and Isabel did.

Jock too, understood how his sons felt. He looked at Dom who nodded assertively. Jock wanted to tell Jeremy and Josh that he heard what they were saying and that he agreed with them. However, he had to glean some responsibility from somewhere and dissuade them from the actions they so clearly wanted to take. "Yes," he said, "I understand how you feel, but we are going to walk away. We have to. We'll report what happened and let someone else be accountable for the repercussions."

They sat on the beach for another half hour allowing the peaceful-ness wash over them, each lost in his own thoughts. Then Dom stood up, stretched and said, "See you later," and without further ado, ambled up the slope towards his old ute.

"I know you said you'd be late but I was just starting to worry. That's why I stuck my head out the door when you got back a while ago," said Isabel. "Was the fishing good? See anyone you knew?"

"No to both questions," they all answered in unison.

*****

A week later, after much nagging by the twins, the four of them went down to the beach. Life had gone on as normal. Nobody had threat-ened any member of the family.

"We need to do it, Dad. I had an idea you wouldn't change your mind," said Jock. "I hoped you would, but knew I wasn't likely to hear what I wanted." Jock and Dom weren't very enthusiastic about the idea because they wanted to protect the boys.

Jock's major argument was that a father should never encourage his sons to undertake something as potentially dangerous as what his boys were suggesting they wanted to do. "No, you won't" he said forcefully. We'll report it and leave it there."

Not to be thwarted, the twins put forward a more powerful inducement, one their father was incapable of doing much about. "I'm sorry to do this to you, Dad, but we will do it on our own if necessary." Josh and Jeremy had discussed this at length and made their decision. "We are sensible enough. If you try to stop us, can you ever be sure we won't sneak out at night when you're asleep? You can't keep us locked up." He grinned. "We're old enough now to make our own decisions, so wouldn't it be better if we were all in this together?"

When Josh and Jeremy talked this over earlier, they knew the older men would insist on reporting their suspicious through the customs hotline. They would insist it was the best course of action. They could walk away from this problem with no one else being any wiser about what they had overheard. However, after days of deliberation, their consciences wouldn't allow them to ignore the situation. They were absolutely certain that there wasn't enough information to pass onto the authorities for them to be taken seriously.

The pair had been over to Boaties Bay the next day and several times since. They'd checked everything out. No evidence of the night's activities remained. By the next afternoon, most of the footprints were washed away by the tides or blown away by the wind. "The beach at Boaties is well used every day. The dirt tracks are always covered with tyre marks. How do we prove which ones belong to Harry's car?" Josh asked his brother.

"And," added Jeremy, "The fishing is good round there so there are always hundreds of footprints at the top of Boaties Beach. New visitors walk over the top of old marks every day. The continual build-up of imprints lasts until the next rainy day or when repeated gusts of heavy wind sweep the sand clean again."

He was right. The sand is so powdery that it's ridiculous to think the customs officers or the police would find anything here other than far too many footprints and tyre marks.

"Just think about it for a while... Dad, Dom, if someone came to you with this tale, what would you think?" Against their better judgement, Jock and Dom had to agree that the boys did have a point.

"Maybe they are right," Jock conceded. "What can we tell anyone? When it comes down to it, the whole story sounds a bit bizarre." All four of them could imagine the resigned sighs as the officials carried out any obligatory questioning. They imagined the talk flowing quick and fast; with bullet-like comments and queries.

"Okay, if you are serious about this, what did the men look like? What was the boat's ID number, the car's rego? What sort of vehicle… what colour? What was their cargo? What date did they say they would be back?"

Jock was forced to agree that, if they reported the incident now, their answers to questions like these would be: we don't know. We overheard something that led us to believe an illegal operation was being carried out but we saw no-one and couldn't see what they were doing. We only heard what they said.

Dom agreed. "You're right, Mate. Even if our unlikely tale was believed, without our knowing when these blokes are likely to be back, the authorities' hands are tied. Their department wouldn't be able to supply the manpower to come here night after night for God knows how many months just in case they found something to build a case on. To begin with, it's a forty minute trip each way to here and back to their office again."

Jock reminded them, "Remember though, I did see one thing: the small oblong containers they were loading onto the boat. They were some distance away, but they seemed small and rectangular. If the yellowish shade in the moonlight is anything to go by, it's possible they were made of wood. Perhaps that is better than knowing nothing at all."

"Yeah, Dad, and you said there was a deckhand on the boat," said Josh

Dom was angry. "The frightening thing is, without concrete evidence, the customs blokes have nowhere to go, no crime to pin on anyone. There's some sort of funny scam happening out there which, if we report it now, with the little amount of information we have, these drongos are going to get away with whatever they are doing. I wouldn't be too happy about that."

"It seems that we haven't much choice, Dom," Jock said. "Josh and Jeremy are hell bent on following this through and I'm damned if I'll let them do it on their own. Maybe we can give it until the next full moon to see if something happens. The biggest problem I have to face as a father is the fact that I'm starting to see where the boys are coming from on this issue, and I almost agree with them. Isabel is going to kill me when all this is over and she finds out."

The twins carefully sneaked a look at one another. They would have exchanged high-fives, if they could. Their slight moral victory felt good.

*****

The next day, Josh and Jeremy sat talking on their front beach. "We should keep a diary, you know." They realised there might come a time in the future when information needed to be passed to the relevant authorities. Their memories couldn't retain all the dates, times and other necessary details. Of course, they wouldn't be able to show their notes to anyone except their father and Dom, but they could use them to maintain an accurate account.

The seriousness of the situation was starting to hit them hard. They thought about the day when they first met Dom and wondered how, from that strange initial meeting, they had become so close to him. He had become one of the three people in their lives whom they trusted most. Shocked, they reviewed what they had asked him and their father to do. "How could we do that to Dom?" Jeremy asked Josh. "He's seventy-two years old, for God's sake! He's getting old."

"Only in years though" replied Josh. "He's still sharp. I don't want to think about doing this without him. He makes me feel safe, and anyway, best mates always stick together."

CHAPTER 3

Thoughts of Dom, took them back to that first day on the beach. The twins had turned eleven years old. They were like most brothers; best mates most times, but sometimes they acted as if they hated one another and were almost enemies. During those instances, the red faces, name-calling and flying fists were abruptly and sharply controlled by a cranky Isabel. These two angry brothers couldn't match terms with, nor have the same authority as their annoyed mum. They put this to the test more often than they should have lately, and came off a poor second best every time.

"What I say goes," she would declare when they rebelled against her rules. If the fight had been a bit too nasty she would puff up like an angry penguin. "You…" She would shout and "You!" She would point, one after the other, at the red-faced pair. "It's time to chill out. Josh you go into your room, and Jeremy into my bedroom – now – and stay there, both of you, for an hour." Then she would charge into each room a few minutes later, dump a pile of comics on the beds and add, "If you can't see your way to being a bit more civil to each other when the time is up, then don't bother coming out until both of you have cooled down completely and are more in control of your manners. You're lucky I'm taking pity on you and am prepared to give you something to read. I shouldn't bother. I should make you stay in here for hours with nothing to do. See how you'd like that. It would be so boring, you'd be crawling the walls. Then you'd see how stupid it is to fight all the time. It's about time you made more of an effort to sort things out amicably before it gets to this stage. You're old enough now to see sense, surely."

The angry penguin then would flounce out muttering about bloody self-centred kids. "Do they think I've nothing better to do than act as a referee for their boxing matches? Wait until their father gets home. He'll sort them out." The boys reckoned they could repeat what she

24

said, word for word, because they'd heard the same comments quite a few times over the last couple of years.

When Isabel told their father about the scuffles, he always gave her a serious smile and said, "Ah well, they're growing up. They're just testing their independence. They'll quieten down a bit in a couple of years." Then he'd go and find his sons and give them both a stern look, tell them to settle down and not to give their mother so much worry, or the next time he'd deal with them both when he got home from work.

When the boys grinned at each other afterwards, their father would say quite firmly, "Careful...! It wouldn't be wise to push it, Boys."

They knew they had gone too far and both shuffled and mumbled. "Yes, Dad... Okay, Dad... Sorry."

Once they'd overheard Jock telling his wife she was quite magnificent when she was angry. "You know, My Love, that auburn hair and temper of yours is the same as your son's. Joshua has inherited your temperament, as you very well know."

"Yes, I do know," they had heard her reply, "...the poor kid."

Although they were born on the same day of the same year, the boys weren't identical. Jeremy was the more serious of the two, while Josh was a little more hot tempered and quicker to become angry about most things. They were tall for their age and not fat, just an average size. Jeremy had wavy, brownish coloured hair, but Josh's curls were the colour of a rusty old water tank – or so his brother always told him.

The days had a tropical feel this summer. Older people in the community had made this claim early in December last year, so the twins thought it must be true. They had lived there long enough to know.

The oldies talked about little else during January and February of the New Year. Any time these local climate prophets ran into one another along the beach, the topic always was 'the weather'. Conversations started with statements such as 'God it's humid; it must rain any day now'. Then there would be the standard answer: the humidity can't go on like this day after day, something's got to give. Someone else would chime in with: *Not today, the clouds are too high, too white,* or alternatively, *the wind's blowing them too fast up there.* All the reminiscing about the climate conditions of previous years came next: *Do you remember that summer of 1976? Boy it never gave up. I had prickly heat for ten weeks that year. Bloody woeful it was.*

When the boys heard these weather conversations, they thought sadly of Great-Nana Blanche who died six years ago. The last time they saw her was on their fifth birthday. When they were all out west, she used to live just down the street with their Grandma. She made up stories for them and, when they were little, there was a favourite. She would start her bedtime story by asking them what they thought the clouds were made of. "Ice-cream," Josh remembered replying, with a giggle.

Great-Nana would tickle his tummy and under his arms. "No, you are not even close." The first time they heard this particular story, they were about two years old. Jeremy could still see her laughing eyes with the crinkles around the edges as she answered him. The magic of these fairy-tales always enthralled the little twins.

The twins ran outside and grabbed their new birthday bikes. A yell from inside stopped them in their tracks. "Jeremy…. Josh…just where do you think you're going?"

"Down to the boat ramp, Mum, we won't be long. See ya."

"Hang on you two. Get back in here."

"Aww, Mu-ummm…"

"Bet she's going to nag about hats," Josh complained just loudly enough for Jeremy but not their mother to hear. They charged through the back door and came to a halt in the laundry where Isabel was tossing clothes into the washing machine. "I can't recall either of you asking me if you could go out and I definitely didn't give you permission to go anywhere. Don't you think that would have be a nice gesture to make? Where are you planning to go?" she asked, giving them a stern look as her words tumbled out in an angry rush.

"We're just going down to the beach for a little while," Josh said. He gave his brother an I-told-you-so smirk behind his mother's back when she asked whether they had sunscreen, hats and water bottles.

"How long will you be? I want you back within two hours, okay? And be careful, we're new here and the place is still unfamiliar. Don't go off the beaten track and don't talk to anyone you don't know."

"Yes Mum. We won't" they replied in unison.

With that over, the twins took off to investigate and discover. Today the sky was an intense blue without a cloud to be seen. "No white sheep or even black ones in the sky," murmured Jeremy, and he remembered Great-Nanna Blanch again. He wasn't quite old enough to realise that associating birthdays with fluffy white clouds was always going to create a small knotted lump at the back of his throat.

They were having another birthday without Great-Nanna. Six years ago she had given them each a book. "You'll be starting school in just over two months' time and you'll be able to read these stories to me." They never did get to do that.

Jeremy was lost in his memories. Just as he was picturing Great-Nana's smile, his twin let out an excited whoop, bringing him crashing back into the present.

"Wow! How hot is this? C'mon lets go down to the boat ramp."

Jeremy had been on the verge of starting to cry when Josh interrupted his daydream, but eleven year-old kids are resilient and their minds dart quickly from one subject to the next. He gave an answering yell of excitement. "Yeah, last one to the top of the beach is a rotten egg." As they spotted the gap in the trees which meant the beach was just a few metres away, at the end of the access road, they hit the brakes, almost in unison. Bringing their bikes to a squealing stop, small pebbles and dirt sprayed out from behind the back wheels.

This was the right track, so they headed off again. Parked just on the edge of the track along towards the beach was an old battered Holden ute. The bravado left them for a minute until they remembered: they had just turned eleven and that's almost grown up. They weren't scared of anyone and there were two of them anyway.

"C'mon", urged Josh, "Let's go down to the water."

On the beach, a few metres past the boat ramp, an elderly man sat in a fold-up canvas chair, his fishing rod poked into the sand beside him. As the boys came closer, he didn't move. Jeremy edged nearer, almost up to the old bloke's knees, and still there was no movement. All of a sudden the old man's head lolled forward onto his chest. The boys hopped backwards in shock. "Is he okay?" whispered Josh. "He's not dead is he?"

Before Jeremy could answer, the old man, having woken with a fright, sat forward in his seat and yelled, "What the hell do you little rotters think you are doing; sneaking up on an old digger like that? Do you want to give me a heart attack? Go on, you young whippersnappers; get the hell out of here. Leave a bloke in peace."

The boys, noticing his red face, turned on their heels and ran like mad to their bikes. Isabel was surprised to see them back so soon. "A quarter of an hour must be some sort of record for you two," she said. "What's wrong? You look a bit hot and bothered."

"Nothing Mum," they replied. "There was some old bloke down there and we didn't like the look of him. Cranky old dinosaur he was too."

"What happened?" their mother asked. "You weren't cheeky to him, I hope."

"No… but he yelled at us for nothing. We didn't do anything to him."

"Hmmm… and while we're at it, I won't have you referring to an elderly gentleman as 'an old dinosaur'. Do you hear me?"

"Yes…We're sorry Mum. We won't say it again."

That night, the twins discussed what happened and felt a bit stupid about their reaction. They decided they would go back tomorrow to see if the man was there again. "Anyway he was old. He must be almost a hundred, so he can't hurt us."

Every day for the rest of the week, they went to the boat ramp before they went anywhere else, but the old fellow wasn't there. Thinking that he wasn't coming back, they had almost given up when, on the following Monday, there he was again, standing up in front of his fold-up chair. He looked different now that he wasn't asleep. From side-on, he had a long nose and really short and very crinkly curly grey hair.

He looks like he's wearing a koala skin on his head, thought Jeremy. This time the man was reeling in a fish. Josh cautiously walked along the sand until he could almost touch the old chap. "What sort of fish is that?" Josh asked.

"A Bluey," said the old man, "But it's too small. I'll have to let it go."

"Can we watch you?" asked Jeremy.

The old bloke nodded and went back to his fishing. They sat in silence for the next half an hour or so watching the man working his fishing rod with each bite. He had dark brown skin like old leather and big hands and feet; almost like a giant's they thought. After a while, the boys said, "We'd better go home now."

The old man nodded again, and without even a sideways glance, continued to concentrate on what he was doing.

After that, the twins would check each day, to see if the elderly bloke was there. Whenever he was, they would sit cross-legged in the sand to watch him fish. During the next few weeks, they hung around beside him patiently and without talking too much except to say hello and to ask what sort of fish it was whenever he reeled in his catch.

28

One day the old chap said, "I'm Dom. Who are you two young scrubbers?" In daily instalments, he told them he had been a fisherman who used to have a beach hut up on the ridge behind where he was fishing. Nearly twenty years ago, he became really sick and spent six months in hospital. When he recovered, he went to live with his brother, two hundred kilometres away.

"I hated the town life," he said and told them the lure of his old fishing grounds had been too much. Dom came back to live in Mingleton, the small beachside town around in the next bay. He bought a new beach house because his old shack at Boaties Bay had succumbed to insects, the weather and old age.

It was during these fishing sessions that the boys came to realise that Dom didn't talk a much, only sharing the bare facts.

"A man of few words, but a good honest bloke," their father commented when he met Dom later that summer.

"Mum and Dad have bought a house here too. Dad works at that big resort down the road," said Josh. "We've just finished Grade seven and after the Christmas holidays we're going to High School. We've never be on a school bus before."

Almost bouncing with excitement, Jeremy added, "I'm going to learn Chemistry. I can't wait."

For the rest of the summer, the two boys and Dom spent a lot of time together. Dom showed them the remnants of his fish traps. Now they were nothing more than oyster covered broken sticks poking out of the mud in the bay. "I had wire netting nailed around the poles and when the tide went out, I'd pick up the fish before the water went out too far. If I didn't, the sun would dry their skin out like leather. I used to throw the small ones back into the deep water on the other side of the fish fence so they could grow up a bit. The really big ones went back as well," Dom said. "They were my breeding stock. I was always careful not to over-fish. I had to think of my future."

The boys asked about the railway lines and old tramway trolley wheels still lying in the mud out past the low-water mark, and now covered in oysters just like the old sticks were. The railway lines were rusting in the sand. He told them the iron wheels were once attached to his boat trailer, and he'd built the short railway track from inside his boatshed down to the low water mark. Early each the morning, he'd haul his fishing boat down to the ocean, and winch it back into the shed again when he'd done with his fishing for the day.

During those last few years before he got ill, he had pushed all the larger rocks aside to construct a channel to allow him to launch his boat closer to the Point. He told them he used a metal garden rake with a galvanised pipe handle to smooth the small rocks and pebbles into a sloping ramp with a channel wide enough for his boat to slide along. He used a tractor and boat trailer on the ramp instead of winching the boat on the old railway tracks, and had removed the top section of railway line to allow the tractor to move the boat in and out of his old boat shed. "That's progress," Dom said. "Things change and we adapt. Nothing ever stays the same forever."

"Where's the boatshed now?" asked Jeremy, looking back across the sand to the scrub at the top of the beach.

The old man seemed sad for a minute and his eyes developed a faraway look before he glanced at Jeremy and replied, "When I came back to the Point, the white ants had eaten all the timber. The posts had crumbled into piles of sawdust and the sheets of galvanised iron – what there was left of them –were lying, scattered all over the ground. A lot of them were missing. I suppose some washed away on the king tides and kids probably took a few bits of it to make cubby houses in the scrub. Anyway, I picked up what was left, threw it in the back of the old ute and took it to the dump."

It was a great summer and the twins reckoned that Dom was the best mate in the whole world now that they had gotten used to him and his sombre manner.

*****

The Christmas holidays finally came to an end and the boys were nervous about starting at a new school. They worried about that first day. It could end up being a bit of a pain being in a class full of strangers. They wouldn't know anyone. They had stacks of friends back home in the mining town where they used to live but, in the six weeks of these holidays, they hadn't met anyone their own age.

They knew they were going to miss seeing Dom as often. This was one of those times when they were glad they had each other. Sometimes being a twin was gross, but at other times it wasn't too bad at all.

The big day arrived. They were out of bed at five o'clock and fidgeted and grumbled. It still hadn't rained and the weather was hot. They rode their bikes to the fork in the road, leaned them against a tree trunk and waited for the bus to come.

When it arrived, the driver welcomed them. "Hello, who have we here? New blokes eh; you look pretty flash in your new uniforms.

It must be your first year at high school by the looks of it." Josh and Jeremy couldn't get a word in so they just nodded.

"Right you are," said the driver. "I'm Ned. Take a seat down the back so the primary kids don't annoy you. They'll be on the bus only for about ten minutes. Their school's on the main drag, just past the turn-off on the highway."

"Yes," said Josh, "We know: Just before you get to the mango farm – where the black miniature cattle are."

"Yep...that'd be it."

Although the bus was empty, they took Ned's advice and headed down the back. As they watched the little primary school kids getting on at each stop, Josh said, "Do you reckon there'll be someone from our school getting on soon?"

When the bus stopped at the front gates of the local primary school, the kids piled out. As they jumped from the bus steps, and before their feet touched the ground, each was shouting to friends in the playground.

"Thank God that noisy lot are gone," Josh grumbled. "Still half an hour to go yet and we're the only kids left on the bus."

"There were more kids out west than there are here," grumbled Jeremy. That didn't last. Every few kilometres, teenagers waited outside their gates beside the highway, some still half asleep and sprawled on plastic stackable chairs under homemade bus shelters. Others mucked about throwing pebbles and lumps of dirt at each other.

Josh thought about the kids back home. When mum or dad drove us to school last year, the kids used to fool around like that too. He noticed some old battered cars parked just inside a few of the fence lines. I suppose those kids drove themselves to the gate. The kids we knew used to leave old cars or motorbikes in their front paddocks all day until they arrived back in the afternoon. Some of the roads into the stations were a few kilometres long. It looks like it's the same here for the cane farmers' kids, he thought.

The twins received a few curious glances but no one said anything to them. "We must be invisible," Jeremy mumbled to Josh. So far, most of the kids seemed to be older than the twins; year nines at least and some in higher grades too they decided. Great, thought Josh, looks like this is going to be a deadly boring place to live.

"Dom said we'd find plenty of friends on the bus," said Jeremy. "So much for his opinion; he's a bit out of touch I think?"

"What would a silly old bloke like him know about us school kids anyway?" Josh's red-headed temperament started to emerge. He needed to blame someone for the way he felt at the moment. Dom fitted the bill nicely.

"Hell Josh, I wish we were going back to our old school don't you? I wonder what Hayden and Blake are doing today?" They hadn't thought about any of their old mates all holidays and now they realised they missed them.

CHAPTER 4

Dom rarely used his mobile phone. He only made the effort when he thought it was important. He hated the useless, under-size article. His fingertips always seemed too big. The compactness of the bloody thing made him feel clumsy and ill-equipped to use it. How the hell could anyone hear him when the little microphone was so far from his mouth?

"Bloody stupid thing," he'd often remark to the twins. "Hello….. Hello… Is that you Jeremy?" he shouted.

"No. Do you want to speak to my brother?" Josh asked as he held the phone a bit further away.

"No, you'll do," was the unflattering reply. "This is Dom. Is your Dad on day shift this week?"

"Hello Dom. Nice to hear your voice," Josh said with what he thought was just the right amount of sarcasm. "Yes, he has Wednesday and Thursday off. Did you want to speak to him? I can ask him to ring you when he gets home tonight. He won't be too late."

Dom's decision was instantaneous. "Not necessary; you can get back to me with an answer when it suits you. I only want to sort out when the three of you can come down to Boaties with me for a couple of hours."

"Okay, Dom. It'll probably be Wednesday afternoon, about four o'clock, after we get home on the bus. I'll get back to you after I check with Dad."

When Jock arrived home, the three of them decided that 3.45pm on Wednesday would be fine. Jock and Isabel planned to go shopping in town that day and collect the boys from school afterwards. This meant the boys would be home a bit earlier than if they'd caught the bus. Jock and Isabel usually treated themselves to afternoon tea in the nice little café in the arcade, and bought a bag of iced donuts and bottles of coke for the twins to have in the car on the way home.

"Wonder why Dom wants to see us at Boaties," said Josh. "He's a pain in the backside when he gets all mysterious about things he wants to talk about face-to-face. The way he acts sometimes, you'd think he was part of a National Security team."

"Yeah, the spy who came in from the Saltpans," sniggered Jeremy. "It's a bit weird though. I wonder what he's up to. If he wanted to go fishing he'd have said so."

"You pair will just have to wait until Wednesday, won't you," said Jock. "Come on; grab a shovel and a sugar bag. Let's go down to the front beach and get some shell-grit for the chooks before it gets dark. Those eggs from the hen house this morning had thin shells. The feather brigade needs a boost of calcium."

To the relief of the curious duo, Wednesday finally arrived. It was a sunny, uncomfortably hot and humid day. "C'mon we'll be late for the bus if we don't hurry," said Josh, grabbing his backpack as he flew past Isabel. "Mum, don't forget, you are to collect us from school this afternoon. We've got to meet Dom."

Josh was hot on his heels. "You know how you usually grab us some donuts from the café, Mum. Well, do you think we could have cream lamingtons today instead, please? The bakery is making them again. The kids at school have been buying them from the tuckshop this week."

The day seemed to drag on. During the final lesson of the day, Reynaud Jackson, the maths teacher, grimaced in exasperation as he asked, "Josh, are you with us? What did I say?"

"Er... Sorry Sir, I don't know."

"Homework ...I repeat, for you and any other inattentive students, page 21 numbers 3 through to 12. With luck, Josh, you'll be back with us in body and spirit after a good night's sleep." Casting his eye over the class, Rey sighed. "Go on you lot, there's the bell. Off you go. See you tomorrow."

Josh, who hated being singled out in class, leapt up from his chair, muttering under his breath, "Stupid teacher ...How come he thinks he's so smart? And who'd want to spell Raynaud with an 'e' anyway? Old Ray Nuts is a pain."

He and Jeremy gravitated toward each other from opposite ends of the school ground. Josh was scowling and pulling at his thatch of auburn hair in temper, a sure-fire giveaway about the mood he was in. He had done this since he was little and, when he was in full throttle, his mother was fond of saying, "You can almost see the smoke pouring out of Josh's ears when he's angry."

"What's wrong with you?"

"Nothing."

Jeremy got the message and left his brother to stew privately. They almost reached the school gate when they heard Jock calling them.

"Hey Boys, the car's over the road beside the Police Station. Let's rock and roll. Dom will be waiting patiently for us at Boaties."

Twenty-five minutes later, they were driving through their front gate after having tooted the horn as they passed the track down to the beach. The twins weren't the only curious ones today. Jock was chomping at the bit to get down to the boat ramp as well.

"C'mon, let's go to meet Dom. We're only going to be five minutes late," said their father. "Sorry, Love," he said to Isabel. "Just put all the cold stuff away and leave the rest. I wasn't thinking straight when I said we'd meet Dom so early. I'll put the rest of the groceries in the pantry for you when we get back."

"What time will you be home do you reckon?" asked Isabel. "We'll be having steak for tea, so I won't start cooking until I see you coming through the gate." Isabel had a university assignment due the next week. She was spending every spare minute she could, to get it finished on time. "Have I got time to work on my assignment, do you think?"

"Yes, I reckon you would have. We'll probably be at least two hours, if not longer" said her husband. "We should be home just before dark. Don't worry about putting the steak on when you hear us arrive. I'll fire up the barbie. The boys can help you throw a green salad together while I'm doing that." The three of them almost ran out the front door to meet Dom around at Boaties Beach, as arranged.

"Hi, everyone," said Dom, "How was your day?"

"Lazy," replied Jock.

"A pain," said Josh and Jeremy together.

Josh told Dom, "I've be trying to work out what you wanted. It made me a bit ratty at school all day. I couldn't concentrate. Mr Jackson gave me a hard time about it."

"I was the same," said Jeremy. "And I almost went to sleep during physics, because the day was going so slowly. What's this all about anyway?"

Dom went quiet for a few moments, then stared at them thoughtfully and said seriously, "There is something important that I want to show you. A secret I never thought I'd ever tell anyone about." The

twins looked at one another in surprise while their old friend continued talking.

"I'd pretty much decided that I was going to die without revealing this to anyone but, with you so hell-bent on investigating the
smuggling racket, if that's what it is, I reckon some extra information
I have up my sleeves will come in handy."

Now the old man had everyone's attention. "There's a very special
place I want to show you, but before I do, you've must promise me
you'll never tell anyone else about it." Looking at the twins, Dom
said, "I'm serious about this. I hope I can rely on you. It would upset
me if you betrayed my trust. Our friendship would never be the same
again and I'd hate that to happen." The boys aren't sure how to take
this, Jock thought with amusement. This solemn man is a different
Dom to the one they're used to.

"It's my family's secret place. It was my mother's refuge, a haven
from possible incarceration. For it to become common knowledge
after all this time would be too much. No one would understand.
Everyone would gossip and my mother would be labelled a crazy
woman. It would rip my heart out to have her memory tarnished.
There is no way I'll allow her feelings to be treated with disrespect.
Just remember that. Her secret is now going to become yours too, so
keep it well."

Dom had wrestled with his conscience all week. He knew that,
unless people had lived in a war-torn country, they could never
understand his mother's uncertainties relating to her wartime experiences. In fact, he found it confusing himself, never having gone
through what she did. "It was bad enough for her as a teenager during
World War I in Italy, but to have the terror resurface in her new
country during the second war was very hard for her."

It began to dawn on Jock what this might be about. Dom was
finding the difference in their cultures an obstacle for the first time
since they'd met him. Maybe this had something to do with Australia's
treatment of 'alien' Italian immigrants during World War II. Had his
mother be in danger somehow?

After worrying about it all day, Dom couldn't seem to stop the
flood of words. "I won't allow anyone to treat her ideas as a joke.
Because she was worried about what effect the war might have on
her family doesn't make her a foolish woman. Although she has
been dead for many years, I won't have her basic need to protect
her children looked on as simply the ranting and ravings of an old
Italian Mama. That's not the name some of the louts used to call us in

those days, but I won't go into that. Some ugly words, spoken with a sneer, were often the start of many bar room brawls." Dom's breathing was becoming a bit ragged so he looked out towards the ocean, as he struggled with his emotions.

Jock moved closer and draped his arm over his mate's shoulder, "Dom, we would never intentionally do anything to hurt you. You have my solemn word on that."

"I wish we'd never gone fishing that night, but we did. That's something we can't change now, and I need to protect Josh and Jeremy just as Mama needed to find a safe haven for her husband and kids." Dom was emotional and unsure how to handle what lay ahead.

Jock knew from past experience, if anything was going to bring Dom peace of mind, it was the ocean. "Let's walk down to the water's edge while we talk, Dom. Our feet could do with some cooling off in this heat."

During the next ten minutes, Dom confessed that this place he was taking them to was the main reason for his returning to live here. He apologised for the stack of senseless things he said to the boys. He knew that they would never betray him but then he spoiled it all by adding, "But if you do ..."

Jock and his sons had known Dom long enough not to be offended by anything he said because of his emotions. They just waited until he'd wrung out his passion and brought it under control. The elderly man had put himself under a huge amount strain since the other day and most of what he was saying was the stress talking. The three of them may have had a long impatient day, but Dom had taken it a bit further. He had created a period of hell for himself.

Jock slid his arm across his old friend's shoulder again and said quietly, "Dom, I'll remind you again. We love you very much, Mate. You are family. If what you are going to show us is important to you, it's as equally important to us." With tears running down his old leathery cheeks, Dom asked them to follow him.

They walked about three hundred metres along the sand before Dom turned abruptly right and headed up into the bushy scrub, just above high water mark. It was a bit of a struggle to push through the tangled undergrowth. At times all four had to bend over at the waist to clamber under low slung branches of the local white cedar trees. Given the network of vegetation they had to negotiate, the bucket Dom carried became a handicap for him. About two metres in, although it felt like twenty, the ground started to dip down into the bowl of a shallow but fairly wide gully. The trees on either side were tall with their branches all pointing upwards to reach for their share of light. By this time, the old Dom that they knew so very well, had re-emerged.

"Hey Dom, I remember this place. You bought us in here a few years ago to show us the scrub turkey's nest," said Jeremy, and with that reminder, he looked over to the left. The large mound was still there.

"The chickens have already hatched this year," said Dom, catching Jeremy's glance towards the small mountain of soil, leaves and twigs.

Both Josh and Jeremy felt a strange regret that they'd only visited once. If Isabel got to hear about that, they could almost hear her saying, "You should have made a bit more of an effort. This is a special thing that not every kid gets the chance to see. Fancy that? I can't believe you never went back to see the next year's hatchlings. Weren't you even curious?"

"Is this your secret? You've already shown us this nest before," smirked Josh.

"Don't act any stupider than you have to," growled Dom, but he'd known the boys long enough to realise they were only trying to lighten the situation. He had been a bit intimidating and grim back there at the top of Boaties.

Jeremy dug Josh in the ribs and whispered just loud enough for Dom to hear, "He's a bit toey today, isn't he?"

Dom gave them a hard look before walking over to a bank of rocks. The largest of these had split vertically. The front slab, about the thickness of a fridge door had slipped downwards about twenty five millimetres and was leaning back against the rest of the parent rock. A flat boulder lying underneath had prevented the broken slab from falling any further.

Back in the car park, before Jock and the twins arrived, Dom had tucked a thin, flat iron bar into his belt and securely covered it with the back of his shirt. Jock, Josh and Jeremy looked at one another with raised eyebrows when they saw Dom take this out.

What the hell is he doing? This big pile of rocks has been here forever and he has never worried about them when he's brought us here before, thought Josh. Dom pushed the iron bar about halfway down, in behind the apparently, unstable slab. With a quick shove, he slammed the flat metal upwards, grabbed the edge of the rock and started to drag it towards his chest.

"Hey, watch out Dom. What do you think you're doing?" Jock yelled, as he frantically rushed forward to stop him. "That rock hasn't got much of a lean on it. It'll fall on you. Be careful, Mate." Dom chuckled and kept pulling at the rock. However, instead of it falling forward, it opened sideways as if on a hinge.

"What the hell is that?" asked Josh. The three of them must have looked like stunned mullets, standing there staring from their old mate to what apparently was now a rock door covering a darkened void that lead to somewhere below the surface.

Jock blinked. "Seriously, Dom, what the bloody hell is that?" He felt his mouth opening and closing like a goldfish's as he tried to think of some sensible remark to make, but he couldn't think of anything. After recovering from the shock, they all shot forward to look into the void in the rocks. On closer inspection, it wasn't a cave, but the entrance to a manmade tunnel.

The rock slab swung on specially designed hinges that couldn't be seen from the outside. Still swinging slightly from Dom's heavy-handed effort with the lever, a metal catch hung loosely on the back of the door. "When the door is closed, this strip of metal slots into a U-shaped holder on the inside of the doorframe to latch it securely," said Dom.

"Wow…!" Jeremy and Josh were gob-smacked. Dom had never seen them so lost for words. Maybe it's been worth my day of anguish just to see that, the old man considered.

"Right," said Dom, "You lot stay here for a minute. I'll go inside and shut the door. See this handle on the back; I can pull the door shut with it. The rock is angled to stop the door from swinging open. If I can't push it out again, you'll have to pull it from outside. I'm just not as young and virile as I used to be," he winked. "Here's the lever. You won't need it because I'm not going to fasten the latch in place, but you could use it to dong any bad guys on the head, if you see any." Still chuckling about this stupid remark, he disappeared into the pile of rocks.

"It's ingenious," mumbled Jock "And I'm willing to bet that we've only seen the beginning of it." Mind you, while Dom might have thought his so-called joke was funny, Jock and the twins, standing and staring at the pile of rocks, began to get a bit edgy. Dom had reminded them about the unfortunate episode the other night. They kept imagining they could hear footsteps on the other side of the bushes. "Quick, go and have a look if anyone is on the beach," ordered Jock. "I don't care which one of you goes, but bloody well hurry up."

When Dom had been gone about ten minutes, Jock looked at his sons and said "He should be back by now. Where the hell is he?

Dom…," he yelled, "Can you hear me?" There was complete silence; no sound at all. "Hey Dom…." No reply.

"Dom, can you hear me?" Jock was becoming edgy now. "D-o-m, for Christ sake, answer me."

"I'm going to open the door," Josh warned. The rock swung easily considering it was so heavy and hadn't been opened for so long. "Dom, are you all right?" called Josh. There was still no answer, only an eerie, unnatural silence.

"I'll just go inside to have a look," he told his father, and he took a couple of tentative steps.

"Yaaahhhhhhhhh!!!" A screeching shape flung itself bodily at him. Josh screamed, turned and took off in the direction of the beachfront, knocking his brother flat on his back in the leaf litter on the way. He sprinted over the top of his sibling's prostrate body and was still running when he heard a gurgling sound behind him. He chanced a quick look over his shoulder and spun around, amazed at what he saw.

Dom was outside the tunnel, doubled over and holding his ribcage because he was laughing so hard. By then, the other two had realised what had happened and they were laughing too, now that they had recovered from the shock. "You mongrels…" was all Josh could say before he started laughing too. He wasn't laughing at the funny aspect of his performance, but because he was so relieved.

In between gasping for air, Dom said with great satisfaction, "I got you there young Josh… payback time. I didn't care which one of you it was, but I had an inkling one of you would be curious enough to open the door instead of letting your father do it."

"C'mon," said Dom in between chuckles, "I'll take you inside. Last one through, closes the door behind you, and slips the latch across. That's a law that's been set in concrete since this place was completed." He was still chuckling, but he thought to himself, those two kids needed to have a fright. They're too cocky about this. It's some sort of game to them, one great big adventure. Maybe now they'll think this over and decide to give the whole idea a miss. I hope so because it could get dangerous. Kids…, he snorted to himself, they think they're invincible.

The tunnel was tall enough to walk through without stooping. The darkness though, was overwhelming. Because it was so long since Dom was in there, he had forgotten he needed to bring a torch. He felt a bit stupid but there was no way he was going to admit to that in front of the boys. "Check along the top of the right hand wall, there are pairs of handgrips along the length of the tunnel. Oh, before we go any further, about two metres along, there'll be a closed wooden door," said Dom. "Don't run into it. The door opens back this way, and behind it, you'll find a small landing and a set of three stairs on the other side. Don't fall down them. There is a handrail on each side of the tunnel as you walk along."

As they felt their way along, Jock found what they were looking for. "Every two metres or thereabouts," Dom told them, "We placed air vents in the walls. The heights are fairly random, to blend into the outside landscape. They are about a hundred and fifty millimetres in diameter. That's about six inches in the good old measurements. We had some decent wet seasons back in those days so we put a bit of a downward slope on them, when we installed them," he said. "That was incorporated in our planning so the tunnel wouldn't be flooded."

Dom went on to explain that the exit end of each of the vent pipes had a different profile. Within reason, he and his brothers wanted the pipes to be the same shape and size as their individual outside stone coverings. "That attention to detail was geared towards an end result that looked as if the whole area was just natural beach scrub with no hidden extras."

With that, Dom pushed the first pair of handles outwards. Suddenly, everyone saw a tiny oval view of the ocean, the mangroves, the beach and the scrub next to the gully entrance. It also allowed a small glow of light into the passageway. In the gloom, Jock felt for and found another vent opening. He continued along the tunnel, feeling for the handgrips at the end of the pairs of thin rigid metal rods protruding about ten to twelve centimetres out from the inside surface of the tunnel wall. As he operated each set of levers, a small sliver of natural light streamed in.

Jock saw that the rods ran through what seemed to be a series of homemade fencing wire eyelets all along the vent. Not unlike the eyelets on a fishing rod, with the line running through them, thought Jock.

Dom explained how the system worked. A small rock is hinged to the top of the vent. When the rods are operated, the rocks push out from the top of the vent, sticking out parallel to the ground below them. Unfortunately, even with the companion rocks scattered around them, the arrangements become noticeable to someone really looking for them. The good news is that people have to look hard to find them. It's not as easy as it sounds. There was nothing we could do about it. It was the best scheme that we could come up with. I guess, in the overall project, the outside ends of those vents were our only small disappointment.

Jock and the boys sensed the tension lessening in Dom's voice as he talked. "I hoped they would still work. The rods shouldn't be too rusty because they're fairly well protected from the salt air. It's a killer on metal round here and the fittings were treated with some pretty thick layers of paint and grease at the time. We probably should bring a tin of WD40 next time we come, though. A spray of that stuff on the placed out in the open where that old that old grease build-up has worn off should help them through into the next century."

"I had no idea that this was here" said Jock.

"Why should anyone but me know about our family secret? God knows, we made sure that it was never going to be found, if we could help it," said Dom. "C'mon, we have to go now. We'll come back in a few days when we have a bit more time. The tunnel is a fairly long one, and if we stayed to find all the vents and open them, it'd be well past sunset. We'll give the rest of the exploration a miss for today. Isabel will get worried if you're not home before dark."

"Dom, is this a cyclone shelter?" asked Jeremy as they made their way towards the exit.

"It wasn't built for that reason but I suppose it could be used as one," Dom replied.

"Well, what is it?"

"It was built for my mother. ...C'mon let's go home," said Dom, in a tone of voice that the boys knew well. He wasn't going to tell them why the tunnel was built, not yet anyway, and they knew today wasn't the day to push him. He'd had a stressful day and he needed a bit of recovery time.

He mightn't ever tell us. He can be a stubborn old coot when he wants to be, thought Josh. Maybe we should just go for the jugular and be done with.

Jock closed the final vent and the four of them inched their way through the dark, back the way they had come. Before opening the door, Dom took them into an extended arm of the tunnel, which Jock and the boys had missed in the gloom. It was curved and roughly crescent-shaped. About three metres long, it branched out at a ninety degree angle past the entrance to the main passageway. "The top-end of it runs almost parallel to the beach. There are a few strategic spy holes in these walls too but they don't have covers."

Jock and the twins found the thin strips of light in the wall when they stood straight on to the openings. There were enough peepholes

42

for everyone to be able to look out over the whole gully. Long narrow glimpses of that end of the beach allowed them to see if anybody was out there.

Back on the beach, Dom had said this place was built as his mother's refuge. He and his brothers thought of just about everything. There has to be a lot more to this story, thought Jock.

Dom looked out through the peepholes, which he helped to build almost fifty years ago and declared, "It's safe to leave now." This was an important ritual which was performed back then and it remained necessary to repeat it on this extraordinary day. "It is an essential practice. It needs to become second nature for the safety of all who are hiding in here," declared Dom.

On the word 'hiding', the twins exchanged a look. They still couldn't comprehend the relevance of it all. When they'd first arrived at the beach earlier this afternoon, Dom, in one short sentence, had told them why the place was built, but they had missed a small clue.

*****

Supper was over and Isabel had gone off alone to the Mingleton SES meeting. Jock had cried off going to the meeting as there wasn't much new business to discuss this month. The group wouldn't even miss him. He wanted to catch up on some reading and get an early night for a change.

Jeremy glanced up from the tide charts he'd been studying. "Hey Dad, if Mum's going to be working at that craft show with Marge both days this weekend, it would pay to organise a full day with Dom. There shouldn't be anyone much around at the boat ramp because the tides are all wrong for fishing."

His son's words delivered Jock felt an uncomfortable jolt. It really upset him to keep secrets from Isabel. He felt like he was sneaking out behind her back, but he decided she didn't need the extra pressure of knowing what was happening. Her studies and other commitments already took such a lot of her time. He knew she'd be beside herself with worry if she had even a hint of what was happening. It's bad enough that I have agreed to go ahead and help the boys with this crazy investigation, Jock thought. His only consolation was that 'forewarned is forearmed.'

The twins held the trump card with their earlier *can't be watched 24/7* comment. The warning about going it alone if needs be rang true. They could be stubborn, and the tone of that declaration contained a small hint of iron. At least, if he and Dom were with the boys throughout whatever was going to happen, Jock felt they could protect the boys as much as possible. Jock and Dom had made a pact to call in the appropriate authorities if things began to look like turning dangerous. No matter how doubtful the evidence was, or how incredulous the story seemed, that was how it would be.

"Hey Dad, are you still with us?" asked Jeremy as he waved his hand back and forth in front of Jock's face.

"What…? What's the matter?" He realised both his sons were looking at him and waiting for an answer.

"Will we tell Dom we'll meet him both days this weekend, or just the one?"

He'd been daydreaming. Cheeky young brats, he thought with affection. "Okay, I'm back with you now. It will have to be Saturday. I'm working Sunday. Give Dom a ring to see if that suits him," said suggested.

CHAPTER 5

Saturday dawned hot and sunny. After waving Isabel and Marge off, Jock and his sons walked to Boaties Beach, arriving just as the old ute pulled up.

"If I didn't know it was hard fact that the first Holden FX, came out in 1948, I'd think the old bomb was older than Dom," said Jock.

"Shh, Dad," muttered Jeremy. "He'll turn around and go home if you make insulting remarks about his pride and joy, and we'll never find out what we want to know."

"G'day mates, lovely day for it," Dom said. Aware they'd been bagging his favourite girl; he gave the ute's rear end a loving tap as he walked past. "There's not many around today, even over at Mingleton. We should be safe to go straight to the tunnel without worrying about being seen."

As they walked along the beach, everyone was busy with his own private thoughts. There was a stiff breeze blowing and the sand was warm and stinging as it whipped across their legs. "Even with that breeze, it's hot today" said Jock.

"We'll be underground. It's always cool down there," said Dom. "In the summer, back in the early '40s, some days when we worked the fish traps, the heat was stifling but we had to put up with it. We always looked forward to the days-off so we could spend a few hours in the tunnel. There were no air conditioners in our homes in the good old days. The December to February months were hard to bear."

"You had electric fans though didn't you?" Asked Jeremy

"Yeah, such as they were. They were pretty efficient at moving the hot air around."

"Isn't that better than nothing?"

"Not really... Anyway, you young blokes today wouldn't have a clue. We didn't have much of a choice. Those bloody fans circulated a bit of air, but you had to have your faces practically jammed up against the fan guard to get much relief. We had to become a bit more acclimatised to the heavy atmosphere, and there's the difference. You young whingers today can't concentrate on your studies unless you have air conditioned classrooms. It must be like sitting in a fridge."

"Yeah, yeah; we know. You're from tough pioneering stock," said Josh, "All that hard work and suffering; no fun and games. What about those dances and parties you used to tell us about?"

"C'mon you three," said Jock, we're almost there. "Give it a break will you? Shut up for a while."

When they had been standing in the gully for several minutes, Josh said, "Dom, where on earth are those peepholes in the crescent tunnel?" As soon as they'd walked into the area, the boys made a beeline for where they thought these openings in the rocks might be, but were having trouble finding them.

"You're close!" said Dom. "There's one about half a metre to your left."

"I think I see it," said Josh. He dragged his hand along the surface and stopped at a long, ragged slot. It looked like a natural gap in where the rocks butted up against one another. "Is this what I'm looking for?"

"Yep," answered Dom, "Good isn't it?"

"Luckily these rocks were in the right places so you could build all this, Dom."

"Luck... Baloney! There were lots of small rocks scattered all over the ground but not many bigger ones when we got here. Only two of the largest ones in the group are original. The rest were carted in by truck, or barrow load by barrow load, from elsewhere, depending on their sizes."

"The area was much deeper in here before we started. It was bloody hard, gruelling work that got this done. My older brother, Aldo, knew what he was doing when it came to working with stones. When we started building, the gully dipped into what my little sister, Rafaela, always liked to believe was an old and very wide, river bed. If indeed, it had been an old watercourse, the banks had eroded, widened and flattened out over time. Hundreds of waterworn rocks collected in there, probably over thousands of years."

Dom's family made use of the rocks, stones and extra soil from around the gully, and then carted more from elsewhere on the property, when it was needed. "We 'killed two birds with one stone' as the saying goes, reshaping the high banks either side of the washout and turning them into vehicle tracks. The over-burden we lugged into this place to use as extra filling."

He nodded towards a small rise. "Look over there, where the bank seems to slope naturally over our tunnel. We created all that. See all those small trees and shrubs, Mama and Rafaela planted them to hold the soil and rocks together. The ancient white-cedar trees just above the high-water mark were already growing there, but a lot of the plant-life in here benefitted from a bit of human help. My mother and sister transplanted hundreds of natural seedlings. It was an adventurous time."

The twins continued to bombard Dom with their questions. "How did you get the largest rocks up on the truck? Weren't they too heavy?"

The answers came flying back, somewhat begrudgingly. "With a lot of backbreaking labour... and yes they were. What stupid questions." Dom was starting to get irritable but the boys kept rattling on.

"How long did it take to build the place?"

"Almost three years, maybe even four, I suppose. I don't really remember and I doubt if we ever really kept track of the total time it took. Time wasn't important. We were treating the job as an apprenticeship. We learnt a helluva lot, you know."

"How did you do all this without anyone seeing you?"

"I still wonder about that."

"Why did your mother want it built?"

"Hey, look at this. Have you had a closer look at the rock above the door into the tunnel," said Dom, completely ignoring the last question. He closed his eyes and, as if it was only yesterday, picturing his young sister standing in that spot. Bending forward, he ran his fingers gently around the tip of a volcanic rock jutting from the top of the mound. "This is Rafaela's idea, a monument to our endeavours. She placed it directly above where the first shovel of soil had been dug that day in August 1940."

"If you stand with your back against the door front and face the ocean, that largest rock on your right- hand side was the original I was talking about. It was standing right there, and we never shifted it." Dom looked at the oversize rock, chuckled and said, "Would you have?" Once we made the decision that it was part of the entrance, this became the spot where it all began. Rafaela, bless her; recorded it for posterity."

"Hey come on. Quit talking, you guys, and let's go down in there to have a look," cut in Jock, who was becoming impatient. He could read Dom's body language and his old mate was looking more than a little ruffled. It's time to call the boys off, he thought. Dom is beginning to find them annoying. Meanwhile Dom, felt like yelling at the twins. He reckoned if they backtracked to what he'd told them that first afternoon, they should be able to figure it out easily enough. The silly young bludgers had been too intent in taking in his emotional outburst to listen properly. Typical teenagers, he snorted.

The trip along the passage was quicker this time because Dom remembered to bring a penlight. The vents were easier to find now they had light to see what they were doing. Some were a bit harder to open than others and the very last set wouldn't open at all.

"Hang on; I'll go out to see what's stopping it," Jeremy offered and took off before anyone had a chance to say another word.

"Wait, I'm coming too" yelled Josh to his quickly disappearing brother.

Dom looked fondly in their direction, as they raced off. They might be young men now, but they still have all the unbridled energy of those two eleven year-old boys I met on the beach five years ago. "Hey, hang on a bit both of you. Not so fast, he called. "You better make sure no one is around out there."

They stopped in their tracks. It was decided Jeremy should go outside alone while Josh monitored his progress by watching through the vents. "You open and shut each one as I walk along out there. That'll give me an idea where the openings all are," Jeremy said.

"Just make sure all your ferreting around the vent isn't too obvious," said Dom. "If we're going to keep an eye on those smugglers from inside here, we don't want anyone to find out about this place." He knew the crooks wouldn't find anything here in the moonlight and that they were unlikely to come here after dark, but Dom wanted to give the boys a bit of a wake-up call. They were a bit over-exuberant. "It's not a game, you know."

Dom's advice had its desired result. The reality of it hit Jeremy like a cold, hard fist in the stomach. He stared back towards his elderly mate. The uncertainties started to raise their ugly heads and begin to take hold. Even though coming here with Dom had been an exciting venture, they were playing for serious stakes."

Jeremy, having trouble finding the last stone that was causing the vent to malfunction, he signalled he was going to take a break. He wanted to check the car park and surroundings anyway. On returning, he signalled that all was clear up top Glad no one was around to see him as they would think signalling to vacant scrubland was the first sign of madness.

Back on the job, he searched and searched, but all the stones looked the same. This is ridiculous, he thought. I won't be able to tell just by looking at them. In front of the vent, he shrugged and extended his arms, palms up, in an 'I don't know' gesture. As he turned to walk back towards the tunnel entrance, he heard a muffled, "Wait".

Inside the tunnel, Josh called Dom. "Lend me the metal torch, please. I want to try some of my version of Morse code."

"Good thinking, ninety-nine," Dom replied with one of his over-used expressions. "Just don't damage the torch."

It took a while but at last Jeremy found the problem and, lying on his belly, he cleared the opening and finished the job by pulling a weird face at his brother. "You idiot, I hope you get scrub itch," Josh responded.

Later, Jeremy raved on about the whole outside set-up. "It really is brilliant, Dom. You can't see the open vents from the beach, I've checked."

"I know, lad, so did we."

"You can't see the individual rocks from that distance. There's not a hope in hell of anyone thinking the whole place is anything but rocks. The tangled scrub is a bit off-putting too. No one would be crazy enough to step any further than two feet into this part of the undergrowth. Have you ever tried to get through it, Dom? It grabs you by the hair, mauls you and holds you back, especially that vine with the vicious thorns. It's amazing really."

"Yes, it was like that back in the early days too. That's why we thought this was a great place to hide.

"It won't hurt to move some of the small branches on the beach front that block the vision from the spy holes, especially the one closest to the rocks which Croaky and Con hide behind," Jeremy suggested.

"Con…?" said their father. "Is that what you called the poor little bloke from the dinghy? Why…? Do you think he's being conned into taking part in the smuggling?"

"C'mon, Jock, they're crooks, no matter what reason each of them had for being there that night. Don't waste any sympathy on that lot," said Dom. "Hey you two Rhodes scholars, be careful with this pruning idea if I'm not around to supervise. The scrub needs to remain natural looking.

"But Dom, the crooks won't be able to notice too much detail in the moonlight," Josh suggested.

"No, but we don't need curious beachcombers discovering anything unusual in the daytime either. You know how gossip gets around. We don't want our cover blown. I've carried this secret for far too long to be careless about it now."

"When they come again, it'll still take a lot of concentration to see those blokes' faces properly," Jock said. "From the end porthole, we can see the whole boat ramp, but only partial view of the rocks where those blokes hide."

"There might not always be as much moonlight as there was that other night either," said Josh

"Aha, but I think there will be," said his father. "I've got a theory about that. I think they operate either on the full moon or the night either side of it, so they have plenty of light to get their cargo from the car to the boat."

Dom, gazing into space and only half-listening, suddenly focussed and stared at the others pensively. "You know what I think? Somehow there's got to be some local knowledge involved in this caper. They seem to know too much about the lay of the land, where all the isolated places are; that sort of thing."

"Yeah; I think you're right, Dom," Josh said. "Harry left a spotter at the gully on Boaties Beach Road. That's absolutely the best place for a lookout. How did he know that?"

"The track has been gouged out by some fairly stupid people bogging their vehicles after rain," added Jeremy. "It's slow-going to get a car around that mess, so there's time to warn the others to be prepared."

Jock agreed. "Yes, it's a bit of a coincidence for a visiting boat, from out at sea, to choose a random pick-up point which, by pure chance, is perfect for their operation. You could be right, Dom. It seems a local has a hand in this."

"Yep, and they'd have a contingency plan. There'll be fishing gear in the dinghy."

"Yeah, it wouldn't take too much effort to look like a couple of locals taking advantage of the moonlight. The fish usually bite well at night."

"Of course, they could transfer the goods on a dark night, but they'd have to use torches. Any local doing a bit of night-time mackerel trolling would wonder what the hell's going on. That would be enough to drag a curious fisherman closer in to shore for a look.

The fishing inspectors run night-patrols sometimes as well. They would check out that sort of carry-on. It stands to reason that the more natural the whole scene appears, the more chance the mob has of acting their way out of trouble."

"It's dark up top where they park the car, and the track to the beach is steep and covered in pea-gravel and pumice stone all the way from the parking area," added Dom. "Not a comfortable slog in the dark, that's for sure."

"Anyway, if the full-moon theory holds up, we've got a couple of weeks until their next visit," said Jock. "Let's get on with learning about Dom's hideout. That's more important at the moment."

Fifteen minutes ago, Dom had walked down to the end of the passage to have a quick look at the hidden doorway in the back wall and had wandered back when Josh asked for his torch. With the twins busy sorting out the vent problem, it gave the older man an opening, to talk privately to Jock. Dom quietly told him about the room hidden behind the tunnel, but he wanted to lead the boys on a bit before he showed it to them. While they waited for the twins to finish with the vents, Dom talked a bit more about the reasons for some of the construction techniques they used.

When he and his brothers were building the place, although they used a dry-stone technique for the walls, they concreted behind them. "You just can't see any cement or mortar from the front," Dom explained. "We didn't want to spoil the effect of the old-style look and we had no choice, anyway. Our little sister, Rafaela, kept saying, 'the stones will all fall down on top of us in the tunnel and we won't be able to save ourselves', so we packed cement into the back of the rocks to keep her happy. The idea pleased Vittorio as well. He had been worried about the sandy soil working its way into the cracks between the stones and leaving collapsed furrows up top, in the covering soil-mounds. The rest of us thought it was overkill at the time, but seeing how well everything has lasted, maybe the extra slog was a good idea."

Jock looked around and smiled. "You've certainly spent a lot of time on this."

"Well, it was wartime and we were too young to join the army, so we had plenty of time to work on this tunnel. Even with the magic of this place, I still have a huge regret. The thing that haunts me is that Mama anguished over something else. It was separate from the internment thing. I'm upset we didn't see it. She wrote a letter to her mother but never posted it. I found it after her death. As the war dragged on, her sons grew older. She worried about them going, one by one, to fight overseas, and maybe to never return. I can't even begin to imagine how she must have felt." With a disgusted snort, Dom continued, "I was bloody-well right there, Jock, supposedly experiencing life with her and the family, and I never even considered it. That's us blokes for you, eh? Ah well, I suppose if I had known, there'd be no answer for it, anyway."

CHAPTER 6

"The nearest town in those days was 60 kilometres away, and the local brickworks almost the same distance away in the other direction." Dom grinned. "Vehicles were a bit slower back then. The few dirt tracks we used were the forerunners of the more solid roads which didn't even begin to materialise for another 20 years or so. There was no bitumen street network at Mingleton in those days. At the time when we decided to build our tunnel, if we'd used bricks, getting them home would've involved lots of long, slow trips."

"Stone was the obvious choice," Dom pointed out. "As our family didn't want the locals to know we were building the underground room, it seemed important to use materials from around here." After giving Jock a wink, he looked directly at the twins and, tongue-in-cheek, said, "In case you haven't noticed lads, rocks are plentiful around here and a far lot cheaper than any other building product we might use. After all, it was wartime and jobs and money were scarce."

The boys weren't concentrating too much on Dom's latest chat about rocks because they were puzzling over his mention of an underground room. To them, it was so obvious there was only a tunnel there. What was the silly old bugger on about?

"Dom, there's no sign of any room down here. There's no possible way that there could be one. That back wall is a dry-stone wall. There isn't even a doorway, let alone a room, anywhere in sight," Jeremy said. "You've got to be kidding if you think you can trick us into thinking this long skinny passage is a room."

"Is that right? Just watch what I do and be prepared for a surprise, my learned lads." Using his index finger, Dom stepped back and traced a large imaginary rectangle in the air in front of the wall. "Believe it or not, there is a large door right in front of you."

"Well, since you are giving us a choice, we choose not to believe it," said Josh.

"Fair enough; let's see if I can prove you wrong."

"How do you think you're going to prove us wrong, Dom? You're standing in front of a rock wall, waving and pointing your finger like you're some sort of magician," scoffed Josh.

"Yeah; what good do you think that's going to do? Are you going to do the *open sesame* thing and hope a hole will magically appear in the wall?" Jeremy added.

Dom chuckled and took a strong hooked piece of wire about the length of a metal nail file out of his trouser pocket. Bending down on one knee, he carefully removed a long spike completely lodged in the rock wall almost at floor level. To get that spike out, he'd inserted the wire into a slot cut into the side of a greenish-coloured volcanic rock.

"There are another two spikes vertically above this one. The second is in the centre of the door and the third one is about 20 centimetres down from the top. Look for the rocks with green inclusions. That's where you'll find them. We need to remove those two as well." The, looking at Jock, he said, "Unless you know they're there, it's almost impossible to see them without using a very strong light." Dom handed the first spike to Jock. It was a solid enough piece of steel with a metal eyelet welded onto its flat end. "I won't bore you with the mechanics of the system, but trust me, these spikes securely lock the door into position on this side of the wall. There's a spare hook, high up in the top corner hidden in a groove under the roof-line in case we lose this one. Hard to find, but it's there."

Jock was looking at Dom with a new kind of respect.

"Here, you two young scrubbers, give me a hand in case the door's gone a bit stiff." With that, he shone the torch beam onto a stone containing a small blob of white quartz. Put your hands somewhere near that spot and shove like mad."

As the twins pushed; the huge door slowly creaked open, turning on a vertical, central steel pole. "Wow...," whispered Josh.

"Is 'wow' the only word you two know?" mumbled Dom, not unpleased with the fact that he had rendered the two of them practically speechless yet again.

They all rushed into the hallway behind the opening. There was another stone wall immediately behind the door. "Right, now we need to shut this door again, quickly," said Dom as he put his bucket of goodies down against the newly revealed back wall. In virtually the same motion as he let go of the bucket's handle, he grabbed a large Dolphin torch from amongst the contents. "There's another quartz-laden stone on this side. It indicates the best spot to push. Guesswork slows everyone down when speed is important. Who wants the torch? Here, hold onto this, young Jeremy, we'll need it soon."

"Way to go, Dom. Any more orders while you're at it?" asked Jeremy, with the sardonic tendency which the twins both reserved specially for the old man.

"Only the same one as before about closing the door as soon as possible; just shut your smart young mouth and push." Jock, standing to one side, chuckled happily. He was enjoying this afternoon immensely.

When the door was shut, it was impossible to miss the metal framework attached across the whole width of the door. Connected to that, a sophisticated, lever-operated arrangement, top, bottom and centre, effortlessly pushed a trio of metal tongues into solid U-shaped brackets on the adjacent door frame.

Once this clasp was slammed home, short of using a battering ram or detonating a stick of dynamite under it, there was very little chance of breaking the door open. "As you can imagine, the room becomes completely secure once we're bolted in behind this big monster," said Dom.

Jeremy found his voice again, although he sounded a bit squeaky when he asked, "Can we go down this new hallway?"

"Be my guests," said Dom. He stepped back to let the other three walk past. "I'll be the rear guard."

The torch beam lit up a dead-end at the top of the passageway that stopped them in their tracks. "Hey, there's no door here, just an open gap. Hang on, what's going on here?" Josh said, swinging the torch beam all over the place. There appeared to be another passage heading back parallel to the one they'd just walked along. "What's this zigzag thing, Dom? Is it some sort of joke?"

Dom started chuckling again as he followed his three mates along the progressively darker new hallway. In this second alleyway, he pulled his own small torch from his pocket. It was dark and the place smelt quite musty, a legacy of being closed up for so many years. Walking through gluey cobwebs in the dark was a weird, not to mention sticky experience for everyone. In the beams of both torchlights, the next entrance became obvious. It offered the same deal as at the other end of the passage. The third alleyway, also parallel to the others, took them back in the direction from which they'd just come.

"What the...?" Josh muttered irritably. "Dom, did you just love building narrow alleys, or what? How long do you expect us to do this walk down, walk back, walk down, walk back, thing?"

"Stop whinging, Lad. Shine the torch through the next door opening you come to and see what happens," said Dom.

No more hallways this time. They stood in the narrow entrance to a room the size of an extremely large lounge room. They saw that this ceiling was much higher than those of the tunnels. A better quality atmosphere made them feel more at ease than they had been in the labyrinth.

"Wow!" said Dom, deliberately imitating Josh. He laughed with pure delight as the chance of getting 'one-up' on the twins didn't come around often. Anyway, despite that small pay-back remark, he really was feeling, just Wow. He hadn't been in this room for more years than he cared to remember. The experience was making him feel like a young man again. He could sense Aldo, Vittorio, Pasquale, Rafaela and his parents standing beside him. It was an emotion-charged moment for him. Emerging from the reverie with a lump in his throat, Dom realised that something was missing "Hey, where's my bucket? Oops!" he laughed out loud. "I put it down to operate the lever on the large door and left it at the head of the first tunnel."

Left just inside the large swing door and temporarily forgotten, the bucket contained a few household essentials, most importantly, a two-litre container of fresh water and a Tupperware container of sandwiches. Jock tossed these two items into it, when they met Dom earlier on the beach.

As he showed the others around Catarina's room, Dom said, "There still should be some candles and other things in those cupboards."

The boys checked out the fruit boxes, nailed together one above the other, to form the 1930s version of a kitchen cabinet. "Every good housewife had one of those, back then," Dom added with a grin.

"Cool," said Jeremy, nodding his approval.

Almost in the centre of the room, up against a stone pillar, stood an old wooden table. Two Chianti bottles stood on it, waiting for the next generation of family to arrive. The straw-covered bases of these candle-holders hadn't been moved from where they'd stood since the Second World War. Each was crusted with multi-coloured wax trails, caked with grimy dust and topped off with a coating of the ever-present cobwebs.

Dom's lighter, cigarette papers and tobacco tin were a permanent fixture in his trousers' pocket. He lit the candles, took out a plug of roll-your-own tobacco and sat to have a smoke Jock, who was itching to check out the tunnels again, wandered off with the large torch to investigate the maze and collect Dom's plastic bucket.

"Ah, you're back with the sandwiches. Come and sit down, Jock," Dom said, looking and sounding, as if all the years had rolled away in the space of half-an-hour.

"It's diabolically clever, Dom," Jock said.

Dom just shrugged and replied, "We had to have some system to be able to open the room and then lock up again pretty damn quickly." Dom made an all-encompassing movement with his arms, saying, "As I've already said, this was for Mama's benefit alone." Dom's eyes became misty as he recalled that past era. "She was a wonderful mother you know."

He took another puff of his cigarette and continued the story. "If anyone did accidentally find the tunnel, we hoped their discovery would end there. The room always was meant to remain our ultimate family secret." He really is in his element down here, reflected Jock, amazed at the change in Dom since they opened that door.

For ages, the four of them remained sitting on an assortment of aged, wooden chairs, around the solid table, eating sandwiches and allowing the atmosphere of the whole place to wash over them. As the twins and Jock sat, taking in everything around the room, Dom was lost again in the precious memories of those special years. Almost unable to believe the evidence of his own eyes, Jeremy was stunned. "It's unreal. We've ridden our bikes over this hundreds of times and never guessed what was buried under us."

"Anyone want another ham-sanger?" Josh asked, and broke the spell for a moment. "There's still four left."

Against the far-side wall, were three homemade double-decker bunks, all designed with a double bed-base and a single bed above, and complete with dusty coir fibre mattress. Dom remembered the fights he'd had with his brothers over that extra double bed. One was for their parents to sleep in; their little sister claimed the second and each of the gangly youths wanted the other. There had been no winners on that one. It became a case of first-in, best-dressed.

"These beds might prove handy," Jock commented. They had to be safely inside this room before the crooks arrived next time. The wait could be a long one. It was necessary to remain well-hidden while they waited. Their lives could depend on it. Might as well be comfortable while we wait, thought Jock.

"Why did you and your brothers build the maze?" asked Josh. "It all seems a bit weird to me."

"Maze...? We never thought of the passages as that. They were just an added precaution," replied Dom. "The design of that 'maze', as you call it, was to prevent any tell-tale light leaks. Light can't travel around corners so the extra walls were made to keep the light inside Catarina's room. Simply put, they are light traps." Dom looked back towards the entrance to Catarina's room and grinned. "I suppose we did get carried away a bit."

"Just a bit, you reckon?" Josh added, with a cheeky grin.

Dom acknowledged Josh's grin with one of his own. "I suppose the light trap is a sort of maze. We relied on it to give us some breathing space to sneak out the back door."

All eyes immediately turned towards the plank door in the rear wall. The message pinned to it, stated bluntly, 'leave the dark behind you.' The double entendre echoed the Bellini family's strong belief in surviving whatever was thrown at them.

"That door is different from the main one," Jock said.

"Everything about this other passage is a more simplified version of what there is in the main tunnel. There's a rock door further down the passage. It has a handle and lock, like a normal door. The hinges are on the left, but there is a difference. We did fit our distinctive security mechanism to it. The light trap, this side of the room, has a different layout, and the tunnel is doglegged and much shorter. The entrance is hidden in a cluster of rocks below the back-corner of the car park, near the mangroves where the land slopes down to Hallies Beach; near where we put our crab pots these days." Dom explained that this tunnel entrance was more exposed than the front one, but had been nowhere near the hard work the other had been.

"Wouldn't the back tunnel pass right under the current road?" Jock asked.

"Yeah, it does. I've stood up there quite a few times and done the calculations."

"So, you reckon it'd be okay to walk through the tunnel now that traffic drives over it? Has the roof been strong enough to cope with the constant passage of vehicles over the years?"

"Yep, our handiwork is about two metres below the track. We figured that depth wouldn't be too shallow. The timber roof is like a good old-fashioned wooden bridge. It's solid, dependable, and has a benefit that a traffic bridge doesn't: it's protected from the outside elements."

"Time wouldn't have weakened the timber, you don't think?

"I can't see why it should have done. Anyway, it hasn't collapsed yet. But I haven't been back under here for about 40 years, so I don't really know. It should be okay. We built things to last in those days.

It's sturdy, and by my reckoning, the traffic only crosses it at one spot at right angles over tunnel. It's a very short overpass, which you'd think would be an advantage structurally.

"Well, Dom," Jock suggested, "Let's go and have a look to see if there's been any damage under here."

"Right you are, but let me go first in case of a cave-in. You boys could go for help, if needs be. Though surely, you'd think it highly unlikely it would collapse the very minute I walk under it after all these years."

"There's no promise it won't either, Dom," said Josh. "After all, you are a bit of a shocker sometimes." The twins began chuckling. Dom gave them a calculated scowl but, turning his back on the twins, he gave Jock a wink and a grin.

"Right you three, stay here. Mind you, like I said, I don't expect any problems. There'd already be a bloody great hole across the roadway up top, if any part of this place had collapsed. A gap in the road like that would be pretty hard to miss, I'd say."

"Yeah, and I reckon the whole of Mingleton would know about the tunnel by now."

They watched Dom's progress until he rounded the corner. Progressing slowly and cautiously, he checked the timber beams in the roof for faults and weaknesses before returning about ten minutes later. "At least I didn't have to check the vents in the first arm of the tunnel."

"Why not?" asked Jeremy.

"Because there aren't any," said Dom, chortling as the boys tried unsuccessfully to find a smart reply to that. "There was nowhere to put air inlets, except in the roof. If we'd done that," he said, "We may as well have put up signs saying: 'Danger! Underground ventilation shafts in the area'. Great secret hideout that would have been, eh?" He smiled with satisfaction. "Everything is fine. The walls and roof seem as good as the day we made them. Want to come for a walk now?"

Hell, thought Jeremy, it seems a bit spooky, walking under the road. Lost in thought about their situation, he jumped when he felt a hand on his arm.

"Do you reckon anyone walking up top could hear us?" whispered Josh.

"Shit, you frightened me," yelped Jeremy. His heart was still doing somersaults.

"Shut up you two," said their father, "Just in case anyone is up there."

59

"Arrrgghh!" A muffled shriek came from somewhere in the dark. It was Jock. "Bloody Gecko; it frightened the life out of me. I thought it was a bloody snake until I realised how small it was."

"I thought you told us to be quiet, Dad. The next thing we know, you're yelling like a Banshee… Good one, Dad," said Jeremy.

"Why didn't you just make this place the exit instead of going to all the trouble of extending the tunnel? You said no one ever came around here without your family knowing about their presence. It seems like a lot of unnecessary work to go right out to the beach with the passageway?" said Jock.

"There was no safe place to hide in the gully if the unexpected should happen," replied Dom. "We would have given the game away, had we been under surveillance. The gully is open to everyone's view from every direction." Their elderly mate went on to explain that the family thought the shorefront was a better choice because of the fringe of trees and undergrowth out there. They also believed that the mangroves, directly across from the exit, gave them an added choice of shelter. In the family's opinion, there were more places to disappear into the natural vegetation out there than back in the gully.

"Now why didn't I realise that?" said Jock.

With the discussion finished, they followed Dom's torchlight along the corridor until they could see what appeared to be a dark, blank wall ahead. "Okay, this is where it could get a bit hairy; the outlook is a bit narrow. This is the exit. We only put two spy holes in here because we are right on the corner of the beach. With only the narrow space between the mangroves to keep an eye on, two openings were sufficient. Besides, remember, in those days, no one came here but us. There are a few blind spots nowadays that we didn't have to worry about back then, but they relate more to the roadway into the car park than the beach."

"Do you reckon? I don't think things have changed all that much these days," commented Jock. "People who park here, ignore that side of the beach. I've never seen anyone peer over the edge into Hallies. They just head for the track down to Boaties Beach. Anyway, just to be on the safe side, don't you think we should only use this tunnel as an entrance?"

"Yeah Dad, that's good thinking!" The boys had caught up with them.

"Well, it's only common sense. This hidden observation-post idea only exists because Dom trusted us with some privileged information. It is going to keep us safe during this foolhardy venture, but we owe him big-time. Anything we can do, to keep his secret, is important. Come on," he said somewhat resignedly, "let's get back inside the room."

*****

"What time is it?" asked Dom…No one knew.

Back around the old wooden table, mugs of water in hand, everyone was thinking about what was to come.

Jock broke the silence. "What's the next move, Dom?"

"Let's go home."

"Shhh… listen … what are those bashing noises?" asked Jock. Then he remembered that, on the way back to Catarina's room, he had heard a rumbling noise and the distant sound of a car.

Jeremy thought he had heard car doors slamming. "Quick let's get into the front tunnel to see what's happening on the beach."

At first the beach was empty, but a few minutes later a family walked into view.

"Hell, that car drove right above us while we were in the back tunnel."

"Shh, let's get back into the room. Quickly! Who wants to take the first guard duty at the peephole?" asked Jock.

Jeremy volunteered and silently hoped that the visitors would be gone in five minutes. That was wishful thinking. Watching the three little kids out there, it looked like they weren't very likely to let their Mum and Dad drag them away too soon. The little boy and his father were searching amongst the rocks directly in front of Jeremy's observation post. Jeremy caught a snippet of conversation between one of the children and its father. "Dad, come and look at this crab. It's all hairy. Can I catch it?"

"No son, leave it where it is. We don't want to hurt it. Come on, let's keep walking." Jeremy breathed a sigh of relief as they moved off.

Meanwhile, Dom, Jock and Josh were busy planning for Croaky's next visit. Trying to be as quiet as possible and unsure whether their voices would carry or not, they decided this would be a good test.

"We should bring some books to read. That'll keep us occupied while we wait."

"Forget the books," said Jock. "We won't be on a five-star holiday, you know. We can't have too much light down here. It's too risky."

"Well, what will we do if we have to wait under here for hours? We'll be dead-set bored, that's for sure."

"That's your problem, Mate. You pair should have thought about that, when you insisted on going ahead with this crazy scheme of yours," said his father, in a slightly satisfied tone. In truth, the boys had used emotional blackmail on him and Dom. They need to learn about patience the hard way, he thought.

Jeremy could see the young mother at the water's edge with her small black dog. At least the dog isn't up here sniffing near the gully, that's a good sign, he thought. They hadn't considered the problem of dogs and their bloodhound habits. He followed the progress of the father and his kids. The youngest girl, not much more than a toddler, was continually on the move. At one stage, she began to run towards the scrub directly in front of Jeremy. "Holly," her dad yelled out "Stop. …Wait for us. Don't go in the bushes, there might be snakes."

When her father ran up to grab hold of her, Jeremy held his breath; they were too close for comfort. although he knew that he couldn't be seen, he still felt vulnerable. There weren't any sounds coming from the room behind him, even as close as he was to the others. Good, he thought. Dom, Jock and Jeremy will be talking and I can't hear voices at all, not even a whisper. The beachcombers were standing very close to the edge of the scrub now. They didn't even look in his direction.

"Come on Elise and Robert, we'll go back now before we lose Holly. We've been here for half an hour already and Mum is starting to walk back with Roscoe. It's time to go back to Grandma and Grandad's beach house. They'll be waiting for us. If we don't hurry up, it will soon be dark."

Jeremy watched them until they walked past Harry's rocks at the top end of the beach and disappeared. There was a lot of giggling and crunching as they ran up the gravelled track. The dog yapped happily and car doors opened and shut. Jeremy heard the vehicle start and then its sound faded into the distance.

"They've gone," said Jeremy as he walked back into the room. "That was good practice. We've now got a bit of an idea about what we will and won't see out there. I lost sight of the family before they reached the car park path."

"That means we won't know for sure where Harry and his crew are at all times. They could be out of sight for longer than we'd like, and depending on where Croaky throws the anchor in, their dinghy mightn't be in viewing range either," said Jock. "At least now we know we can hear footsteps in the gravel up to the parking area, but once they get up there, we've got Buckley's of knowing exactly where they are. That's good reason to be grateful for the unexpected arrival of that family today, I guess." "So, that settles it. We can't afford to use the back tunnel, except in an emergency, or unless we're absolutely sure it's safe to do so." He glanced around the table and asked, "All agreed?"

Come on, let's call it a day," said Dom.

CHAPTER 7

It was a Saturday morning again and there was another boat anchored out from the Point. The twins gulped down their breakfast and Jeremy, after a quick glance at his brother said to Isabel. "Do you need anything done this morning, Mum? We thought we'd go down to see what's been washed up by the tide over the last few days."

Given the all clear, they grabbed their bikes and pedalled the quarter mile to Boaties Beach. Whenever they saw a vessel out front these days, the twins took the long way around. The possibility of a crew member from the cabin cruiser seeing the twins suddenly appear on this beach every time the boat arrived was a risk they didn't want to take.

"The need to think about that bloody boat and having to be careful about everything we do when we go to Hallies and Boaties lately is a bit of a pain. Sometimes I wonder what we've started," Jeremy said to his brother.

"Yeah, the whole thing is starting to get at me big time. I get a bit keyed up when we're going to check out a boat now. This is number four already this week," agreed Josh. "It's just the waiting; the suspense of it all. I wish they'd hurry up and come again."

As they pedalled over Dom's tunnel, at about a hundred yards or so from the parking area, they planned to slow down and listen. Jeremy, ahead of his brother by about 20 metres, brought his bike to a stop and waited for his brother to do the same. "You'd think there would be an echo or something wouldn't you? There's just nothing, no difference. The ground sounds the same as anywhere else around here, when you ride over it."

64

There were no vehicles in the parking area so it was a huge surprise to walk over the rise and be confronted with a crowded beach. People were fishing all along the water's edge, each person absorbed in what he or she was doing. A few looked back over their shoulders, giving Josh and Jeremy a nod as the twins scrutinised the most recent tidal debris. However, most of the visitors were too busy making sure their lines didn't get tangled together in the ebb and flow of the waves to take too much notice of the twins. It was an example of wall-to-wall fishing at its very best.

"How can they put up with it?" puzzled Jeremy as he kept his eyes on the debris ahead of him "It would drive me insane."

"No Luck today, Josh; no fishing lures or marker buoys, only mangrove leaves, seaweed and plastic bottles."

Just ahead, Jeremy watched as the tip of someone's rod dived towards the sand. "C'mon; let's see what he's caught."

"Hi," said Jeremy to the young fisherman. "What do you reckon it is?"

"It nibbled and played around with the prawn bait before it picked it up and took off. Whoops! Hey, it's off again," said the young bloke, playing his line out. "It's probably a Mangrove Jack or a Sweetlip," he said as he concentrated on the job at hand.

They watched the rod tip moving up and down as the young fisherman played his quarry. He had a bit of a fight on his hands. The fish must be at least pan-sized, considering the light gear being used. The fish would 'run', the angler would turn it, wind it back a bit, until the fish, with a renewed surge of power, took off again. It took a fair while, but eventually a 40 centimetre Grass Sweetlip flapped furiously to the foamy water's edge.

"You bee-yooty!" yelled the young fellow. He dealt with the fish, threaded new bait on his hook and cast his line back into the waves. With that done, he had time to talk, while waiting for the next bite.

"I'm Graham," he said. "Are you visiting or from around here?"

"We're locals. I'm Josh."

"And Jeremy," his brother chimed in as they extended their hands for the obligatory handshake. "What's the big occasion? Why are there so many people here?"

"It's our club's annual fishing competition. An away-trip this time," said Graham.

"Looks like you got a reasonable turnout," replied Josh, looking up and down the beach. "There must be about twenty people here."

"Are those blokes out there in that dinghy part of your lot as well?" Jeremy innocently inquired.

"Yep, we towed the dinghy behind the truck. The mob of us drew the winners' names out of a hat and I lost out again. That's why I'm on the beach and they are in the dinghy What's new? I'm never real fortunate when it comes to anything involving luck."

"You're like me," said Josh. "It's a waste of time even buying raffle tickets."

"Two of the older blokes hit the jackpot this time. They work hard for the club, so everyone was happy for them. In fact there wasn't much whinging about it this time at all, thankfully."

Josh, with what he thought was an ultra-subtle enquiry, said "I suppose they know the area pretty well."

"No, they don't," said Graham. "They've only been here once before. We've got the weigh-in station round at Mingleton in the Council's Picnic Area and an old bloke, who was driving his tractor along the beach, towed our boat and trailer down to the water. He suggested that we follow the shoreline round here, so a few of us did, but a lot of club members stayed behind. The local bloke told us that there were a few big rocks and other obstacles, but the tide is going out so we'd be okay to walk around the water's edge. Local knowledge is always handy and much appreciated. We've been fishing the tide out along the way but it'll be dead low soon. We'll fish our way back on the incoming tide."

The trio chatted for a while. When Graham got another nibble, Josh said, "Nice to have met you, Mate. We'll take off now and leave you in peace to concentrate. Good luck with the competition." With that, they collected their bikes and headed home to spend the rest of the day catching up on their school assignments and generally just mucking about around the yard. It was pointless going back to the beach. They had eliminated today's boat from the suspect list.

*****

On Sunday, they went off on their own again. "Well, at least we've been home a bit more lately. We won't have Mum wondering what we're up too by going off to meet Dom so often."

"I hope it's a bit quieter today. I wonder if we can get from the track to anywhere near the tunnel entrance without being seen from the beach. Let's go check it out."

The place was deserted.

"We need to find a marker – a reference point – of some sort, at the top-end of the gully to guide to the tunnel entrance. It should be somewhere close to the car park so we can get straight down into the tunnel without being seen from the ocean. After walking along the beach for quite a distance, they turned and headed into the scrub. Not stopping at the tunnel door, they continued towards the back of the area and climbed the rise to reach the concrete slab of Dom's old hut. They kept walking along the car park roadway towards Dom's 40 year-old Bowen mango tree and a solitary clump of lantana, and took more notice of the little things they usually ignored.

"Perfect," Jeremy said, "Now we'll walk back towards the junction of the tracks into the bays and then retrace our steps. That's when we forget about anything else other than sorting out the rest of the markers. After that, we need to find out if we can get into the tunnel without anyone out near the boat ramp, seeing us."

Too easy!" said Josh. "Here's the intersection. Now, let's turn back and see what sort of map we can make of the landscape." A few metres along Boaties Bay Road, they veered off to follow some well-defined wheel marks through the bladey-grass until they reached the quarry. The short easy walk across bare earth, crushed aggregate and past the heaps of discarded scrap-metal, ended at the crudely-formed side exit, pushed through by locals to create a shortcut to the car park. A lumpy burl on an old gum tree, a favoured and well-used wallaby trail which led towards the ocean and a Cocky-apple tree with a U-shaped trunk were the final choices for landmarks. Despite the grasstrees scattered everywhere, plenty of clumps of bladey grass and a few dead branches to move out of their way; the going wasn't too bad at all.

"Once we get used to where we're heading, we won't need to worry too much about landmarks, especially after we show them to Dad and Dom."

"Okay, let's go home for lunch and come back later this afternoon."

At about two o'clock they told Isabel that they were going out again. "Just over to the quarry and probably to down Boaties to see if there's anything interesting going on there this arvo." Once they were back in the scooped-out hole that constituted the base of the quarry, they checked out all the old car bodies dumped there over time by the local louts. There was rusty red, upside-down Torana which almost hid the car track. They found it this morning, and, at the time, thought it was too good a marker to ignore. It had to be tagged as another landmark.

Josh dug a stopwatch out of his pocket. "Lucky I remembered to bring it," he baited his brother. As they took the first step away from the rusty Torana, he pushed the timer button. "It will make it easier for Dom and Dad, if we give them a time-frame to follow."

Jeremy had to admit that his brother did have a point there. It took fifty-eight seconds from the Torana to reach the Cocky-apple tree. Once they timed that leg of the trip, Josh put the timer back in his pocket, and smirking, pulled out a notebook.

"Don't even think about saying any more," said his brother. "I get the message. You're really well prepared. Well, whoopee doo," grumbled Jeremy.

From the start of the gully, the twins couldn't see the beach or the ocean, so they assumed they couldn't be seen from that direction either. They walked on steadily and soon reached the mango tree and the clump of lantana. From there, they could see the end of the point and the white caps beyond it. It was a bit choppy out there today.

"Okay, this is the stage where it could get a bit dicey." The cement slab was on the left and there was an awful lot of beachside scrub between it and the sea. The problem was an open patch about the size of a football field they needed to sneak across. They might just be lucky.

"Hang on, Josh, you've got a red T-shirt on so, how about you stay here, and I'll go down and stand in the middle of the boat ramp? The tide's a fair way out. I'll yell 'yes' any time I can see you."

"Right; when you reach the boat ramp, yell out *ready'*. That's when I'll try to get down to the tunnel without you seeing me. Watch this spot like a hawk and we'll see what happens." It was about four minutes before Josh heard the shout. He took his time getting there and by the time he was standing in position to jam the lever behind the rock he still hadn't heard Jeremy call out. After standing for about five more minutes in front of the tunnel entrance, he went out to the beach through the undergrowth. As he stepped out of the brush onto the sand, Jeremy yelled, "Yes, I can see you now."

"Cool," said Josh when Jeremy came up along the sand to meet him. "You really couldn't see me in there at all? Are you sure you were concentrating?"

"I didn't take my eyes away even for a second," was the injured reply. "That's why I was so long before I yelled 'ready'. I couldn't see you at all from the boat ramp, even when you were standing exactly where I left you. I searched and searched, but red shirt and all, you were invisible. There must be something solid, blocking the view.

From up there at the waterfall rocks, we can still see over whatever it is, towards the sea. Weird, isn't it?"

"Cool," said Josh again. "Let's go home."

*****

"Hurry up, here comes the bus." Josh raced down the road and jumped onto the running board, just as the driver was about to take off. The bus slowed to a stop as Jeremy reached it.

"I didn't see you two coming. You'll have to wake up a bit earlier," grumbled Ned. "I can't have all this unnecessary stopping and starting, and don't jump onto the bus when I'm about to drive off. It's dangerous."

"Yeah, yeah, we're sorry," apologised the twins as they made their way down the aisle.

"Whinging old bastard," Josh said to Jeremy. "What class have we got today, just before lunch?

I've got physics, so that means you've got geography."

"Bummer; our class won't finish on time. It never does. Old Jessamy will have some work he expects us to finish off before the bell, and there's always someone who can't get finished on time. I thought that was our schedule but I hoped I was wrong. The usual thing will happen. What's on tomorrow then?" asked Josh.

"What's this, 'twenty questions' time? I'm not so excited about my lessons, that I have the timetable printed inside my forehead, you know."

"Give me a break, Jeremy. Stop whinging and grab your work diary."

"God, why can't you do it yourself? We've both got a double English class," Jeremy said after flicking through the pages.

"Hmmm, tomorrow it is then. We'll go down to St.Vinnies at lunch time to get some dark clothes for everyone."

"Lucky none of the kids are around to see us going in here," said Josh, as they walked through the doorway of the local opportunity shop the next day.

"Here's a black T-shirt" said Jeremy.

"No good; we need something with long sleeves."

They ferreted around in the racks and found two scruffy black nylon tracksuits and a couple of hardly-worn 2XL Rashies. One was dark grey, and the other was black with a hardly noticeable sports logo on the upper left chest area.

"They'll be perfect. They won't even make us too hot when we're wearing them. All we need now is two more pairs of long pants."

After a search of the next rack, they settled on some black, elastic-waisted fishing trousers.

"Seven dollars for the lot; what a bargain we've got. Don't show any of the guys at school though. They'll think it's a great laugh. These aren't the most upmarket outfits, are they?" Josh was all fired up. He checked no one was in hearing range before saying aloud, "Come on then, Harry, hurry up and get here. We're ready and waiting."

"I don't know about those Rashies not being upmarket. I'd be happy enough to wear one of them when we go fishing," Jeremy admitted.

That afternoon, when they were showing Dom their purchases, Jeremy laughed and said, "It's getting a bit exciting now, don't you think?"

Dom looked dolefully at them, shook his head and grunted.

Not the least bit put-out by Dom's reaction, Josh said, "We thought it would be a good idea if we left the stuff in your ute. That will give us with one less thing to worry about if we have to move in a hurry."

"C'mon Josh, we better go home and start our homework. What do you reckon though, Dom? Good gear, eh?"

"You've done well. I couldn't have done much better myself. No actually that's wrong. I would have been a bit more discerning than you've been. I didn't realise you two were so old-fashioned." And he smirked.

*****

Josh looked up from writing in the diary. "I can't believe we are doing this. We must have been crazy to push the idea onto Dom and Dad."

"Well, it's done now. We've have to live with it. It would look bad if we backed out now."

"What about the set-up at Boaties'? Dom and his family are legends aren't they?" Jeremy was still gobsmacked at what Dom had shown them.

"Yep, that bloody old git, Dom… What about this arvo? I could have punched his lights out. …Old-fashioned…!" spluttered Josh. "I know he was only baiting us, but it's the way he smirks when he does it. That gets on my goat sometimes. He knows how to push the right buttons, the old mongrel."

Jeremy laughed at his brother's irritation. "He knows how to flick your switches anyway. But getting back to this weird scheme of ours, if the underground room wasn't there, I think I would have wanted to bail out about now. At the beginning, it seemed a responsible thing to do, but now I'm getting really toey. I wish there had been more clues, so we could have dumped all this on the Coast Watch guys."

His brother was only half-listening. He was more focussed on Dom's surprise revelation.

"Can you believe how hard it must have been for Dom and his family to build that place? What about the big door and the maze? How clever is that? ...Jeremy, you do realise that, if we'd gone to the authorities that next day, we would have missed out on something incredible. I'm happy to sacrifice my nervous stomach for that."

"Yeah, I suppose so. You've got to hand it to them. It's tremendous."

CHAPTER 8

Isabel called out, "Boys, breakfast is ready." Every Sunday, they sat around the table on the front patio to eat their bacon and eggs. It was a family ritual, come rain, hail or shine. Well, with the exception of any morning when a cyclone was bearing down on them.

"It's a pity Dad has to work today. Look how glassed out the water is. It's like a millpond." Josh took a sip of his orange juice and casually said to both Isabel and Jeremy, "There's a cabin cruiser anchored out off the Point. I wonder if we should take a leaf out of their book and see if Dom wants to take the dinghy out to do a spot of fishing." His quick glance at his brother was a bit more calculated though.

"Good idea," said their mother, "We could do with some nice fresh fish for tea. I'll prepare some coleslaw and a potato bake when I get home." Isabel never doubted that they would have fish for tea when Dom was in the boat.

"Let's give Dom a ring," suggested Jeremy. In next to no time it was all arranged for ten o'clock. "He says that we're just in time to catch the last half hour before the top of the tide and then we can fish the outgoing. We'll ride our bikes over to Dom's place. He offered to come and get us in the ute, but I said we need the exercise."

"Don't forget the Sun-block," advised Isabel. The boys rolled their eyes. "I can hear Marge's car out front. See you this afternoon. Have a good day and tell Dom I said thanks for babysitting for me." With that, she grabbed her bag and went out the back door chuckling quietly to herself.

"That's really funny," muttered Josh. "It must be time to chuck that joke away. It's well past its use-by date."

By ten-fifteen, Dom was driving the purple Ford Dexta across the sand. The boys were standing on the carry-all with the dinghy on the trailer behind. They were all set for a pleasant day on the water. Their ulterior motive wasn't going to spoil their day out. The old tractor wasn't going to be alone on the beach this morning, either, by the looks of it.

"Twenty two parked here already today, Dom. I hope there's some room left out there for us."

Once the outboard was cutting smoothly through the water, Don grinned and asked, "Where do you want to go first

"What about the Point?"

"Be a bit crowded there today, wouldn't you think?"

"We'll chance it. Maybe that boat is gone by now." When they rounded the rock spur at the edge of the small tidal island, the boat they wanted to have a look at remained anchored across the bay. Dom motored over slowly and gave them a wave. They acknowledged his gesture, so Dom cut his motor and slowed to a stop. Once their wake had settled, the dinghy didn't move much in the oily-looking water.

"Catching anything?" He asked the two blokes in the other boat.

"I've had a few nibbles" said one of them.

"Bit shallow here, I think," said the other. "We're thinking about moving. We've be here just pottering around for an hour or so. We thought we'd move into deeper water to catch the first of the outgoing."

"Yep, that's what we thought we'd do too," said Dom. "You know the area do you?"

"Not really, we're here on holiday. We've come down from up North. One of our mates has a place down here in Mingleton, in Currajong Street."

"Not Ron's place is it?" asked Dom. "He built it himself; white painted, cement block place. Now what the hell did he tell me he does for a living?" Dom pondred.

"He's a mango grower, from up our way. He's my next door neighbour actually. We're staying at his beach house for another week yet."

"That's right, I remember now. Tell him that Dom the fisherman said *g'day* when you see him. Want to know a good spot?"

"We'd really appreciate the help, Mate. We know our way around Lucinda, but we're a bit lost when it comes to this area."

"Well, there's a big pile of bombies in the middle of the next bay. They're in deeper water and, if you go around the back of them, you'll find a good rocky ledge. It's going to be our first port of call for the day. Good spot for trailing for mackerel too, if they're running." Dom yanked the rope on his pull-start outboard and called, "See ya.

The boys and I are heading over there now. You can follow us if you like. There are plenty of spare spots," and then to the twins he said, "Ahoy, me hearties, off we go."

"What's up with you this morning, Dom? Anyone would think you'd won Gold Lotto or something."

"Nope. It's a great day, I'm in good company, and have my favourite fishing line. What more could a man want?" chuckled Dom.

"C'mon, you're laying it on a bit thick now. The thought of babysitting us, as you often put it, doesn't always make you this happy. Why are you so chirpy?"

"Does a man have to have a reason to be happy?" Dom grinned. "Well, for starters, the blokes in that boat over there are not our suspects – wrong voices – and they were too free with their information. There's no reason for them to be here other than for the fishing, that's for sure. What a lovely, lovely day to spend with such nice young fellows. I'm glad you thought of coming out here."

"Thank God we're almost at the rock ledge," said Jeremy. "If we have to listen to you raving on with all that 'what a lovely day and such good company' crap for much longer, I think I'll either puke or swim ashore, sharks and all."

"It's a shame Isabel's not home," said Dom continuing with his mad mood. "There is your place. You could have given your mother a wave as went flying past," he said. "C'mon, smile. It won't crack your cheekbones, you know," and with that, he burst out laughing.

The seagulls squawked and chopped and changed positions on their rocky perches as Dom's dinghy nosed in closer to their chosen fishing spot. After finding their favourite anchorage, the trio settled down to listen to the gentle wash of water against the hull of their boat. After waiting for well over twenty minutes without a bite, Jeremy's mind started to wander. We'll need a couple of stools in the tunnel, he thought. We can't risk getting fidgety, so we'll need to be comfortable. Wonder where we can get some?

"Whoops, I've got a bite. Hey Dom, Josh, I've got the first fish. Hah, beat you two."

They ended up catching half-a-dozen stripy bass, three really large blueys, two wire-netting cod and three really good-sized sweetlip. The fish were biting well now and a stack of under-size parrotfish and a rock barramundi were returned to the water until they 'grew up a bit'. The small tomato cod around here never grow much bigger than what anyone would term as 'miniature,' so they always had a free feed at everyone's expense before they were hauled in, de-hooked and unceremoniously chucked back in disgust.

"Well, that's enough for a couple of meals. I think we should call it a day? It's not a good idea to get too greedy," said Dom.

The blokes in the other boat had taken their advice and it looked like they were catching fish too. "See ya... and thanks for the tip," they called as Dom and the boys motored past.

"What'd they just say, after 'see ya'?" asked Dom.

"I think they were thanking us for dropping them onto a good spot," said Jeremy. "They were smiling anyway."

Back in the yard after they'd washed the tractor, cleaned the boat and filleted the fish, Dom said, "Take these home for Isabel, I've got plenty in the freezer."

"Mum will expect you to come for tea anyway, Dom. The usual time, about six, okay?"

"Right you are. Tell her I'll bring some of her favourite gelato for dessert. I bought a new flavour this month."

*****

The four blokes cleaned up for Isabel after tea. "Go and do some work on your patchwork quilt, while we do this," they'd told her.

"You must be inspired after the craft show," said Dom.

"How was it, by the way?" asked Jock.

"Great. Do you mind if I take you up on the offer? I'm not trying to be anti-social. It's just that I have to get it finished for next month and there's not a lot of time left. Thanks for the fish ...and the gelato, Dom. It was lovely. You need to buy that particular flavour again." Isabel smiled at him and said, "Give me a yell, will you, before you go home?"

They left Isabel to her sewing and wandered down to the little beach in front of the house. Sitting on the sand, Dom lit up a smoke as they brought Jock up to speed on today's investigation.

This brought to mind what he'd be thinking about when he was sitting in the boat this morning, so Jeremy suddenly asked, "Dom, have you got any spare wooden stools at your place? We haven't got any."

Dom looked at Jeremy in amazement and thought, away with the fairies, that's what he is. We're talking about more serious matters, and he's worrying about bloody furniture. Kids...! Out loud, he asked, "What the hell do you want them for?"

When Jeremy explained, Dom, feeling that he may have been a bit hasty, told Jeremy that he had one with metal legs, but he'd try to get another couple at the local Op Shop when went into town sometime this week.

They chatted for a while, but decided that, other than tidying up the hideout, that's all they could do to be ready for the next time their suspects visited. They couldn't make too many plans at this stage, so there was nothing for it but to play the waiting game. …And the next full moon was only a week away.

*****

On Tuesday afternoon, the twins pedalled around to Dom's. Jock didn't have a day off until Thursday so the twins weren't completely forthcoming about where they were going. They told their mother they were going around to Mingleton to treat themselves to a Mars Bar from the caravan park shop kiosk, and then they were going to walk along the main beach looking for lures and floats washed up by the tide. They planned on being away for a few hours at least, and thought they might end the day at the estuary, catching up on a bit of the tourists' fishing gossip.

It was Isabel who had made the suggestion that they call in to visit Dom. "I've made him a chocolate slice and some jam drops for his freezer. Drop them off for me please."

"Hello you two, what are you up to?" Dom was out in his backyard collecting the day's eggs from the fowl house.

"…Want to drive us round to Boaties for a while? It won't be dark for two hours yet." They bundled the stool from Dom's shed, into the back of the ute and the boys squeezed in the front beside him. "I haven't been able to find you any more highchairs yet," he said. "The lady at the Op-Shop told me that I had to be pretty lucky to get them. They are popular and seem to be snavelled up as soon as they walk in the door."

"That's okay. This one is good, and one is better than none."

Along the track into Boaties, Dom had to move off to the side of the road a bit, to make room for a battered old Toyota sedan to pass them. "There's Blue," he said and acknowledged the elderly bloke with a downward thrust of his index finger as they passed. "It looks like he's been fishing off the rocks around here. Luckily, he doesn't go fishing after dark because of his eyesight. I don't know what would happen if he came upon Harry and the mob. He'd just about have a heart attack, I think."

"He's a good example of a local guy who could drop in quite innocently on those crooks one night. That's why we have to be able to give the authorities enough to work with," said Josh. "We have to get rid of those mongrels from our area."

When he parked the old ute and got out, Dom started to head towards the usual dirt-ramp onto the beach.

"Hey Dom, wait. Come over this way, past your old cement slab. Let's go in the back way." They headed for a spot they'd always called 'the waterfall rocks' and followed along a recently carved-out creek bed. It was fairly easy walking, even though Josh kept snagging the stool's long-legs in the bladey grass and on other rubbishy shrubs.

"Some mothers do have 'em," said Dom, shaking his head after the second mishap and expecting a few more to be in the offing.

Down at the edge of the main bowl of the gully just below the lantana bush, Dom got them to move a few of the flatter rocks into a sort of haphazard pattern. "Stepping stones," he said. "Don't be too obvious. You know what to do, don't you? Vary the height and distance between them. They need to look natural – six or so here, and one or two there. That'll give us a solid walkway so we don't leave too many footprints. And, for God's sake, put that blasted stool over beside the tunnel door before you fall flat on your silly bloody face," he said irritably.

They spent a good hour or so removing any snags that would be a problem in the dark when they had to get into the gully with a minimum amount of noise.

"Right," said Dom, "We've spent more time than we should have on moving these rocks. We'll have to hurry. You wanted to spend a bit of time on the front beach at Mingleton today, looking for lures and gutsing out on Mars Bars, didn't you? Isn't that what you told Isabel?"

With a cautious look in the direction of Boaties Beach, they walked over to the tunnel door. Dom handed Josh a penlight. "You race inside and put the stool in the passageway. We'll wait out here for you."

Later, back at his house, Dom gave Jeremy two small torches. "I bought them the other day. Give one to Jock. You keep the one I gave you to use in the tunnel today, Josh. We all need to get into the habit of taking them with us every time we go down there. And buy me some spare batteries, I ran out of cash the other day."

"Hurry up, Jeremy," said Josh. "Let's go and find us a couple of lures and lead sinkers and maybe chat to a tourist or two, if there's any around today."

"When you're finished, call back to my place. I'll drive you home, but don't expect it every time, okay? You pair are just lucky that I want to see Isabel about something."

The twins knew that Dom tried to be tough about a lot of things but he was a big softie underneath. "I wonder what question he'll invent to ask Mum when we get home?"

Later that evening, as they walked across their backyard, Dom was calling out to Isabel. The twins waited for a chance to get a word in. "Hey Dom, in case we forget to tell you before you leave, we're going around to the bay tomorrow at about four-thirty. See you there if you feel up to it."

"Feel up to it?" he spluttered. "What do you think this is, you cheeky young bludger? I'm not an old codger yet. I'll be there."

As they looked out to sea from the front patio the next morning, they noticed another boat anchored out near the Point. "Nothing we can do about it, Josh. I wonder if Dom will come to the bay this afternoon. C'mon, hurry it up or we'll miss the bus."

With so much on their minds, school was looking very ordinary. The day dragged on. By the time they got home, the boat had disappeared. One less thing to worry about, they thought.

That morning, Isabel had said she was going to spend the morning baking. The boys suggested 'some banana muffins would be nice'. As a result their mouths were watering as the raced through the gate at 3.40pm looking forward to a nice smoko.

"Wow, banana muffins and cherry butter cake. Can we have some straight away Mum?"

"As soon as you wash your hands and faces," she said, "and don't eat it all. Leave some for your father."

When they finally arrived at the parking area at Boaties, Dom was busy on the beach. He'd brought a bucket to collect some shell-grit for his chooks, so he wasn't too cranky about them being late. He had things to do while he waited.

"Hello Dom. Here, put this in the ute. Mum has sent you a chocolate pound cake, just baked this morning. She said to tell you to cut it into four or five slabs and freeze them. Just thaw out a section at a time. Oh, and there's a box of Anzac biscuits too."

As he stored his parcels in the cab of the ute, Dom began to whistle happily. "Thanks, and tell Isabel that this is the best surprise I've had all week."

"Hey, did you see the boat this morning, Dom?"

"No; do you think I've got X-ray vision? How could I see it from my place?" Dom looked out past the boat ramp. It couldn't have been the boat we're waiting for anyway, because it's gone now. It was probably someone from the Resort Marina. Quick... there's no one here. Let's get into the tunnel."

They started off down the beach. "Hang on a bit. I was so busy stashing that cake away that I forgot something. Come back and give me a hand." Amongst the provisions Dom brought with him, there were some Mexican-looking rugs and two more stools from the Op-Shop. "I was lucky today; the stools were donated while I was standing at the front counter. I don't think they even touched the floor before I grabbed them."

Although they shared the load between the three of them, Dom opted to carry the heaviest stuff. The soft beach proved to be a handicap. He stopped and started a few times. "Must be getting older," he grumbled. "Who'd have believed it?"

In the tunnel, they arranged the stools beside a couple of the vents.

"Is this what you wanted?" asked Dom, while secretly thinking the younger generation was getting far too soft. "Too much TV," he'd say, "And these days, the young bludgers are like loose-limbed sloths, lolling all over the lounge chairs. Someone needs to explain the difference between beds and seats to those kids. A bit of hard work, that's what they need. Give me a week with any of them; I'd sort them out quick smart."

With an hour to spare, they sat around the table with a cup of tea each and tried to work out some sort of method of attack.

"I wish Dad was here," said Josh. "We might get him down here tomorrow. It's his day off."

"You'll need to start being a bit more careful. We seem to be coming down here a lot more than usual to meet one another. Isabel will start to smell a rat," said Dom.

"No, it's cool. It was Mum's idea for us to call in on you the other Tuesday afternoon. She wanted us to deliver the baked goodies to you."

"Yeah," added Jeremy, "Since we made our decision about the investigation, we're very careful not to let her think we're getting together more often than usual."

79

"She knows about seeing you today though. That's why she sent another cake and some biscuits." Josh looked at Dom's waistline and said, "Anyway, look who's talking. You're the one who needs to be a bit more careful, Dom. You don't want to get your calories up too much. I hope that's not a pot-gut we can see developing from all the extra cakes and sugary things you've been eating lately."

"Don't you worry about me. I'm fitter than both of you put together. Now let's get on with this detective lark you silly bludgers cooked up."

"Croaky and Harry 'cooked it up,' not us. …And talking about those creeps," said Jeremy, "Are we ready, do you reckon? Have we come to any conclusions about how to get any useful information when they return? A car registration number or boat ID would be handy."

"In that case," said Josh, "One of us probably should stay outside. We might pick up a few more clues, that way."

"That might be a bit tricky. One false move and we're in trouble," said Jeremy. "It'd be our luck for the poor stutterer to make another bumbling mistake and trip over one of us in the dark. What did we end up calling him in our diary? …Con."

"I shudder to think what would happen if he did. He'd scream blue murder and then that Croaky mongrel, will have us by the scruffs of our necks. I don't fancy coming up against that guy at all."

The trio spent the next hour, cleaning up the room and placing more candles in bottle-holders around in strategic spots. They dragged the mattresses out into back tunnel, and belted as much dust out of them as possible. Back on the beds, the scruffy old things looked as good as new dressed up with Dom's rugs from the Op Shop… sort of newish, anyway.

"Let's move the fruit boxes over beside the front doorway," said Josh. "Just on the left as you walk in. We don't want to be feeling our way across the room to find the torches or the matches to light the candles."

"Come on, time to lock up," Jeremy said. "We want to do that test outside again."

"Dom, will you help us out with this? Go out the front way and stand in the middle of the boat ramp. We'll wave to you from the cement floor of your old hut, and then go out the back and up over the waterfall rocks. Yell out when you're down there," said Josh.

Ten minutes later, the boys walked out of the gully onto the beach and gave Dom a whistle. He spun around, looked in their direction, gave them the thumbs up, and pointed towards the car park.

At the old ute, Dom said, "Great going, lads. I lost track of you after you walked off the track up near the concrete slab. You got into the gully without me being any the wiser. Toss your bikes in the back of the old ute and I'll give you a lift home. I'm going to have a beer with Jock."

Jock was home by the time they got back. "Hello Jock; how was your day?" Dom greeted him.

"As good as can be expected when I can't go fishing, Dom."

"...And yours, Isabel?"

"Good actually, but I'm late getting tea ready. I've been working on that assignment and got carried away."

"How's it going anyway?" Isabel was studying externally towards a Bachelor of Arts, which included an English Literature unit. She was enjoying the experience.

"Not too badly. I got a good mark for my last assignment so I'm happy. ...Are you going to stay for tea tonight, Dom? We'd love you to."

"Only if you let us blokes serve up the meal and clean up afterwards while you continue what you were doing on your assignment."

"That's a fair exchange," she said laughing as she went to add the vegetables to the casserole. "This won't be cooked for about three quarters of an hour yet."

Jock and Dom grabbed some drinks and set up some fold-up chairs about a metre from the beach.

Now showered, the boys wandered into the kitchen and looked around. Puzzled, they enquired, "Has Dom gone home already?"

"No. He's staying for tea. He's down near the front beach with your father."

"Great. Can we have a can of coke each if we promise to eat all our vegetables," Josh asked Isabel with a big grin.

"Go on the pair of you. It's still another thirty or forty minutes until teatime. Go and annoy the men. I want a bit of peace to do some more assignment work. I'll call you when tea's ready."

*****

"Definitely not," said their father when Josh suggested someone should stay up at the top of the beach to check out Harry's car, when he arrived. "It's early days yet. We'll find a way to get all the information we need without doing anything stupid and, quite frankly, what you're suggesting is bloody ridiculous."

"I agree," said Dom. "That mob might have some unexpected rituals that we don't know about. We could get caught out big time."

"Yeah," Jeremy said to Josh, "What if Harry always goes behind the tree you're hiding behind, to have a pee before he leaves? Who would get the biggest surprise, you or him?"

"Why would it happen to me?" asked Josh. "I never said it was going to be me up there looking for the number plate, I just thought someone should do it."

Jeremy spluttered and fumed, "You're kidding me aren't you?" When he saw his brother's expression, and realised that Josh was serious, he spluttered a bit more. "That's right... Bloody typical; it's the same as the usual crap you come up with: *great idea of mine but don't expect me to be the one to do it.* You always seem to expect someone else to be the silly idiot risking life and limb. Good one..."

"Come on," Jock warned them. "Don't start sniping at one another. No one will be doing what Josh suggests anyway."

Thirty minutes later, they heard a shout. "Isabel is standing at the top of the lawn waving her arms at us. I think it is teatime. Come on everyone." Jock slapped Dom's shoulder "It smells like lamb shank casserole, your favourite. C'mon mate, let's go and get stuck into it."

Later, when he and Jeremy were lying in bed, Josh said, "I'm sorry about what happened earlier. Sometimes I don't think enough about what I'm about to say before I open my mouth, do I? I wouldn't put you in danger, you know."

"Yeah, I do know that. It's just that you make me really mad sometimes, brother."

CHAPTER 9

As Dom drove home from Jock's place that night, his mind wander back through the pages of their family history, back to a time when the idea for a 'Catarina's Room' first developed. It was an emotional trip back down memory lane for Dom, but one he had to take. Recent developments had seen to that. So much time spent in the tunnel and Catarina's Room brought it all back. He remembered it well…

The crush had just finished for another year. December 1941 was only days from becoming past history. In Europe, for two years now, the war continued to rage on. An end to the bloody conflict, of that human insanity, seemed to be no closer.

"Whata you know Giovanni," said Catarina. "Some of our friends in Townsville gotta sent to da camp for aliens."

"What? They can't do that. These people live here now," replied an outraged Giovanni. They are Australian citizens now, they aren't aliens."

"You and our bambinos, you be orright. I am born in Italia, I will be put in a da … 'ow they say… in a da internment camp."

"Don't be silly. You will be all right, I promise you. Practically all of our family was born in Australia. It is absurd that the authorities should think my wife, and the mother of our Australian children, could be a threat. Just being born overseas, doesn't mean you have no allegiance to this country, Catarina. Our whole future is here. Why would you be classified as a danger to this country?" raged her husband.

"Maria, she says all a' her friends say we a gonna go to da camp. Well, all a da boys are in de army. Da boys fight for da country, but da parents still might 'av to go to dat place."

Giovanni was puzzled. "I don't think that could be right. Why would the Government think that the average Australian would have any secrets to give away? Do they imagine parents would betray a country that their boys are actively fighting for?"

"Well da Government dey do think dat."

"If they do, then it's ridiculous. Surely the officials would realise that parents would never put their own sons at risk. Maybe whoever told you that got the story a bit wrong?" suggested Giovanni. He tried to console his frightened wife but she still remembered how things had been in the Old Country during the Great War. She didn't have any pleasant memories of World War I, none at all. Bureaucracy, as far as she was concerned, was treacherous and untrustworthy. "I won't let them take you away, Cara Mia," he promised her, putting his arms around her, hugging her tightly and gently smoothing her hair.

But Catarina wouldn't be pacified. "Ow you gonna stop dem?" she asked. "Dey come in da autobus one day when you not be home and dey take me to dat place."

"Don't be silly; I won't let them do that. I'll hide you somewhere rather than let them take you away from us. But they won't single you out. You aren't a security risk."

"Dey will. I am having da big bit … ow you say… big bit of da fright. 'Ow you a gonna hide me? Dey finds me and dey takes me away. Dey looka everywheres in da scrub and dey finds me."

"No they will not take you away from your family," vowed Giovanni. To calm down his panicked wife, he gave voice to the idea that was running through his mind; a grandiose plan to construct a safe place. One that was impossible to find should an internment look imminent. "Would you like us to build you an underground room, so they will never find you? Will that make you feel more secure, my Sweetheart?"

"A-a-h-h; *si Caro, grazie*." Catarina sighed and burst into uncontrolled sobbing.

Giovanni held her tightly until she settled down. "We love you, Catarina. I will never let anyone separate us. The children need you and I need you. Just you let anyone try to take you away from us and see what happens. Not one of us will sit back quietly and let that happen," he assured her.

He told the boys how frightened their mother was. "Who knows, maybe she is right. They may want to put her in an internment camp until the war is over. This is a civilized country, so I wouldn't think she'd come to any physical harm. But if your Mama was separated from us, it's anybody's guess what sort of mental stress she would suffer."

Dom confessed, "I never knew she was so scared."

"If the truth be known, she is absolutely terrified," said Giovanni.

"Well, from now on, no matter where any of us are, we'll race straight back to the house, whenever we hear a car along the track. Mama will be okay. We'll make sure of that."

"That's for sure," agreed Vittorio. "We won't leave her alone. We'll give her all the moral support we can."

"Let's build your Mama a hideout, somewhere to take refuge when she feels threatened. Where's the harm in doing that?"

"But Pop, Mama is safe here with us, without going to all that trouble.

"I know that," said their father, looking earnestly at his sons. "And you know it as well. We're all confident about her security, but she's not convinced."

"It doesn't matter what we think will or won't happen, Vittorio," Dom said. "I would be happy to build the place Papa's talking about, even if we never need to use it."

With a sense of purpose, Giovanni said, "I'd do anything to make your mother feel safe." He had struggled to understand what her life had been like; living with such fear during the war in Europe but it was beyond his comprehension. Sometimes, he shared her waking moments following the nightmares that left her drenched with sweat. He would hug her tightly until the trembling stopped, and she recognised the lacy curtains of her Australian bedroom, but beyond that he felt helpless. His life experience provided no answers to help rid her of her demons.

Giovanni was so proud of his wife. She had left her own family and travelled such a long distance to begin her life with him in a foreign country. A fisherman's life isn't easy but she coped brilliantly.

As the boys grew older, they helped to bring in and prepare the catch for sale. Like their father, the older boys, as they came of age, worked on neighbouring properties when short-term employment was available. On Sundays, Giovanni's days off, he worked around the fish traps, mending them and scaling and gutting the fish. For the remaining six days of the week, he spent long backbreaking hours, cutting sugar cane.

He often thought his wife must feel isolated, during the six long months, when he left at daybreak each morning and didn't return until after dark. Catarina and the children had no means of transport during the day, but fortunately, none of their family was reckless or foolhardy. Accidents rarely happened, and when they did, they were trifling events.

Luckily, Giovanni worked on a nearby property. Many of the other cutters lived in farm quarters but, because he lived close by, he was spared that separation from his family. Giovanni was grateful for the fact that he could help with the children in the evenings. Spending as much time as he could with his family was a priority.

My lovely Catarina has never complained, but she must miss her parents so much, Giovanni thought sadly. She must yearn for all her family in Italy. It was difficult enough for me to leave all that was familiar, and come up North. I really can't imagine what it is like for her to be so much further away from her parents than I am from mine.

He smiled proudly when he thought about Catarina and their kids. His regret for separating her from her provincial countryside was very real, but having the children around them, helped a lot.

Aldo was 16 now, Dom was 15, Vittorio 13, Pasquale 11, and the baby and only girl, Rafaela was nine. Catarina hadn't been back to Italy for over twenty years and none of her family had seen any of their children. It was very hard for her to bear at times when she thought of her mother and her father. She had a brother, three sisters, her Nonna and Nonno and a large extended family to whom she was very close; aunts, uncles and cousins. She constantly prayed for her nephew, Enzo who had joined the Regio Esercito in July 1940, a month after Italy entered the conflict. After this war is over, I will take her home for a visit, he promised himself.

*****

Once Giovanni started planning the tunnel, the whole family was keen to get on with the job. "You are old enough to give us a hand with this, Rafaela, if you would like to. You can tackle a little bit of the lighter work. What do you reckon, Cara Mia; do you want to help us?"

"Yes Poppa, it will be lots of fun."

"Good girl," said Giovanni. "It might be fun, but it'll be a lot of hard work too, Sweetheart."

"That's okay. I can do it," the determined young girl promised. Giovanni had tugged his daughter's plaits and thought how like her mother she was.

Before war was declared, Aldo had begun working in the sugar industry with their father, while Dom looked after the fish traps and the crab pots. He was the perfect person for the job. He loved fishing. Volunteering to work at home was no hardship, as far as he was concerned. He'd bring in the catch before it could dry out in the hot sun, gather the day's supplement of oysters and attend to any other necessary chores, except for just one particular task. He left the job of dealing with the customers who arrived at the cottage almost every day, to Catarina and Rafaela.

His mother and little sister loved attending to the sales and meeting new people, while he wasn't keen on this aspect of their business at all. His reserved personality established early in his childhood, and became a lasting integral part of his temperament.

The Bellini family worked hard and life was good. There was a load of love and laughter and, to Giovanni and his brood, this was everything. Catarina was kept busy looking after her home. She loved the closeness they all shared. Having seven people to cook, wash and iron for was a huge job but someone always hopped in, and gave her a hand whenever they could. The two younger children helped both Dom and their mother in the afternoon, whenever they weren't exploring along the shoreline.

"My bambinos must have freedom. When I was a signorina in Italy, the war in Europe was horrible," Catarina would comment but say no more. Her memories took over. She refused to speak about her experiences and the things she had seen during those dreadful years. When she was alone, she whispered to herself, "I will never tell the kids about that horrible, horrible war. They need to grow with happy memories. The sons of our family, they left home to go to fight and never, ever came back." She refused to even think about some of the other atrocities she witnessed, or heard whispered about, in the village.

Vittorio had just finished school and he wanted to go out to work, but Giovanni preferred the boy spend another year at home before he had to face the hard labour of the cane fields. The lad was a tremendous help in the steadily growing business. Word was getting around about the Italian family and their fish traps. Most importantly he worked hard, was full of enthusiasm for everything he did and always seemed to be happy and content.

The entire family was excited about building the hideout. They had never done anything like that before so, in their eagerness, they were almost impossible to hold back. "Where will we start the tunnel, Pop?... and when?" asked Dom.

They spent quite a few weeks walking over the land about a quarter of a mile behind the home cottage and discussing their plans. Catarina had never made a secret of the fact that her Domenico intended to build a small shack of his own one day 'nearby to his fish traps near the boats shed' as she told her customers.

During the nightly planning discussions, it was decided that the cement floor of Dom's rough hut would double as the roof of an underground room. Dom would get his little hut earlier than he ever thought he would. The bottom line being, it would provide the perfect cover story, the ideal excuse for the menfolk to be down at the boatshed all day. Earlier, during the designing phase, Giovanni had said, "We'll have to use thick timber slabs over the underground room to support the concrete floor of Dom's place."

"It will be like a cellar," said Vittorio, "But without a proper cellar door. It will be no use putting a tunnel entrance inside the shack. That's the first place anyone would look for it."

Giovanni agreed with his fast maturing son. Another concern, was keeping the project secret from the growing number of daily visitors. Giovanni would have to make sure that no one saw any change in their daily routine. Catarina would worry about that. "How can you build a secret room without people knowing? They come here any day of the week or on weekends to buy fish. They will see you digging and carrying rocks."

"No Mama, I disagree. It won't be all that difficult. We usually get a bit of warning," said Aldo. "The track into our place is rough so people have to drive slowly. We can hear them coming for miles. The fish traps are far enough away to give us plenty of time to sort our story out." The three boys nodded in agreement. They knew when someone was coming because they could hear the engine for almost five minutes before the car finally arrived.

When the eventual site was chosen, they were all relieved. After such prolonged discussion each night, the boys were keen to roll up their sleeves and get on with the job. Talking didn't get them anywhere fast. Action was needed now.

"It's in front of that bit of high ground in the next bay, near our second lot of fish traps. The walk across the rocks and through the mangroves on either side of the beachfront is virtually impossible for most hikers," said Giovanni. "That'll make it easier to be a bit secretive about the job.

"Is it somewhere near our boatshed" asked Pasquale.

"Yes, that's exactly where it is, directly behind the old shed." Because of the secret place they were about to build, Giovanni was glad he and Catarina had chosen to build their home on the secluded headland, rather than in the beach settlement, a couple of miles away.

The tiny community of Mingleton hadn't existed when Giovanni and Catarina first arrived in the area. The Johnson's hut was the only building round then. It wasn't until the following decade that a dozen squatters' cottages sprang up.

Giovanni and Catarina decided to build on acreage in the next bay to his boss's beach property. The inshore seabed was much more suited to the types of fish traps the couple wanted to make. Besides, on the headland they had selected, there was plenty of good soil for gardens and it was high and dry enough to allow their animals to roam. In addition, it had great scope for expansion.

At the time, Giovanni had been able to push a vehicle track through the lightly timbered bush, linking up with the roadway into the Johnson's beach house. This enabled them to share vehicle access with what would soon become the small township of Mingleton.

When the newly-weds first arrived in the area, Giovanni began cutting cane for Joe Johnson, and remained his farmhand for many years afterwards. Joe's farm was about seven miles from the ocean, and on the main road. His weekender was a two bedroom high-set house with a kitchen, a sleep-out across the front, a lounge room, and verandahs round the other three sides, not forgetting an outhouse way down the back yard.

Joe was of the same opinion as Giovanni about cyclonic surges so he had chosen wisely: a site on a small rise and which provided lovely island views. His passion was fishing and, when he discovered that Giovanni came from a long line of fishermen, he offered the young couple the use of his beach house until they could build their own home, on the condition that he and his wife, Evelyn could come down and stay some weekends. Joe wanted to spend time fishing with Giovanni. Catarina was so excited. The Bellinis slept in the sleep-out part of the house, leaving the bedroom free for the Johnsons when they came for the weekend.

In gratitude for all that these treasured friends had done for them, Giovanni saw to it that during the crushing season, when Joe couldn't go fishing very often, he and Evelyn had fresh seafood on the tea table every Monday night. Joe never expected repayment, but Giovanni never thought of this as remuneration, just a gift for a good mate, freely and gratefully given.

Giovanni and Catarina spent almost two years in the Johnson's house while they prepared the site for their own home and established their fish traps. During the crushing, Giovanni cut cane for six days and then worked on his own property on Sundays, preparing the land, getting a large vegetable garden underway, fencing it to keep the scrub turkeys, wallabies and bandicoots from eating his food, and then digging the house foundations. He cemented thick wooden poles into the ground to support the walls of the house and prepared to lay a stone floor in the best Italian tradition. After eighteen months of concentrated work, often with Joe Johnson's help, a three-room home with a sleep out stood proudly on their chosen land. A Queenslander's home wasn't complete without a verandah which included a roomy sleep out.

They could now concentrate on the fish traps. He wanted these ready for the not-so-aptly named Slack season, the period between late November and early June when men worked just as hard, catching up on the necessary chores at home. The young couple with their two sons moved into their new home just before June that second year at the start of the new crushing season. The new little addition, Domenico Bellini with his thick cap of almost black hair, had been born on 23 May 1924 and was then one month old

As the years rolled on, a few more bambinos, one by one, joined the family and eventually, so did a couple of milking goats, a billy goat, three cows and a gentle old bull; some pigs, guinea fowl, chooks, geese, ducks and turkeys. Life was great ... until the clouds of the Second World War showed on the horizon.

CHAPTER 10

It was Sunday and the whole family was enjoying the usual day off. "Pop, I think I've found a suitable track. I reckon we can widen it so we can drive the truck down to the gully behind the boathouse. The trail starts at our old mulberry tree." Dom took his father along the wallaby trail and down into the gully that was washed out a bit during the previous wet season. "There won't be a lot of work involved. The banks need a bit of trimming for us to drive comfortably through it, that's all." Dom was happy enough with his idea. He knew it would work. "I went that way yesterday to check the traps. A new track through there will shorten our usual walk. I have to admit though, there are a few problems other than the deep-sided gully," Dom admitted with a wicked grin, "But I think it'll do after some modifications."

The chosen building site was about a quarter of a mile away, not too far but well away from prying eyes. "The idea of secrecy, as far as visitors were concerned was good on the face of it but, if we can't get a vehicle down there, what's the point?" Dom had uttered this statement so often he was on the verge of boring himself to death with it. "There'll come a time when we have to move loads that are too heavy for us to carry to the boat shed, and then what will be do?."

"Yeah, Dom," Vittorio always agreed, "And as for the lighter stuff, if we have to carry everything, every bloody day, there and back, we'll be too tired to work anyway. What would be the point of worrying whether visitors can see what we're up to, or not? There'd be no construction happening."

Giovanni admitted they had a good argument "Well Dom, you're always badgering me about a roadway. So we better have a look at this track of yours. Come on let's walk down there now."

As luck would have it, most of the larger trees in that area were far enough apart to manoeuvre the truck between them. The remaining obstacles weren't insurmountable. A hundred yards past the deep wash-out, two gigantic rocks sitting side-by-side created a corner which was too tight for vehicles to negotiate but, if a few saplings were removed, that problem could be sorted out. The final and biggest problem, was located at the second rather large, wash-out. The track could curve neatly around the edge of it, provided a certain large gumtree was chopped down. It was this small matter that caused Dom's wicked grin.

Their father usually refused to allow any of the large trees on the property to be cut down. Whether he would come to the party on this one or not remained to be seen. Unless it was absolutely necessary, their father considered the removal of mature trees as pure vandalism. Today, Giovanni merely grunted, nodded and said, "Okay." That his father was prepared to fell this eucalypt without a murmur, wiped the anticipatory grin instantly, from Dom's face.

The reason Giovanni was happy with the suggestion was because the tree was tall and straight. In fact, it was perfect for use as a ceiling support in the underground room. Sometimes it is necessary to make compromises, he thought. Once all the obstacles were overcome, it didn't take the family long to create a navigable track for everyday use.

Anxious now to begin building Catarina's refuge, Giovanni was standing behind the boatshed surveying the proposed building site. He'd had a gut-feeling from the outset: This would be the most suitable site. Most nights over the meal table, they spoke at great lengths about the whys and wherefores of the construction location.

It had been those nightly discussions and the concerns his brothers raised about moving the thousands of rocks needed for the project, which prodded Dom to actively seek out a suitable roadway for their faithful old Chevrolet.

*****

"We'll begin with some light work today, but next Sunday, we start in earnest. We can have all our materials and gear set up down here by then, and it'll be full bore ahead," Giovanni declared.

Dom said, "Before we start, I think we already have an issue to consider. If we build the tunnel and the underground room at ground level, we would get a good high view over the beach. But that's a helluva lot of soil, we have to fetch from somewhere to cover all the stonework. The soil is really sandy and extremely easy to dig. If we excavate down about five feet and sink the bottom two-thirds of the tunnel below the existing surface level, then we'd be left with only a couple of feet of tunnel roof that needs to be covered with soil. That makes a lot more sense to me."

"It would look more natural when we're finished too, just an insignificant rise in the natural landscape," added Aldo.

"Yes, we easily still could see everything on the beach I reckon. The vent pipes will still be high enough to overlook the beach and be effective."

"Why not work a compromise between both ideas?" asked Giovanni. "Build the first three or four feet of the tunnel completely above ground. That would make the door to the entrance simpler to build. Then drop down about three or four feet deep, and add a set of stairs."

"Yeah, that would work. In fact, by the time we reach the front of the actual room, the ceiling height we anticipate will be just about spot-on. It needs to be much higher than the ceilings in the passage-ways," was Pasquale's enthusiastic contribution. "It should be just about level with the top of the shallow elevation behind."

"Why don't we work the tunnel in small sections, say, four feet at a time, and throw soil from each current section back over the work, just completed," said Aldo. "There would hardly be any double handling then; and, by creating fully-finished segments like that, we'd be able to reassure Mama there are small boltholes to hide in."

"No matter what though, there will be a lot of rocks and soil to carry over to the job, won't there?" Pasquale said mournfully. He couldn't seem to get 'the carting rocks phase' out of his mind.

"Yes; lots of heavy work," agreed their father with a sigh, "But not straight away. Remember, to begin with, we'll find a lot of our material around here close and handy."

*****

The following Sunday, with the new map tacked to the wall of the old boatshed, everyone stood outside with their shovels and a couple of wheelbarrows.

"Right the sooner we get started on the front wall of the tunnel the better," said Dom.

"Can we put a pointed stick in the ground where we dig out the first bit of soil?" asked Rafaela. "Then when I grow up I can come to look at where we started the tunnel. That would be nice."

Dom hammered a marker-peg in beside that first shovelful of excavated soil, and directed an extra-special smile at Rafaela.

Everyone was impressed with her idea. In fact, each one of them wished he'd thought of it first. They soon found the initial work was moving at a fast pace because they had discussed, and planned, their design to such a degree before picking up the tools. Dom had found those lengthy, tea-time conversations, long-winded and frustrating at the time, especially when Aldo 'held the floor.' Now he begrudgingly acknowledged their value.

About 11.30, Giovanni paused and listened intently. He grinned and patted his youngest son on the shoulder. "Can you hear that, boys? There's a car coming. There's to be no work done here until someone checks what's happening with any visitors up at the house. "I'll just run back and see who it is," offered Pasquale. It seemed that no sooner had he raced off, he was back. "It's only Mr and Mrs Castellini."

The Castellinis left after lunching with the Bellini family. Catarina immediately changed from being the sociable hostess into an agitated woman. "How long before you finish the tunnel?" she asked. "Tommaso Castellini told me that, even if you were born in Australia, you are put in the camp."

"Surely that can't be right," said Giovanni.

"Si, his wife, Gina, said her cousin who he lives in New South Wales told her some of his friends from the ship they came out on are now in a camp in Western Australia."

"Mama, we started the tunnel today. I'll take you over there after I collect the fish. Please don't worry. None of us is going to be taken away, especially you, we promise," said Dom.

Giovanni admitted that he had been aware that the Federal Government had created a National Security Act in 1939 to allow the internment of 'enemy aliens' who could pose a threat to this country… but our Catarina? No way. Vittorio said, "We've been going well so far and now we've got a reason to work faster."

"I wouldn't be too worried," Giovanni soothed his son. "We are so isolated out here and your mother is the only one of us who wasn't born in Australia. Did you take note of a couple of points on the Government policy's bottom line? It targeted those who could pose a threat to this country. The document was formed also to calm community attitudes. Can you honestly tell me the description could apply to your mother? People like her, no matter what ethnic group our customers belong to. On top of that, what top secret information is she privy to? That's so ridiculous, it's laughable. Anyway, I really think that half of the stuff we hear might be slightly blown out of proportion. You know what gossip is, when it's been passed along by a lot of different people. After half a dozen repeats, the story probably doesn't bear any resemblance to the original."

Catarina remained shaken and worried, so her thinking soon shifted to her own sons. "My bambinos, you will not join the army," she spoke softly with a worried catch in her voice.

"Don't worry about that. We can't anyway," said Aldo. "We're supposed to be between 20 and 35 years old to join the AIF. I'm too young, unless I falsify my age, and Pop is too old."

"Eh! Come on, I'm only in my mid-forties," grumbled Giovanni, slightly insulted about being cast in the 'too old' category.

His wife grabbed Giovanni fiercely by his upper arm and glowered at him, "You are not going into the Army," she yelled. "I will not let you. I hate the war. It takes people away. You never see them again. You are not going ...*Capisce?*"

"C'mon Mama," said Dom, "That stuff Gina Castellini told you about her cousin's friend in Western Australia; it will never happen to you. The war might be over soon anyway. Have hope. We are building your room. Even if we only finish the tunnel stage, soon there will be a secret place for us to hide. It might be a bit cramped with all of us lining up along the wall though," Dom chuckled.

Later, Dom and Catarina strolled over to the construction site in time to see the two younger boys tossing rocks into the wheelbarrow and pushing them back to the tunnel at breakneck speed. They were having the time of their lives. What an adventure this was for them. Aldo turned towards his young brothers. "While you two are stacking rocks over there, Dom and I will make a start on constructing a short passage, connected to the main tunnel, and parallel to the beachfront. We found a small unforeseen glitch. When we are underground, we can't see if anyone is standing in front of the main doorway. We need to know who's out there so we can safely leave the place. C'mon Dom, let's get started."

"Is it really necessary to build this section you're talking about? Can't we concoct some sort of spyhole over the front door, instead?" Dom asked.

"Yes, it is essential, and one spyhole isn't enough either. Seeing who's in front of the door isn't the only problem we have. We can't we see what's happening at this end of the beach from most of the other vents either. The boatshed is in the way."

"That's true. I hadn't thought that far ahead," replied Dom. "Well that's a couple of lengths of pipe we won't need to fabricate. It would be a waste of effort."

"No, I don't agree. We should build the vents anyway," said Aldo. "We'll need to let as much air and light as possible into the passageway."

"What sort of observation outlets do you suggest we need for this new section you're talking about? The design of the others won't work there."

"I was thinking about using the large rock beside Rafaela's marker, as part of the new tunnel arm. You know; the original one that has been here virtually since the ice age. I reckon the way to go would be to bring in some other bigger rocks and butt them against it. We can create a couple of barely discernible slits at the junction where they each lean against one another. The larger boulders won't need to be covered completely with soil, only the rear portion of them. When we're finished it will look convincing enough. The largest rocks will jut out from the bank in a natural formation. It's safe to assume that a series of niches would form where the rocks cram against one another.

These small apertures will be perfect. Just wait, they'll be an example of my dexterity," said Aldo, grinning and preening like the proverbial peacock.

*****

The 1942 crushing season, had been in full swing for about a month, giving the family only one spare day a week to work on the tunnel project. In a week's time, it would be the end of August, so they figured there was almost four months remaining, maybe even five, before the unpredictable monsoon system came down from the north. Giovanni hoped that would get reasonable weather during the latter part of this year, so they could work solidly every Sunday, before nature heralded in the New Year with its expected all-out and merciless attack.

Through January and February, the floods came and went and then work resumed in earnest. They needed to put a full-time effort into the construction before the 1943 crushing season began. As the months went by, quite a bit more of the tunnel was constructed. When the very first section of the roof was built, Aldo said, "Yep, and the planks will benefit from some long bolts through each end so that they can be anchored into cement to hold them in place. Scratching his unshaven chin, he said, "I'm glad Pasquale started us thinking about using the reinforcing cement. It definitely is helping."

It was important that, despite the initial extensive round-table planning, the family remained open-minded. They agreed that it was valuable to be amenable to new ideas: To always treat the job as a work-in-progress. The question Pasquale asked about the tunnel leaking and Rafaela's fear of possible crumbling rock walls was heeded.

Aldo assured them that wouldn't happen because they would buttress the roof timbers tightly together, side by side, and put some bearers in from floor to ceiling to support the walls." He suggested they put a couple of inches of cement slurry on the outside over the joins to keep any dirt and moisture out and, although the stones would be securely interlaced together, the concrete would lock them in as solidly as if they were a brick wall.

As the work continued, the vent pipes were laid out above ground and the external shell of the tunnel was covered by a crust of cement about an inch and a half thick. Most of the family thought the end result looked like a weird, stiffened caterpillar with its rigid matchstick legs sticking out along one side. Dom was the exception. He thought it looked like the head of a yard broom warped in the sun and with most of its bristles missing.

When Vittorio first saw the strange arrangement, before the top-soil was dumped over it, he hadn't stopped to think about what he was going to say. "It looks so odd. How will that cement wormlike thing remain a secret? You'll be able to see straightaway that it's not natural." As soon as the words were out of his mouth, he paused, looked down at his soil-stained hands, and said, "That was a bit stupid, wasn't it? I already know the answer? A covering of soil and small stones will make the artificial bank look genuine, even before the next stage has started and Mama and Rafaela will be along with their seedlings and watering cans."

*****

When the full length of the first new tunnel was completed, the family decided to add yet another line of rocks to create a second passage-way. These shorter corridors were only sixteen feet long, the width of Catarina's room. Not content with that, one silly day when the Bellini world was particularly beautiful, the idea of a third was debated.

These three short passageways, tucked in between the main tunnel and the large room, formed an efficient light-trap. They zigzagged back and forth between the concealed door in the main tunnel and the entry to Catarina's Room.

With the start of the year's crushing season, work returned to a Sunday-only basis. Giovanni, Aldo and Vittorio worked on the construction of Catarina's Room, happy to sacrifice their one day of rest for Catarina. During the week, Dom helped his mother, sister and youngest brother with the revegetation behind the boatshed. The war was playing havoc with their profits but customers still spasmodically turned up at the house. Dom left Catarina and Rafaela deal with them as watching over the progress of the newly planted vines and shrubs was more his line. "The root systems will become so matted together; they will form an effective, and waterproof, protection above the tunnels. That will be a tremendous help," he often told his mother as the plantings developed into a healthy covering.

The biggest worry was the unfinished front door at the tunnel entrance. It was covered with a sheet of iron and was still as well camouflaged as it had been at the very beginning of the build in late-1942.

The end of the cane-cutting season for the year saw the menfolk resume construction work fulltime. Every few days, if the latest patch of bare earth wasn't quite ready for cultivation, Catarina, with Rafaela's help, would advise the crew she wasn't coming to the gully that day, choosing to stay home and concentrate on selling fish instead.

CHAPTER 11

Catarina missed her family in Italy more then than at other times of the year during the lead-up to Christmas. She sat quietly on a rock on the other side of the gully absentmindedly watching scrub turkeys foraging for food and scratching leaf litter everywhere. Rafaela left her mother to her thoughts and looked the delicate sea urchin skeletons, which washed up on the sand at this time of year.

During Catarina's quiet moments, Giovanni and children felt helpless in the face of her distress. Her mood related to the plight of her parents and other family members once again living in a wartime environment. Each of them knew that Catarina just needed some personal space, to be alone with her memories, especially during the Christmas period. Wartime was difficult but so was separation from loved ones and, being so far away, there was nothing that any of them could do.

The Australian internee camp issue was an added stress. Thankfully, Giovanni's idea of building Catarina an escape room seemed to have helped. Her anxiety levels were dropping. However, with the work dragging on longer than they realised it would, the rest of the family was becoming a bit edgier. The odd bit of nit-picking slipped into the boys' conversations, and other small flaws started to mar the family's natural cheerful dispositions. Giovanni and Vittorio had disagreements and Giovanni, who rarely swore, peppered their discussion with curses. The job had become a massive task. What had started as a tunnel and a room kept growing.

The project kept the boys out of mischief, but Giovanni was concerned about the surfacing behavioural developments – including his own. It wasn't only because the job had been taking so long to finish. There had never been a finishing date. It was the bloody war. It continued to drag on. Everyone expected it to be over by now and each time the new casualty reports came through, especially if they included any of the young local lads, the entire community's morale took a huge hit. There was little anyone back home could do. It was a ruthless situation, with no visible end in sight. Giovanni doubted any of the young men understood what they were letting themselves in for when they volunteered for active duty overseas.

Catarina, watching the job drag on and seeing that morale so low, tried to lighten the mood whenever she could. During the long months, as the artificial banks continued to grow into more natural looking scrub, Catarina and Rafaela often helped with the wheelbarrows. They rearranged a lot of the soil the menfolk were digging from the excavation site, continuing to add to the volume and integrity of the artificial embankments. Catarina and her young daughter worked at their bush garden with a feverish intensity. They collected leaf litter from wherever they could find it to use as mulch, and this gave them an unexpected bonus. The decomposing plant material contained lots of viable seed. Before long, the newest bank was sprouting plants everywhere and looking as natural as the rest of the area.

The weather wasn't quite as sunny as it had been in previous months. There were sporadic sprinkles of rain during the night and a sun shower or two during the day. It was enough to cool the days, but not enough yet, to stop construction progress. The showers had the newly planted area growing rapidly. When five weeks of wetter weather arrived and caused work to be shelved, board games, smoko breaks and afternoon naps became an everyday reality. Although frustrating, it was, the holiday everyone needed. Body batteries slowly recharged and good nature returned. In two weeks it would be Christmas. Catarina was down in the dumps until Vittorio told her, "Well Mama, it's too wet for anyone to drive out to collect you for the camps. They'd get bogged in the Four Mile crossing. We're stuck with you for a bit longer yet."

After having spent the day doing an annual spring-clean in preparation for their Christmas celebrations, Catarina was exhausted. Last year the wet weather came earlier than expected and she wasn't ready. This year though, she would be, she had vowed. Rafaela and Pasquale planned to make some crêpe paper chains to decorate the small she-oak sapling which Catarina intended to ask Dom to find for her. Every year, finding just the right shaped sapling or a straight well-formed branch with needle-like leaves, was important. Dom felt the same about the Christmas tree as his mother did, so it wasn't difficult to convince him to put aside his chores for a few hours to scramble around in the bush to find exactly what they wanted.

*****

"Any ideas yet, about that blasted door down in the scrub? It's been over a week since we sat outside and talked about it. Nothing has eventuated. We need to make a cover for the tunnel entrance immediately, if not sooner. We've left it too long already," groaned Giovanni in frustration. "Surely one of us can come up with a solution? How can it be so difficult?" He stood up and stretched his tired back "I'm off to bed. I'll see you all in the morning. Don't forget to close the back door when you are finished. Bloody possum got into the potatoes last night. Mama almost went ballistic."

With eight days to go to Christmas, the torrential rainfall cleared for a while. It was during this period, the downside of living in the beautiful tropics became evident. The heat was almost unbearable. It was so hot and sultry, everyone was crossing fingers in the hope there wasn't a cyclone on the horizon. All the signs were there.

If the weather turned bad on them, special Christmas food wouldn't be too much of a worry. During those lean war years, Giovanni and Caterina's hard work had produced a state of near self-sufficiency. They still had to shop for certain items such as flour, salt and the occasional pair of gumboots, but they were doing very nicely even so. To add to that, they'd just shopped to boost the annual stockpile of provisions, in case of a cyclone.

The house site they chose all those years ago was proving to be the best decision they ever made. The twenty acres of arable soil, on a good-sized headland which never flooded was an ideal set-up for the animals. The abundant straight trunks of the native tea-trees provided timber for the many shelters, pens and coops they needed. To top it all off, their fish traps and the oyster beds were almost inexhaustible.

Their goat herd was invaluable. The billy goat and his harem kept producing kids, some of which were used as food. Spare females were swapped with other farmers, to keep the herd from in-breeding and the goats' milk was used for cheese making and cooking. A couple years ago, Giovanni acquired three dairy cows and a bull. There were always new chickens; so plenty of roosters grew into roast dinners, while the hens and other birds provided eggs. Two galvanised rainwater tanks at the house and two beside the boatshed provided sweet drinking water. The garden harvest was regular and prolific. Rainwater wasn't wasted on the gardens. Two 44 gallon drums were filled from freshwater sources nearby to preserve the tank water for drinking.

During the last week before Christmas, most customers didn't arrive until late in the afternoon, but business was becoming slower every month because of the war. Dom quite often opened the traps during the daytime tides, to let fish escape.

Added to the worry about the weather turning foul, the immediate problem was still what to do about *that bloody entrance door*. "The unprotected opening is right out in the open. It's noticeable and is a potential open-drain waiting to channel floodwater. We'll have to come up with a clever design soon," Giovanni was heard to say after every evening meal, as the chat session was about to begin.

Although the topic was uppermost in their minds, no-one had come up with a brilliant solution or, for that matter, even a half-workable idea. Giovanni and the boys sat outside the house in a cool place beside the water tanks to have a specially convened council-of-war. They were waiting for their father to come up with a last minute suggestion.

"This situation is ridiculous, My Lads," he said, "We're still no closer to a resolution. The monsoon rains, and maybe, even a couple of cyclones aren't necessarily out of the equation. Just because we didn't get a big storm last year, doesn't mean we're not tagged to be the next chapter in old man Weather's notebook this season." A spike in Giovanni's blood pressure was causing his face to redden. "That covering over the tunnel is looking more and more like a natural bank every day, except for the bloody gaping hole we know is hiding under the camouflage. The manmade shaft, the hardwood timber ceilings and nice flat stone floor, not to mention those beautiful dry-stone internal side walls will raise a few eyebrows, if discovered."

"Yes," agreed Dom, "And I guess the door which opens onto a set of wooden steps, four foot along the hallway, won't keep anybody guessing for too long, either."

Giovanni shook his head in frustration. "We have been lucky so far that no one has landed on Boaties Beach to answer a call of nature or to do some beach fishing."

"It would be a brave bloke if he did. No one would be game enough to land on Dom's front beach, right in front of his fishing traps would they?" asked Pasquale, tongue-in-cheek.

"We have to get a door on that tunnel and it has to look like a natural rock face. Not only do we need to safeguard our hidden shelter, but we have to protect the work we've done already. A few inches of water collecting in there when the rain sets in, will take ages to dry out. Remember what happened last year. There's a lot more tunnel now than there was last December, and there's a wood-framed ply door in there now, which will soak up any water. We could end up with a warped mess on our hands."

After half an hour of wasted chat, the group stood up disconsolately when Catarina called them for their evening meal. Giovanni gave the largest galvanised water tank an angry whack as he stood up. The little bantam hen, which spent her nights there, squawked and flew out in fright. She cackled, fluffed up and strutted around the tank stand. Giovanni, knowing she'd take half an hour to settle down said, "Sorry, Fluff Chook, I know exactly how you feel."

At last Christmas Eve arrived. The men's usual chatter session had almost finished when they realised that Pasquale was speaking to Rafaela and the pair of them were giggling unrestrainedly.

"It was the night before Christmas, and inside the house,
a possum went prowling. The potatoes went missing,
and you seriously can't blame the mouse."

"Cool" said Rafaella, breaking into another fit of excited chuckles, "But you aren't really a very good poet, Pasquale." That set him off again.

"Hey, you two young ones, I forgot you were still sitting there," mumbled Giovanni. "Look at the time. Mama won't be too pleased with me. Off to bed with you right now or the possum won't be the only poor bugger your mother yells at.

When the family woke on Christmas morning to the parcels under the small decorated sapling in its crepe-paper wrapped kerosene tin, Dom said cheerfully, "Well, at least the reindeers were able to fly over the flooded creeks. Who's coming out to see if we can find their hoof-prints in the mud?"

CHAPTER 12

It was a few days ago that Dom took the afternoon off to go looking for his mother's Christmas tree. Like small terriers, nipping at their brother's ankles, Pasquale and Rafaela nagged and nagged, to go with him. Dom wasn't at all happy with the idea, especially as the younger pair could get side-tracked easily. Going by past experience, he knew those two were more of a hindrance than a help. At some stage Rafaela would plead, "Bring it for us Dom, please," her large brown eyes, round and serious. "I'm so little and this is too heavy." Dom knew he was being conned, but 'the look' got him every time – but not this time.

He laid down the law. "Right, you can come, but I will not be carrying anything back for either of you. Do you understand what I am saying? I have promised Mama that I will collect a tree for her, and I am going to get the biggest and best one, I can find. That'll be all I can carry. " Dom was quite firm about his decision. His two young siblings knew better than to try to push the issue when he was in this mood. "Those are the rules. If you behave yourselves, you can come with me, otherwise stay home. It's your choice." As he was laying down the guidelines, his young siblings looked at one another, and pouted. Dom wasn't impressed by that carry-on. "You did hear what I said, didn't you? When I say we are going home, we will be doing exactly that," he repeated, firmly, "Got it?"

"Yes Father Dom," Rafaela said cheekily. "We will do what you tell us. We promise."

Now the Christmas tree, standing in a clean, rectangular four-gallon kerosene tin filled with coarse river sand, looked festive. Paper chains hung decoratively from the branches and a silver-frosted, cardboard star topped it all off. Purple crepe paper, sepia-coloured envelopes and pages of black and white newspaper had been recycled for the purpose. Dom believed they looked better than any store-bought decoration he'd seen. It had been standing in the family room for four days now. This ritual was a gentle reminder that Christmas Day was just around the corner. By the time the big day arrived, the tree would be shedding brown leaves all over the floor, but no one seemed to worry about that small matter.

On this particular night, the air was oppressively hot, and finding somewhere cool to sit after tea was difficult. The family was winding down after a busy day. Pasquale and Rafaela were as jumpy as all get out and brimming with excitement, over the large rock they had seen up on the headland. Pasquale was going to tell their father tonight because they were quite certain it was 'the one'. Rafaela was hopping from one foot to the other in her delight. So much so, that her mother sidled up to her, asking quietly, if she needed company to go the outdoor toilet.

"Oh M-u-u-m-m – No, I don't," she said, and stopped her enthusiastic bouncing. "Pasquale, Pasquale... Tell everyone what we found. I am busting for them to hear about it." Her youngest brother looked sourly at her. She'd spoiled his secret. He had intended to break the news slowly, not have it thrust into the open like this.

In exasperation, he said, "Pop, we know where there's a rock that might make a good tunnel door," said Pasquale.

"Do you really?" His father spun around, his attention focussed on Pasquale. "Where was it, Mate? You may have hit the jackpot." Giovanni was positive that, if his son thought the rock was suitable, then it probably was.

"You know those ti-trees up along the front of the lookout, there's a big boulder over behind them."

"Yes Poppa," interrupted Rafaela. "We've seen it lots of times. It's got a big split from the top of it right down to the ground. It's been broken into two pieces; a real skinny bit and one great big fat lump," she said, and renewed her excited bouncing.

"It might be okay. I think you'll like it," Pasquale added, trying to appear casual about the whole deal. Since he and Rafaela first discovered that particular rock about three weeks before, Pasquale had been obsessed with the rock and thinking about the tunnel door. Because the conversation every night, had been about the urgency of finding a rock such as this, he wasn't about to admit to having discovered it weeks ago.

Pasquale just knew that he and Rafaela had found what everyone was looking for. But, until he repeatedly looked it over, he was ultra-cautious about mentioning it. With Vittorio always ready to ridicule him for the smallest reason these days, it was important to take the time to be positive, he reminded himself at the time. There's no point in making myself look stupid by jumping in too early. "It's good isn't it, Raffie? You said it would make Poppa pleased when he saw it, didn't you?"

"Yes, it must have been like that for years and years…and years, because it's got dirt and grass, and a little tree growing out of it," said Rafaela, feeling more important every minute. For so long everyone had looked for such a rock, and there it was. She and Pasquale had discovered it.

"What size is it?" asked Dom.

"…About the same size as our old truck door. Dom, you remember when you yelled at us to hurry up because Mama's tree was getting heavy, well, we were looking at it then. There are some stones and a bit of scraggly scrub around it."

"What do you mean by 'scraggly scrub' Pasquale?" Vittorio asked, trying to make his brother feel stupid.

"I thought you'd be smart enough to work that out without me having to tell you," Pasquale replied calmly. "There aren't many bushes around it and they're only small and thin, more like large weeds. The ground is flat as well. Pasquale was confident that he'd handled the situation coolly enough, but he took a deep breath and continued with his story. He and Rafaela had found the missing link, he was sure. He wasn't going to be put off by his stupid brother. "We can drive the truck up close," he said, looking directly at his father and pointedly ignoring Vittorio.

"First thing tomorrow morning, let's go there to see whether the rock is suitable," said Giovanni. "It sounds exactly like what we're looking for. Good work, you two."

*****

The next day, standing in a circle around the split rock, they discussed their options. "You two young ones have saved the day," said their father. "It is just perfect. What a find." Giovanni checked the surroundings. "We can reverse the truck into this spot from that side of the headland," he said, pointing in the direction behind Vittorio.

"Yeah," said Dom, "But we'll have to cut out these two small saplings. Luckily the smaller stones, scattered everywhere, are all weather-worn and none are too large, or sharp enough to puncture the tyres."

"Come on, let's get moving. With a bit of pushing and shoving, we should be able to lever the bloody thing onto the tray-back." Giovanni was all business now that they finally had a tunnel door after such a lengthy search to find it. "Hurry up. Someone go and get the truck. Let's give it a go." After all the meanness he aimed at Pasquale, it was Vittorio, who excitedly raced home.

The sides of the vehicle's tray back – two large timber planks – doubled as a ramp. Securely tying the winch- rope around the narrowest chunk of rock, they heaved and pushed, with much grunting, groaning and sweating, all round. It wasn't that the rock was overly weighty. It was embedded in the soil, and the small tree growing in the gap between the two pieces sported a mature root system which seemed to be glued on. The previous year, Giovanni installed a hand-operated winch behind the driver's cabin. It had more than proved its worth on a number of occasions. After a crowbar dealt with the minor problems, Aldo jumped onto the back of the truck and soon had the winch working its magic. Finally, the front section of the rock was on board.

"That's just about the best Christmas present I could have asked for," said Giovanni, beaming broadly. "It didn't prove to be such a hard job, after all, did it?"

"No, and it'll be a lot easier getting it off," said Pasquale, as he wiped his sweaty face. They all grinned at that little gem of an understatement.

Luckily Dom had seen the need to make that track into the construction site. Vittorio drove the truck slowly while Rafaela sat in the cab beside him. Their brothers and father followed, walking slowly on either side of the track, throwing any rocks and stones they found, onto the tray. Then, down in the gully, the 'front door' was unloaded and placed in its temporary position.

"Right," said Vittorio, voicing the collective question. "How will we fix this onto the frame at the tunnel entrance?"

"Fixing it will be the easy part," replied Aldo, who now considered himself the stonemason in the family. "The hard part will be drilling, and chopping, small slits into the rock so we can cement a set of hinges in place in such a manner that the mechanism won't be seen from outside. However, I reckon I'll be able to do that, and I've already made three hinges that will work."

"That large split rock must look completely natural when we're finished," Giovanni reminded them.

"What are we going to use for the door frame?" enquired Aldo. "We keep referring to the tunnel-door frame, but we haven't really got a frame, just a front opening."

"What about walking the causeway over to the island when the tide's out tomorrow to see what we can find?" suggested Dom.

Not to be left out, Rafaela said, "There's lots of good stuff over there, all sorts of long, skinny rocks."

Pasquale agreed. "Big chunks are breaking off those flat ledges all the time. We're sure to find something." He and Rafaela were experts on where to find most things lying about on the foreshores. There was hardly an inch of land that they hadn't walked over in their inquisitive wanderings.

*****

"Poppa, Poppa... come and look at this," called Rafaela. "Another part of the rock shelf over near the oyster beds has broken away since we were here last. The front piece has fallen forward and split into four. These bits look just about right."

After examining the rocks, her father agreed. "They are just perfect, My Angel." Giovanni looked at her with pride. He never ceased to wonder how he and Catarina had been so lucky to produce such a delicate, beautiful little girl and four strong, handsome boys.

"How will we get them back? The mud flats are the shortest distance across to Boaties Beach, but there's no way we can walk through that quagmire carrying these heavy things," said Aldo disconsolately.

Giovanni was of the same opinion, "...And that is the problem... the weight of them. How do we carry them through that sludge?"

"Hey everyone, you are forgetting our most valuable piece of heavy equipment," said Dom. It would be just perfect for this job."

"What are you on about? It's not possible to use the tractor or the truck on the soft sand and the thick mud flats between Boaties and the island," Aldo said.

Dom smiled as he reminded them about their fishing boat. "The boat; now why didn't I think of that," asked Vittorio?

"Duh," muttered Pasquale, "Because you aren't as smart as you think you are."

"Enough" roared Giovanni. "You two have been backbiting for days. It's over and done with now. Do you hear me? NO more."

Dom gave the two antagonists a dirty look. "Are you two settled now?' he asked. "Tomorrow, we'll wrap a chain around each rock and connect it to a large float. The floats will pinpoint our objectives at high tide. The plan is to haul the rocks into the boat, motor over to the beach and drop them onto the trailer in front of the shed," Dom explained.

"Won't they be too heavy for the boat?" asked Pasquale.

"Who knows?" shrugged Dom. "I don't think they will be, if we carry them, one piece at a time. We can always try towing them behind, if we run into problems with hauling them onto the boat. We'll have to wait and see."

"Towing? I don't know how well that'd work. What if they snag on the bottom?" asked the hot-headed Vittorio, who'd now settled down a bit.

"We know the seabed around here like the back of our hands. It's mostly sand and mud. There are hardly any rocks large enough to snag anything on," said Aldo.

"The few bombies that are out there aren't in the direct line we'll need to take," said Giovanni, frowning as he concentrated on a mental-map of the familiar territory. "Like Aldo said, we know exactly where the snags are, so that part won't be a problem."

"It'll be a very slow trip," said Aldo. "If we go too fast, we'll create a huge drag on the rock. We don't want to swamp the back of the boat."

"Yeah, there's that risk," Dom agreed. "I've never tried to tow a half-submerged rock before, so I don't really know what will happen. I must admit, I'm not happy about the thought of it."

"It'll be like trying to fly a kite upside down," said their father, "And, having said that, my old brain is starting to kick into gear. We don't want the rock to corkscrew through the water. That could snap the chain or worse, flip the boat on its side, before we get across the bay."

"Well, even if we have to make three, slow trips and it takes all day, then that's the way it'll have to be" concluded Dom.

And Pasquale, with the optimism of youth, said, "That's all right. We've got plenty of time, and anyway, we'll get those bits of rock on board the boat, just wait and see. I can't see what you're worrying about."

The next day, full tide occurred just after midday. This gave them practically all morning to prepare for the job. The narrow channel separating the island from the mainland is only a couple of hundred yards wide, and an easy walk at low tide. Transporting the rocks shouldn't be a big deal. It wasn't such a great distance. It was the unfamiliar nature of the job that had them worried.

Giovanni woke them bright and early. "Only bring what's necessary. Chains are not the lightest things to carry and we've got tools and other things to take as well."

At teatime the night before, Catarina said she wanted to come with them, to pick some milky oysters. An omelette entrée followed by almond-crumbed whiting fillets, a fresh garden salad, and all washed down with a crisp, white Lambrusco was just the ticket. Catarina believed her men were overdue for a few special treats and Christmas was only days away, so why not start early with the classy meals.

Pasquale said, "We can leave some of our stuff over there tomorrow night, if we need to. It'll save us carrying the gear each day."

"Yes Poppa, we can put it in our little cave," said Rafaela.

"It's just a cavity between some huge rocks but it's close to where we'll be working and fairly hard to find, so everything will be safe. No one will pinch it," said Pasquale.

Over on the island the next morning, three of the most suitable rock pieces were prepared for transport. When they had secured floats on all three rocks, they hid the tools they had needed for the job and helped Catarina and Rafaela pick the oysters.

Everything had gone smoothly, so they could have motored across on that same afternoon's tide, but the boat trailer wasn't quite ready. Next day, Giovanni and his sons launched the boat and tied it to their mooring buoy, out near the mangrove saplings in the bay. Securing the sheets of iron onto the boat trailer, they dragged it down to a point just above that day's predicted high-water mark and hurried over to the cottage for an early lunch.

"Well, boys," said Giovanni patting his stomach and burping quietly, "Your Mama is the best cook in the world." Before sitting down to the meal they had convinced Catarina to do the unthinkable, to leave the washing up, until they returned that afternoon.

"C'mon, let's get a move on. The tide is on the way in and there will be enough depth of water to take the boat across to the island."

They motored across the now flooded causeway, and approached the first float. Dom was happy to see that the water was almost glassed out today. The job would be a lot easier because there were no waves to bounce the boat around. You've got to have a win occasionally, he thought.

"Well, come on," said Giovanni, "Let's get on with it. We'll see if we can drag the first one on board, otherwise it's on to plan two, the flying *an upside-down kite strategy"*

Dom was the skipper for the day, so the job of manhandling the first rock fell to Aldo, Vittorio, Pasquale and Giovanni.

"Right Aldo, grab the float and we'll start to haul it in," said Giovanni. They slowly heaved the rock up, through the water and soon had it dangling against the side of the boat. Vittorio and Pasquale kept the strain on the end of the rope and, on Giovanni's word, started edging towards the middle of the deck as Giovanni and Aldo tried to balance it on their side. It took a few minutes of swearing, manoeuvring and sorting out the boat's balance, but the rock finally was aboard.

"The boat seems to be handling the weight well. We could probably cope with loading another one, as well," Dom suggested, but Giovanni preferred to play it safe and just take one at a time.

With the rock safely on Boaties Beach, Vittorio said, "That was much easier than I expected, thank goodness."

"Yes," agreed Dom. "I wasn't looking forward to having to tow it."

"Me too," said their relieved father; "Me too."

*****

By Christmas Eve, the rocks they'd fetched from the island were cemented into place on either side of the tunnel entrance. This latest operation had been played like a game of chess between the Bellini family and the weather gods. The cement had to be protected until it became touch-dry. Everyone was aware that, before it reached the point where it was 'set', the concrete mix remained fragile. The rain could do some damage, so lots of breath-holding was the order of that day.

The doorway looked good but the rock they secured across the top of the door frame, seemed slightly unnatural. It would have to be disguised. Dom and Rafaela said they'd plant some native-grass runners around it and encourage it to grow into the crevices. There was no getting away from the fact that the door frame could give the game away. It was one of the few bits of the entire job open to public view. They'd had no other choice, but to assemble it in several pieces due to the weight they'd had to deal in transporting the bloody things. It stood to reason camouflage was a forced necessity.

*****

Three days before the New Year, he made a start. He took his time. There was no kudos in being overzealous and risk damaging the rock, not after they'd taken so long to find the precious door. He was relatively lucky though. These particular rocks from the island had a large amount of sandstone in their makeup. Softer than the flint variety near the boatshed, they were easier to chip and drill. Attaching the door was the last essential job needing to be completed before the expected flooding set in. After observing Christmas and Boxing Days with due respect, Aldo began the difficult process of drilling into the solid matrix.

With the preparation finally was completed successfully, all that remained was to cement the hinges into place. This wasn't as easy as it sounded. The weather had made the task more uncomfortable than it should have been, and the gang had to build a temporary frame of saplings with sheets of roofing iron nailed on top to protect the site. Indications were for the onset of the 'big wet'. It was a race against time, but soon everyone could take a deep breath after a job well done.

CHAPTER 13

Towards the end of January Aldo, invited Giovanni and the family, to gather in the tunnel. He pulled the new door shut with an understated fanfare, revealing a totally unexpected side of him. Everyone had expected some histrionics, but he was so proud of the job, he wanted it to speak for itself.

"It's been a time-consuming job, and it hasn't been a picnic, has it? You've made me a very proud man, doing all this for your Mama," Giovanni said with misty eyes. "Thank you so much. Now the tunnel is as water-resistant, as we've been able make it. We can relax until the flood season is finished." Showers, while still spasmodic, were becoming more serious every day. The tunnellers were lucky that the deluge had held off so long.

The secret doorway into Catarina's concealed room was ingenuity at its simple best. "It is beautiful," said Giovanni with pride. "Aldo, my man, you are a genius."

Still more work remained to do on Catarina's Room and this resumed in earnest when the ground was still damp underfoot. It wasn't until mid-March that landscape started to dry out. The large flat rocks, lying everywhere on the beach were brought in to create a cobblestone floor.

*****

There was cause for celebration on the 3rd September 1943. Italy signed an armistice with the Allies. Catarina was overjoyed at the cessation of internment of the Italian population in Australia. Her Italian family was no longer an enemy of her adopted country. After the news filtered through, she walked around for days, smiling happily and singing at top volume. Her sons had mixed feelings. Not about the armistice, but about the room they hadn't finished, and which was now basically a white elephant. Vittorio, in particular complained loudly. "What a load of hard work that was… and what for? Now we've got a bloody unfinished construction that we don't need anymore."

Dom looked at him with distaste. This brother of his could easily graduate from an elite school of whingers, with first-class honours. This time, he had crossed the line big time. This was his worst misdemeanour, as far as Dom was concerned. Dom roared, "Get over it, Vittorio. When we started this job, it was for one reason: Mama's well-being. I, for one, will never regret that. We will finish the place even though it's now unnecessary. And by heck, we'll have some great times down here."

"Yes," said Giovanni, "It will always remain our secret. We'll sleep here occasionally, especially during summer. The temperature under here is so comfortable all year round."

Towards the end of October, the second section of the room was finished and they were about to start on the third. "Finally, the last stage of our mother's underground home is about to commence," Aldo announced with an over-the-top flourish of his arms and taking a deep bow to the imaginary audience he envisaged standing on the cement slab of the soon to be built fishing hut.

It was too much for Dom, first Vittorio's unnecessary carry-on back in early September, and now this. He grabbed Aldo and told him, "Get over it, Aldo, you're giving every one the shits, Mate – especially me." Vittorio and Pasquale nearly wet their pants with glee. It was so unexpected of their normally calm, unruffled brother.

Giovanni gave everyone a very stern and, warning everyone to settle down, said, "Grab the shovels. We need to pour the cement roof and finish it, pretty damn soon. We're starting to work in more open country now. It's danger time and the sooner we get the whole thing covered the better."

As they sat in the drawing room after tea that night, Giovanni looked deflated and said, "You know what…? We have been so busy working against the clock lately, we have completely overlooked one essential aspect. We aren't quite as close to finishing as we thought we were."

"C'mon Pop, you are joking…aren't you?"

"I wish I was. It struck me immediately this morning when we started to work on the back wall. We can't have a subterranean room with only one entry. If we really did have to rely on the tunnel for safety, what would happen, if the front tunnel was discovered while we're under there?"

"Bloody hell, Pop, we would be trapped like rats in a sewer. We need to be able to get out. We need a safe exit."

Over the following weeks, there were many anxious moments when visitors called at the house and asked whether that lad of theirs had started his building yet? Several long-term customers had said that they would have to bring their walking shoes next time so they could 'pop over for a look.' "Don't be in too much of a hurry" Giovanni would reply. "It probably will be the end of the year before we get a chance to do any more to it."

If Dom was within hearing range, he would add to his father's response. "Yeah, I intended to finish my shack, but the weather had other ideas. Our fishing traps in both bays copped a bit of a hiding during the last wet season. Rough seas and wayfaring logs, took their toll on the wire netting. We're busy reinstating them now, and it's proving to be a big job.

Six months later, the slab floor of Dom's new hut proudly awaited a building to be constructed on it. Their secret underground room was now successfully hidden from the world. What a relief to everyone concerned.

Catarina had reverted to the happy carefree mother she had been when the children were small. Knowing that she was no longer in danger of being taken away from her family, had made a huge difference, but the hideout was important. She always reminded them that there had only been twenty-one years between the Great War and the World War II. There was no guarantee another War wouldn't happen as quickly. She always believed power-hungry people were unpredictable.

It was all over. Down in the room, the door in the back wall sported two handwritten notices, nailed on with roofing nails; *Shut this bloody door before you open the other bloody one* and *Leave the dark behind you.*

Dom said, "I guess we knew when we had successfully buried such a large construction without being caught in the act, *the sky was the limit after that.*" Giovanni looked affectionately at his son, the dedicated fisherman, and smiled. He noticed lately, that Dom had developed a new habit. He's begun using a lot of Australian idioms. I don't know where he picks them up from. He hardly goes anywhere to mix with other people. Ah well, I guess it's just a phase he's going through. It probably won't last."

Aldo swung his bone china cup, filled with hot tea, up in the air saying flippantly "Let's drink a toast to Catarina's room."

"Be careful with that boiling water," his father warned Aldo. He looked at Dom. "Since we're proposing toasts," he raised his cup of tea, carefully, "To Dom's dream home. May it be a happy one… well, that is, when we get around to building it."

"Thanks Pop," said Dom. "The skills we have learned during these last two years have been invaluable. I plan to take my time building the hut from the floor up but I reckon I might use hardwood timber and galvanised iron. There's no way, I want to face another stone wall for a long, long time."

"What do you say everyone?" said Vittorio, "Will we have a week off, then get a move on with Dom's hut?"

"Might as well," said Pasquale. "We've got nothing much else to do now."

A few weeks later, sitting quietly after tea, Giovanni observed, "It's February 1944 already. Where does time go and why is the War still carrying on? It's been a very long four years and five months."

CHAPTER 14

"Hello Dom, it's Jeremy here. There's a cabin cruiser out at the Point. It arrived, towing a dinghy behind it, at about four o'clock this arvo. I have a funny feeling about it. That time we walked across the mud-flats, Croaky and Con's dinghy was being towed behind a cruiser. Remember…? We saw them heading across Hallies Bay."

"Hang on…Can you hear me? Hang on a minute, I'm down the back and the bloody neighbour's dog is barking. I can't hear properly. Hello, hello…I can't hear you. Wait a minute."

Jeremy stood for a couple of minutes, staring out to sea while he waited. "Hello, hello, can you hear me now?" Dom could never get used to any of 'that damn new technology rubbish', as he polite-ly called it. What he impolitely called it doesn't need mention. His mobile phone would almost ring out while he fumbled for the ON switch with his large fisherman's fingers.

"Dom, I could always hear you. It's just you who couldn't hear me because the dog was barking. At the risk of repeating myself…" Jeremy said in a half-smart tone, "I said, there is a boat with a dinghy out on the bay this afternoon. For some reason, I think it might be Croaky and Con."

"Towing a dinghy you say? You could be onto something there, Lad."

Jeremy stifled an impatient sigh and rolled his eyes. "I got the binoculars and checked. There didn't seem to be anyone on deck and I couldn't read the name of the boat either. …And before you say anything about that," Jeremy said snappily, "I made sure I was standing in complete shade so there wouldn't be any chance of the sun glinting off the lens."

Dom heard the exasperation that Jeremy wasn't making any effort to hide. He wished he was within striking distance. My hand's just itching to give the young smart arse a back-hander. The thought was

117

laughable because Dom was all talk. He would never hit the boys, no matter what. It wasn't in his nature. "Okay, we probably should get down there tonight to check it out. Where's your mum? And don't give me cheek just because I'm too far away. You're never too old to get a clip from me when I catch up with you, My Lad."

"Sorry, Dom, I didn't mean it. You know that. Anyway, she's outside in the garden with Dad."

"You go outside and I'll ring back soon. Don't you or Josh answer the phone though. Leave it to either Jock or Isabel."

Their parents were enjoying a late afternoon in the garden now that the days were getting longer. "Do you think I should put another Grevillea just here beside the birdbath? I was thinking the other day that the corner looked a bit bare. Oh bother! There's the phone. I'll go and answer it, won't be long."

"Hello. …Oh…Hi Dom. We haven't seen you all week, how are you going.

"I've been a bit slack lately and the old joints had been getting a bit stiff. I thought it might be time to get a bit of exercise. That's why I'm ringing. The tide this afternoon was fairly low. There's a king tide tonight so I reckon it could be a good time to put the pots in."

"Do you want Jock and the boys to go with you? We haven't had a crab meal for ages. Hang on, I'll yell out to him. Jock, Dom's on the phone."

Jeremy had filled his father in on the situation, while his mum answered the phone, so Jock was prepared for the call, which to anyone overhearing it, sounded like two men planning a crabbing trip. "Yes, you're probably right. They should be about, especially with the huge variation between high and low water; great conditions for crabs. Hang on I'll check with Isabel." Jocks held his hand over the mouthpiece as he spoke to Isabel. "Dom wants us to help him with the crab pots. Did you have anything you wanted us to do?" She shook her head. Joke spoke to Dom again. "No worries; Isabel wants to get some more sewing done. Why don't we go fishing as well tonight, and leave her in peace. We may as well fish the tide in. Will five-thirty do

Isabel immediately went inside to make them a thermos of coffee and a pile of sandwiches for their supper. As they waited on the front patio, Josh said to his father, "What do you reckon, Dad? Check out the cruiser out front. It's about twenty-four foot long, half-cabin, painted white with a red stripe along the water-line. Is there anything about it you recognise?"

"I suppose it does seem familiar, but the mind can play tricks. I didn't take in a lot of details that night. I didn't think I had to, more's the pity. I was too nervous about being seen. You know, with the full moon and all; I wasn't about to stick my head out up too much."

The boys piled in the back of Dom's old ute and kept the smelly crab pots, two yabby pumps and a battered old tin esky company, while their father sat in the front with Dom. At the Boaties car park, the four of them grabbed the pots and the food and set off towards the beach. They had two pots each, all baited up and ready to go.

At the top of the rise, it took a lot of effort not to stop dead in their tracks. A dinghy was anchored close in to the mangroves on the other side of the boat ramp and directly in front of Dom's underground hideout. It was so close to shore, the large plastic registration numbers were clearly visible from where the group stood. The bloke in the dinghy was facing the other way and intent on trying to catch Mangrove Jack or Bream along the seaward edge of the trees.

"Shit," said Jeremy, out of the corner of his mouth, "Do you reckon that's him?"

"It could be," said Jock. "Let's get into the mangroves while he's not watching."

"Bloody sand-flies," said Dom, slapping at his arms. "If the crabs were as plentiful as those little white-winged bastards, we'd get sick of crab sangers."

"I'd lay an odds-on bet that's our mate Croaky out there. It all seems a bit too much of a coincidence. I'll bet he's aware of us, but he won't want us to see his face. It works both ways."

They spent about 20 minutes tying their pots in the mangroves. Then they walked along the sand, keeping their faces turned landwards most of the time in case the bloke in the boat looked around. They stopped, looked across the top of the boat ramp towards the island and slowly scanned back across the waves, until their eyes landed on the small boat. Although they deliberately kept it casual, their inspection was quick and thorough.

Josh raced back to the ute and grabbed the yabby pumps so they could vacuum the yabby beds to collect the bait they were after. Now well out of the fisherman's hearing, Jeremy said quietly, "By the way, Dom, I think I saw Con on the cruiser in our bay. There was a weedy looking bloke on board. He looked like he'd have a squeaky voice, just like the little stutterer."

"That's a bit of guesswork isn't it?" his father added and glanced across at the dinghy. "You can't tell a person's voice by his appearance."

Josh agreed with his brother, "That dinghy over there clinches it for me. There's no outboard. He's using oars. I doubt he'd row all the way from Mingleton."

"It could be them," Jock agreed, "But not because you think a weedy bloke would be a stutterer. The 'no outboard' factor makes me think we should spend an hour or two in the tunnel – just in case."

"You're right. It certainly won't do any harm" agreed Dom.

Before walking back towards the boat ramp, they spent another half hour collecting the soft-shelled yabbies which were excellent whiting bait and threw damp sand into the bucket to cover them to keep them fresh for the next day. Then Dom hurried on ahead of the others.

"C'mon, hurry up you lot. What's holding you up?" Dom turned around and yelled at them, "Time to go. We'll check the pots again in the morning. It's going to be a good tide, so I reckon there's a fair chance we'll have crabmeat for lunch tomorrow." They stashed the small bait-bucket in the empty esky and drove off.

In next to no time, they turned into the back of the local dump. The council blokes had stockpiled truckloads of sandy loam along the eastern boundary. Dom parked between two mounds of it after edging the ute in as closely as he could. He passed the twins their bag of clothes and the extra supplies he'd brought. "Your father took ours out as we were driving along. Get dressed quickly. Rub some of that charcoal on your faces and shove the burnt corks in your pockets. Oh, and put your wristwatches in your backpacks too. They shine too much in the moonlight."

The twins peered at the blackened wine-bottle corks sitting on top of the clothes. He might be almost eighty but he's still pretty cluey, thought Josh. Their watches went into the backpacks, but not before checking the time. "Near enough to six-thirty; it will be nightfall in about twenty minutes," Josh announced.

With tonight's the full moon, the place would be lit up like a lounge room. They all knew they'd have to be cautious. There was a good ten minute walk ahead of them, and within the next half-hour, the evening would be as dark as it was going to get tonight. Just what the doctor ordered, thought Jeremy, using one of Dom's favourite expressions.

Their timing was right. Everything was going to plan, but now they were closer to the beach. They could hear the waves. Their stomach tightened with nervous tension. "If our instincts are right, then this is the real thing and not a dry run," said Josh in a quivering voice. By the time they reached the top of the waterfall rocks, the twins felt like giving up and going home.

"Dad, I'm really scared. What about you?"

"Don't think you're Robinson Crusoe, Mate I've never done anything like this in my life before. I'm probably feeling worse than you two are. After all, I'm responsible for your welfare. I pretty much violated my duty-of-care towards you pair when I allowed you to take on this hare-brained investigation."

"C'mon," said Dom, "We've got this far, there's no turning back now. It's too late for guilt trips and the 'we shouldn't be doing this' scenario. We have to get this over and done with without getting hurt. Anyway, you little mongrels…," and the twins were treated to one of Dom's seriously-black looks, "…You came up with the hare-brained scheme. You dropped Jock and me, right into it, so forget about being namby-pamby little sooks. You've got no one else to blame. You'd better man up, real quick, My Lads."

"Dom is right, boys. It's too late to back out now. Take a couple of deep breaths and we'll be off. Keep your wits about you and we'll be all right."

They had decided there'd be less chance of making too much noise by walking into the darkened gully one at a time. Whoever went first would be responsible for opening the door. "I'll go first. Give me a three-minute start and then the next one can start off," said Jock. He took the iron lever from Dom and walked off cautiously to soon disappear into the trees and shrubs at the edge of the gully. "So far, so good," he murmured and let out a thankful sigh to relieve the build-up of pressure as a result of his strained breathing.

"I'm next," said Jeremy, and went off on quivering legs. When he reached the tunnel entrance, Jock was nowhere in sight. After a quick glance in the direction of the beach, Jeremy pulled the door open just wide enough to edge into the security of the passageway.

"Did everything go okay, do you think?" came Jock's whispered question from the dark interior. "Let's see how well we oiled the hinges on the vent covers. I'm opening the first one now."

"Not a sound," said Jeremy. "What's happening out front, Dad? Can you see anything at all?"

"There's nothing doing out there yet. How about working your way down to the last vent? If anything strange happens, come straight back and tell me. I'm not moving from the doorway until Josh and Dom get here safely.

Josh had started his journey. He wasn't as lucky as the other two. He made it halfway down into the gully, when something suddenly shot out from the bush in front of him. With sheer willpower, he only just stopped himself from screaming out at the top of his lungs. He sank down onto the ground, his heart hammering like crazy. Only then, did he realize that the moving form was so small; it couldn't possibly be a man.

He stayed there a few minutes until the jelly wobbles settled. He heard another rustling noise as he was about to stand up. Keeping as still as he could, until his eyes became more accustomed to the gloom, he kept watch for the body accompanying the soft footsteps. "Dom…," he murmured, when he recognised his elderly friend.

"What the hell? Josh, what has happened are you hurt? You were supposed to be in the tunnel by now." Dom bent forward to check him out.

"Yes, I know but I just got the biggest fright. I thought I was going to black out so I had to wait until the dizziness passed. A bandicoot ran out, practically from under my feet. I wasn't expecting that to happen."

"Shit," Dom whispered, "You did extremely well to keep quiet. I never heard a thing."

"I think I was so petrified my vocal chords froze. I'll never laugh at the girls at school again when they say they feel light-headed after a fright. It's definitely not just a girl thing."

"Well come on, I'll give you a few minutes start. You go ahead of me."

Back in the tunnel, Jock was quietly panicking as he wondering where Josh was. He should have been here almost five minutes ago, he thought. I'll give him another couple of minutes and then go looking for him.

"Dad, are you there?"

"Thank goodness," whispered Jock. He grabbed his son in a huge bear hug the minute, Josh stepped inside the entrance. "What happened?"

"If you let me drag my face out of your shirt," Josh said in a shaky voice, "I'll explain."

"Sorry, Son, that was just a split-second reaction. You had me worried."

A few minutes later Dom arrived. "Last one reporting in. I've locked the door behind me. How are you feeling now, Josh? Settled down a bit?"

"Yeah, I've just finished telling Dad about it."

"Right, we'd better get a move on. Jeremy should have opened all the vents by now," Jock said.

"Nothing is happening yet, is it? What's the time, do you know?"

"…Don't know; I'll open the big door. We can use a small torch inside the room when we need to find out small details like that. It might be a bit of a challenge to remove the spike in the dark, so bear with me. I could be a few minutes. We can't risk using a light to see what I'm doing." They left Dom to get on with the job. A whispered 'Aha' was heard along the corridor a few seconds later.

Jeremy couldn't be separated from his stool so the others left him at his observation post.

"It's about seven o'clock," said Dom.

"I wonder how Isabel is. I absolutely hated deceiving her earlier. She believed we were going off safely on one of our usual night-fishing jaunts, so I really feel like a louse," her husband admitted.

"Yeah, I know," added Dom. "I feel the same but, if she had been told about this, she'd want to come with us. As capable as she would have been on this job, we need her to be at home. She's our safety net. At least, if anything does go wrong, we'll have someone reliable, and sensible to help us."

"Yes, said Jock. "She'd be more skilful in a tight situation than we are. It's for that reason she's our perfect backup." He paused for a second. "Did you bring the phone, Josh?"

"Yep, sure did."

"Have you got that vibrating thing turned on, so it won't make a noise?" asked Dom.

"Hell no, I forgot. It's in my back pocket," yelped Josh. He grabbed for the mobile, as if it were red-hot and hit the off button as soon as he had it in his hand. "I have now. Boy, I was lucky, no one rang."

"Yeah," said Dom grimly. "If we need to have slip-ups, it's just as well it's when our friends are still out on the ocean."

"Is your mobile turned off, too, Dom?"

"No, but it's not here anyway. I left the useless, mongrel thing at home."

Jeremy came into the room. "There's movement. A dinghy's heading our way."

"Well, it doesn't look like there's any mistake about their identity does it? Do you want anyone to take over from you yet?"

"No, I'll be right."

"We'll be out to join you soon. Let us know when they almost reach the shore please, Jeremy. Hang on a minute, before you go back to the spy-hole. You can't see any candle light from out there, can you?" asked his father.

"No, there's nothing. That light-trap system really works, Dom. Because of all the blackness behind me, it's almost like I'm looking through a window into a bright room."

Jeremy went back to his stool to continue watching while the other three worked on their plan of action.

Jock was going to stand behind Jeremy at the first porthole while Josh and Dom were going to keep an eye on proceedings from the next one. About ten minutes later, Jeremy came back into the room and nodded. They blew out the candles, made their way out to the tunnel and took up their positions.

"No use going to any of the other outlets, they're too far along to see this end of the beach," Dom informed them in whispered tones.

"Sshh! Can you hear them? That's someone talking, isn't it?" asked Jock. "Yes, I think it is … Listen! They don't seem to think they need to keep their voices down."

"T-t-the s-s-sea was a b-bit ch-ch-choppy to-n-n-night," said Con.

"Hurry up. I can see the headlights already. Don't worry about covering the boat ID, just get up the beach quick smart," snarled Croaky. "Come on. Hurry up. We've already talked about you needing to bloody well lift your game. I hope you were listening properly. We don't want things to go wrong because of your clumsiness, you stupid little sod."

The pair walked along the narrow width of sand until they reached the rocks at the top of the beach, before sinking down out of sight behind them. The breeze must have been blowing towards the tunnel because Croaky and Con sounded as if they were almost in the room with them. In what seemed only a few seconds, a soft rumbling sound seemed to vibrate through the room.

"That'll be Harry arriving," whispered Josh so quietly, he could hardly be heard.

Suddenly, many curlew cries came from the beach. Croaky began talking. "How ya going, Harry? You're on time. That's bloody nice, for a change."

"There wasn't any traffic tonight," Harry replied in a clipped voice. "It's all right for you. You're lucky you haven't got to worry about too many boats on the water. This is a quiet area. One of these nights you'll be late and I'll have great pleasure in whinging about it, just like you do."

"All right, all right, keep your hair on. Can't you take a joke? Let's move it, eh?"

Croaky, Con and Harry had only walked half way down the beach with the first load of little boxes when there was a scraping sound and a loud thud, followed a few seconds later by another metallic, grating noise.

"Hell!" Croaky yelled. "What's that? Oh Shit… Dylan, you stupid little twerp, you didn't anchor the boat properly. There's a bit of a swell coming through and it's swinging the boat around. You bloody little idiot; can't you be trusted to do anything right? The dinghy is rubbing on those rocks."

Josh smirked to himself. "Dylan? That name doesn't suit the squeaky little runt."

"S-s-sorry B-b-boss, but y-y-you t-told me to h-h-hurry up and t-to g-g-get up the b-b-beach and h-help H-h-h-harry so I th-th-thought I w-was r-r-right," Dylan whined.

"You thought, you thought…! That would be the day," Croaky spluttered. "You little half-wit, I should take you apart limb by limb."

"Come on," Harry said, "Give it a break. There's no time for fighting. Put the boxes down beside the rocks. We'll have to wade out to the dinghy and fix the problem. We can't leave the boat floundering like that. There'll be no profits, if any of the travellers get tossed into the surf. Just cool down and let's get on with it."

CHAPTER 15

Dom couldn't believe his ears. "Well, well... how about that. Who would have thought it? This is the first of our lucky breaks, and so early in the piece. It'll take that lot, more than a few minutes to get the mess sorted out." Spreading his hands apart, palms upward, he hunched his shoulders into an amused shrug and said, "We wanted to know Harry's number plate, didn't we? I'll just go up there and get it. I won't be long. This is an unexpected gift. You got to get lucky sometimes, I suppose."

"Be careful," warned Jock. "We weren't expecting this sort of unplanned opportunity. Don't get sprung."

"Don't you worry about that. You're looking at a car park chameleon. If that lot even look like coming up the beach, I'll be out of sight quick smart. The three big gum trees up there have plenty of undergrowth where I can hide. I'm not real hero material. The number plate is important, but not at the expense of my health."

"Just be bloody careful, Dom."

"If anything goes wrong, don't come looking for me. I'll meet you at my place. You go back through the quarry to get the ute," he said, handing the keys to Jock. "Just remember, I know the area better than they do. They might see me but they have to catch me. I'll be quite safe."

Dom was gone before the rest of them could even blink.

"That's what I call confidence," said Josh, "And you know what? I reckon he could do it too. He's a wily old coot."

"Dom is a legend," agreed Jeremy. "Don't we always tell you that?"

Their father smiled and looked towards the beach. "The three blokes are almost at the water's edge now. I can see two of the boxes they carted down from the car, but the others are out of sight.

"They were talking about travellers," said Jeremy, "So, whatever's in the boxes must be alive. Some sort of small animal or reptile, do you reckon?"

"…Or maybe birds," said his brother" "They're worth a fortune on the black-market."

Jock was concerned for his elderly friend. "Dom should be up top, behind Harry's car by now.

"I know, but we can't afford to think about Dom. We need to concentrate on what's happening out front. What can you see, Dad?"

"Harry and the big fella are holding the boat as steady as they can while the little bloke is fooling around with the anchor rope. The waves are bouncing the dinghy up and down." Jock began chuckling as he watched the performance. "It's a bit of a circus. That poor little bludger really is hopeless with the anchor. At least Dom will be safe for a while. They've got plenty on their minds at the moment."

"Hell, what's the little bloke's name? Dylan? He's just started to walk back towards the beach, but thankfully the others are staying with the boat."

"Oh shit; it looks like he's going up to the car."

After what seemed like a lengthy half-hour that was in reality all of about four minutes, Jock exhaled quietly. "Dylan is racing back down the beach. What's he been up to, I wonder?"

I'm going over to Josh's peephole for a while said Jeremy.

"Ah, look what he's carrying. He went to get a sand anchor. The poor little blighter wasn't having much luck with the pick anchor in the rough surf. That's really strange though. Why would Harry be carrying a spare anchor in the car?" Jock found it very puzzling

Dylan had almost reached the boat. "God, I can see why old Croaky thinks he's a useless little twit. He's dropped the pick anchor in his hurry to get to them, and now he's having trouble finding it under the surf. Croaky is almost blowing a fuse."

"Move over. I can't see properly" said Jeremy giving his brother a bit of a shove.

"You should have stayed where you were."

"Settle down you two, and drop your voices a bit. Your whispers are getting a bit loud."

"Croaky is taking over. He's tying the new anchor to a rope he's pulled out of the bottom of the dinghy. It looks like he doesn't trust Dylan to do it properly."

Everything out front finally was sorted. The trio waded through the shallow water to start the job which they normally would have finished by now.

"That took them well over three quarters of an hour."

Jock sniffed the air. "What is that smell? Did anyone else get a whiff of it?"

"No," replied Jeremy, his mind completely focused on the sight out front. "Dylan is clumsy with everything he does. The poor bloke isn't all that reliable. I wonder why they bring him."

"I don't think he'd be that bad normally. More than likely he's frightened of his boss," said Jock. "Poor little bloke. He probably doesn't want to be here. Maybe his boss is bullying him into helping."

"Whatever," Josh said. "Croaky is not the only one who's cranky. Harry doesn't seem to be happy either. Anyway, that's their problem. They made it easy for Dom to check out the number plate."

"Croaky will be spewing about things taking too long to happen" said Jeremy.

"Good God, there's that foul smell again." Josh turned towards the open door to see if he could find the source. "Is that what you were talking about before, Dad? It's really strong now. God, something stinks to high heaven."

No sooner had that been said, than Dom walked in behind them.

"Mongrels," he said. "Don't know why the little idiot had to come up the beach. I hope they get the bloody book thrown at them if they get caught."

"Don't you worry, Dom. If we have anything to do with it, they will get caught," said Jock stifling a grin. His forearm was pressed firmly against his nostrils and he was breathing through his mouth.

"They've got a white Toyota Land cruiser fitted with a moulded plastic canopy. I got their plate number. I wrote it down in that book on my way through. I hope we nail those mongrel bastards to the wall," he muttered, with a touch of venom.

Dom was never happy if he thought he was made to look stupid. He was in a ripe old mood.

"That smell is pathetic. What happened to you?" asked Jeremy. "You stink to high heaven."

Dom scowled at the twins. "I don't really want to tell you pair of know-all little bastards. You'll think it's hilarious."

"C'mon, Dom, tell us. We won't laugh, we promise," said Josh nudging Jeremy in the ribcage with his elbow and stifling a chuckle.

Dom gave them a hard look and said, "When the little squirt started back up the beach, I flew down the slope and jumped behind a bush. The only trouble was that it was right beside a puddle of putrid mud. I didn't see the bastard, until it was too late."

It turned out, because his shoes couldn't get a grip, Dom kept sliding back into the centre of the stuff, and not only once either. Every time he tried to get traction, he couldn't get a solid grip on anything useful. He eventually grabbed a clump of grass, took a deep breath and scrambled out of the morass. By then, the little bloke had almost reached the top of the beach. It had been a close call.

"What did he come up for anyway? I couldn't see what he was up to," Dom grumbled.

"Phew, you smell like dead tadpoles and rotting frogs Dom," whispered Josh with a muffled snort.

"And mouldy decomposing leaves and dog shit," said Jeremy quietly, while finding it extremely difficult to keep a lid on his laughter.

"C'mon lay off, you guys," said Jock. "It appears Dylan came up to get another anchor."

"What?" That gave Dom something else to think about other than his indignation. "Why would Harry be carrying another anchor in the car? That's not usually found in a standard vehicle toolkit."

"That's what we can't work out," said Jock." What did you find out up there, anyway?"

"Not as much as I would have liked. The canopy windows were open but covered by locked security grates. I was a bit pissed about that. If I'd been able to shove my arm in the back to feel around a bit, I reckon I could have found out what was in there. I had plenty of time up my sleeve, as it turns out."

"Well, you got something else up your sleeve instead, Dom," and with that, the twins almost doubled over.

"Yeah, have a great laugh. The main thing is that I got what I went up there for: the vehicle's registration number. I couldn't see the boat ID. The dinghy had swung around the wrong way. Shame, because those plastic numbers are pretty big. I'm sure I'd have been able to see them, even from up there," grinning at the boys, he continued, "It's lucky we saw them earlier this arvo, isn't it?"

Jock asked whether Dom had heard any sounds in the back of Harry's vehicle.

"…Only some scratching sounds and slight movements. That's the first time that young bastard got something right. He locked the bloody door again, after he found the anchor."

"Dom, come and have a look. You can see two of the boxes pretty clearly. When they were being carried down the beach, they seemed to be all the same size."

Everyone moved over to the next vent so Dom could see properly out of the first one. It had nothing to do with getting further away from the smell. Well, not much, anyway.

"Yes, small pine crates of some sort," Dom said, "And, without doubt, the same size as those in the back of the vehicle."

"That's what I thought. They look a bit like tomato boxes," said Jock.

"Might be a bit deeper though, and newer," commented Dom. "I think these might have been specially made for this job. Look out; here they come again."

Croaky was still at it. It seemed he never gave up on poor little Dylan. "You are a first class idiot, Dylan. I don't know why we even bring you."

When Croaky, Harry and Dylan had started to move higher up the beach and closer, Josh raced over to the first vent and started tugging his brother's arm, signalling for him to move over to the second vent with their father.

Jeremy was livid and shrugged him away but Josh was determined. The blokes outside were getting too close. Jeremy had to give in for the sake of silence.

Jock could see the tightness of his son's jaw as Jeremy edged in beside him. "God, now there's going to be an all-out brawl later."

Josh and Dom had the chance to see Harry at close quarters when he picked up the two cases in full view of the vent. They tried to memorise his likeness as best they could. Unfortunately, the other two watchers had moved out of sight, but all four watchers were able to concentrate on the voices from close range.

"We'll have to step the pace up now. We've lost too much time. I have to be out of here and home by midnight for an important phone call," said Harry, who still sounded ill-tempered when he spoke to the other two. He hadn't seemed to loosen up at all. If anything, he seemed increasingly tense. There's no love, lost there, thought Dom. Harry's spitting chips about everything that has happened, and he's having trouble suffering the other two fools.

When Harry, Croaky and Dylan finally waded through the water to stow the first lot of cargo in the dinghy and were well out of hearing distance, Jeremy exploded. "What the bloody hell were you playing at, Josh? Who decided you were the boss?" Jeremy wasn't talking much above a whisper but his body language was a sure-fire sign of his mood. He kept sounding off until he felt his father's hand on his shoulder.

"Just settle for a minute, son. Josh might have had a good reason for what he did."

Josh, knowing from past experience it's was best to ignore the tirade, said, "You two take the second shift while Dom and I go back to the room to compare notes. We have to write it all down."

"Write it on what? We haven't got any paper. Seeing you're so much in control, maybe you should have brought the journal," said his ill-humoured brother.

"Well, I did bring it. I grabbed it at the last minute as I ran out of our room. I shoved it in my backpack and promptly forgot about it. From the time Dom picked us up, it's been full-on action. I only just remembered the notebook when we first got into the tunnel and you were out here watching them.

"That's right," said Dom." I watched Josh put it on the table. I mentioned writing the number plate in the book when I first came back from up top. Don't you remember?

"That's why I wanted to get the clearest view possible," said Josh.

Jeremy calmed down a bit when he realised that his father was right. There apparently was a good reason for what he considered his twin's bad behaviour. "Well, I didn't hear you, Dom."

"No, Mate, you were too busy making fun of my entertaining mishap to keep your mind on the job."

"I knew that, if we swapped places," said Josh, "I'd get a better look at those blokes out there. You and Dad can watch the second transfer, compare notes and go back to the big room to write it up in the diary. That way, we don't miss anything. Our facts will be spot-on, if they're fresh in our minds when we write them down."

"Good thinking" said Jock.

"I'm sorry about what I had to do Jeremy, but it couldn't be helped. They were too close by then."

"And," said Dom, "Lift your game, young Jeremy. You pair wanted to do this, so there is no place for childish sulking. If you don't start thinking straight, you risk putting us all in danger. How bloody old are you, six or sixteen?" This time, Dom wasn't allowing the boys, the latitude, he usually did. He was angry with Jeremy, and when Dom was angry, he didn't hold back.

When Josh and Dom reached the candle-lit room, Josh got his first good look at the old man. All down one side, from his face to his shoes was muddy. Dried mud had caked into Dom's shirtsleeves, while bits of slimy rubbish still slowly dribbled down his muck-encrusted trouser leg.

"Yuk, you stink, Dom. Over there is a four-gallon drum of water," he said and pointed towards the drum, "and beside it, there's a cleaning rag in your mother's old enamel bowl. Why don't you have a clean-up before we start to write this stuff down?"

Dom, still in a bad mood, swished water savagely over his face and hands. He tried to remove most of the solid matter from his clothes. "I'll have a shower when I get home. That garbage has soaked right into my clothes anyway, so I'll still pong even after I've washed my face and removed the junk hanging off me."

"Yeah, and in the meantime, I've got to put up with you," grinned Josh.

"Lucky I've got my other shirt and strides in the ute. Anyway, what's wrong with you?" He was drying himself with a scratchy old towel. "Can't you handle a little bit of a foul smell? Come on, let's get on with it."

Later, when Dom and Josh were back in the tunnel, Jeremy apologized to Dom. He had let the romance of the idea of an underground shelter take over. It was almost like they were involved in a fictitious story rather than a real one.

There was silence for several minutes after that as they watched the scene outside. Harry, Croaky and Dylan were on their third trip up and down the beach. "That's six boxes. I wonder how many there are all together," said Jock.

"Not too many, I hope," said Jeremy, trying to make amends for his bad behaviour. "Josh is still cuddled up to Dom although the smell is still pretty foul," he said with an attempt at humour.

Well, Dom thought to himself, this one is still alive and nipping. "Should be fun for him," Dom grinned, nudging Josh in the ribcage.

"He is loving it." The droll reply barely covered the stifled gurgle that threatened to erupt. It was a chuckle of relief rather than humour, as Jeremy tested the waters.

The laughter will soon disappear when he realises that he hasn't done his homework thought Dom, and he felt little sympathy. The two little blighters forced our hand and it serves them right if the teacher gives them the rough edge of the stick tomorrow.

They watched the rest of the transfer take place in double-quick time. Croaky and Dylan were huffing and puffing as they hurried up and down the beach.

"Did you notice that Dylan is bandy?" asked Jeremy.

Jock felt sorry for the poor little blighter. His boss bullied him, and now these two were making fun of him. He hoped that Dylan had no choice but to be involved in the scam. If so, he thought, the Judge might hand out only 'a tap on the wrist' in his case.

"Yes, and the bloke you call Croaky, has a slight limp that becomes worse, the faster he walks," said Dom.

"Harry's description is the problem. It's quite difficult to define his appearance." Jock was very pensive as he spoke. "I don't think I've seen him before but there's something bugging me. Some sense of memory that I can't bring to light. Lucky we have his number plate to follow up on."

"Don't rely on that," said Dom. "It will be false."

"What do you mean?" asked Jeremy.

"It means that vehicle will be wearing an incorrect set of plates, borrowed from another vehicle, probably a stolen or abandoned one. I checked the bolts. They are more threadbare than they should be.

"Why not just cover the number plates when they are on a job? It would be easier."

"And what do you think would happen if a random highway patrol spotted them?

"Yeah," added Dom, "The Force has stepped up the surveillance lately."

"What will we do about Harry's car if you think the number plate is suss?"

"I guess we have to work out a plan of action for that one," said Dom. "Perhaps we'll have to follow Harry home after his next visit."

"I don't know if that would be safe, Dom."

"Well, I reckon he's local. We know what his car looks like, so we'll have to search for it around the place when we're out and about, won't we?"

"It's a common make and colour around here, and everyone sticks a canopy exactly like the one you've described tonight on their 4WD. We couldn't really be sure which one is Harry's."

"We could, you know." Dom grinned craftily. "I always carry my trusty pocket knife with me so I scratched a small, but very deep 'H/y' through a few layers of paint and metal inside the rear left side wheel arch, right down towards the bottom of the car body. It won't be noticeable to Harry, unless he feels it when he washes the car. By the look of it, he doesn't do that too often. I had time to make a thorough job of it too. It's almost like a professional engraving, it's that good."

"I'm glad you're on our side." Jeremy remarked.

"Listen," said Jock. "They sound as if they might be finished for tonight. They're talking again… not as loudly as they were before. They're still a fair distance away…but…Shhh! Concentrate."

"Well, that's it then," said Croaky. "See you next month."

"Yeah, okay then, Basil. See ya. Hey Dylan, like I said, that anchor is yours after you get the boat unloaded. I picked it up for half-price at the bait and tackle shop yesterday. Lucky I forgot to take it out of the car. I must have known something, eh?" With that, Harry started back up the beach, stopping for a moment to yell back at young Dylan. "Don't let that slimy mongrel standing beside you take it off you, orright."

The group in the tunnel were amused by Basil's antics. He looked very much like he was about to race him to do a bit of damage to Harry's face.

"Basil…," snorted Jeremy. "What sort of moniker is that?"

"Be careful what you say," growled Dom. "When I was a kid, one of my best mates had the same name. It's a good, old-fashioned English name. You young blokes think that any of these new-fangled names, are any better? Some of them are pretty weird."

"We should have called him Herb, instead of Croaky. That would have been closer to the mark."

Basil and Dylan waded through the shallow water to the dinghy. "Hop in. You get the sand-anchor. I'll pull the other one in and start rowing. Bloody hell, Dylan, pull the chain in tighter and hold the boat steady. You're letting the back of it drift over towards the rock again. Christ… hold the bloody thing steady, will you. Work with me, not against me, you stupid little idiot." Basil's whinging, continued to drift across on the night air, as the pair rowed away. Meanwhile, the sound of Harry's car was becoming more distant.

"God, I really feel sorry for young Dylan," said Jock. "And the riddle of Harry's spare anchor was so simple. We were trying to make too much of it. That's probably a good lesson to have learned anyway. Don't over-think things."

Another half hour passed before the cabin cruiser in the next bay started up and, towing the dinghy behind it, headed in the same north-easterly direction as it had the previous month. "That's another successful operation they think they've gotten away with," said Dom. "They'll have a bit of a shock coming, someday soon."

"You're enjoying this aren't you?" said Jock. "Catarina's Room is finally being used for something other than family sleep-overs. Since the boys made that crazy decision to investigate that episode at the point that night, we have benefitted from its existence."

Dom looked intensely at his mate. "I think you might be right. It is exciting for me, but I'm scared for the boys too. Now that you've pointed it out, it does almost feel like some sort of justification for all the hard work Pop, Mama, Rafaela and the rest of us, put into building the underground room."

"Your mother would be proud and happy, wouldn't she? Her room has come full circle. At the end of 1941, when the news finally filtered through to her, about the interment of people born in Axis Alliance countries, she considered her underground sanctuary to be the solution to maintaining her freedom. She could hide there, from the stupidity in the world. You were offended when your brother questioned the need to complete the tunnel, but the family over-ruled him on that." Jock believed that Catarina would be satisfied when, half a century later, her son was using the underground system again, to protect others.

"I never thought of it like that. All I could think of was those two silly young buggers and their gung-ho idea. I was so worried, I didn't sleep at all that first night after they told us what they intended to do. You've probably hit the nail right on the head, Jock. I did want to keep them safe."

Dom and Jock sat for a while in the silence, before Dom began speaking again. "We changed the subject before I got around to telling you what I thought I could smell up there. Bird's smell… feathers; I got a whiff of them in the back of Harry's 4WD. The smell is distinctive when there's a bunch of them together. You can't mistake it."

"If that's the case, I'll bet anything you they're probably parrots of some kind."

"Come on, Jeremy, let's write our evidence into your journal," suggested Jock. "I'm curious to read what's been written so far. We'll have a look at it when we get a quiet time at home. It will be another month before we see that lot again."

"Do you think so? That might not be the case," said Dom. "It could be earlier. You never know."

The others looked at him enquiringly. "I was almost convinced that they were trafficking defenceless birds, and when you thought my suspicions had merit, Jock, I joined the boys. I'm afraid I'm in it for the long haul now. The birdsong in the old days was integral to our existence. We loved the parrots, the scrub turkeys, sea eagles and curlews – all of the species around the place. They deserve to live in freedom, just like my mother did." Dom was off in the past again for a few minutes. "A little bit of quiet nosing around here and there won't go astray. Sooner or later, we're going to find Harry's car, and when we do, we'll have the basis for some more groundwork."

"Dom, before we talk anymore about what we need to do, can we go soon? You stink to high heaven," said Josh. "You need to get cleaned up before we have to fumigate the whole place?"

"I know my tantrum back in the tunnel, was a bit much for the rest of you to put up with but you haven't improved any, Dom," agreed Jeremy.

They made their way cautiously to the back of the gully and climbed up through the dry creek bed until they were walking in single file. "I'll go first this time," said Dom. "When it's safe I'll give a whistle."

By the time they reached the back of the quarry, the four of them had started to feel a bit more secure. There was no sign of Harry and Spot, his lookout.

"Right," said Jock, "We'll head back to the dump. If you hear anything coming, don't panic. Calmly merge into the tree shadows and stand still, just in case it's Harry."

"I don't think we'll have any problems with them." Dom was almost right, but not quite. There were no difficulties until they were within a metre of the open gateway into the dump.

"There's a car coming," said Josh.

They were caught out in the open. All the trees around the perimeter had been cleared, and replaced with a chain-wire fence. Running like mad, they threw themselves between two heaps of soil just seconds before headlights raced around the corner. Glaring spotlights and the thumping of over-loud music shattered the quiet night. It was just a mob of young kids, almost spinning out as the car skidded around the corner. Gravel spewed out in every direction, showering the soil in front of them with stinging pebbles.

"That was a close one. They could have collected one of us. Bloody young louts," whinged Dom. "God, a man must be getting old," he said, suddenly feeling every one of his seventy-two years. "I haven't had to run that fast in twenty years. It's enough to give a man a heart attack."

The tyres screeched as the car circled around the community bins several times. Smoke from the burning rubber formed a ghostly image in the moonlit scene.

"Cool. Those donuts are impressive," said Josh, unwilling to look at Dom as he said it.

The high-spirited youths chucked a bag of empty stubby bottles into a bin, as they drove past. "Good shot, Jase," someone shouted. The car completed the circle and headed down the road again.

"Do the parents know what their kids are up to?" mumbled Dom, still huffing and puffing a bit. He really hated badly-behaved people, especially young ones who should have been taught from an early age to be more considerate of other people. No excuse for it. They were noisy, drunken little gits.

"C'mon, Dom, they're gone now," said Jeremy, who knew it was pointless right now to point out that the lads were just having a bit of fun.

"Yeah, and if I ever catch you pair acting like that, I'll clip you in the ears so hard, your eyes will water."

The twins grinned at each other and Jock had to smile as well. If Dom had anything to do with it, these boys were going to grow up into well-adjusted adults.

When they reached the ute, the boys jumped into the tray and said, "We're glad we're going to be sitting in the back."

"All right...all right...you've made your point. I'm getting changed right now," Dom assured them. "We'll go back to my place first so I can have a good scrub down. We can't have Isabel seeing me with mud all over my face. Our explanations mightn't sound convincing." Dom stood beside the ute and changed his gear. Then, before the twins realised what Dom was going to do, he chucked the smelly gear into their laps.

After Dom came out of the shower smelling of soap and shampoo, he said "I want to grab some fresh fish to take to your mother. Isabel will think it strange if we didn't catch any tonight after we raved about the good tides. Lucky I had a good fishing trip this morning. I caught some beauties. I left them whole, only scaling and gutting them in case we needed them for tonight. Josh, grab a bag of party ice out of the chest freezer in the laundry please, while I get the fish out of the fridge. We'll ice them down so they look like we've just brought them in from the dinghy."

*****

"Sorry we're a bit later than usual, Love," apologised Jock. "The fish were biting steadily towards the end and we couldn't convince ourselves to wind the lines in. Thank goodness they eventually went off the bite."

"What did you catch?" asked Isabel looking into the esky. "O-oh, lovely; they'll make a nice meal. Those sweetlip are a good size for baking whole. Want to come around for tea tomorrow night, Dom? We haven't done the 'posh' dinner party thing for some time. Let's do that for a change, eh?"

"You're on, Isabel." Dom had an excited gleam in his eye. "I'll wear my new mauve shirt and purple tie." He winked at the twins. I'll pick up a couple of bottles of good-quality champers too."

The boys rolled their eyes at the thought of a glammed-up Dom. "The mind boggles," they told him.

Jock wrapped the fish in Gladwrap and stacked them in the fridge. "I reckon we might get a couple of muddies in the pots over the next few hours as well, so we'll have a nice seafood banquet. I'll see if the chef at work has a couple of spare avocados. I spotted some triple-cream brie in the fridge. We can make some canapes for starters, if you're supplying bubbly, Dom."

"I'll be off then," Dom said. "I'll see you tomorrow night." With a glint of mischief in his eyes, before he turned to walk out the door, he dropped the clanger he'd been keeping up his sleeve all night. "I'll check the pots in the morning on my own, if you like. With going fishing after dark, you lads wouldn't have had a chance to get much homework done. You'll be too busy to come with me when you wake up I expect."

"Hell, I haven't finished that essay," said Josh.

"And I've still got work to do on my Chemistry assignment," moaned Jeremy.

"And a couple of other things," they mumbled. "M-u-u-mm… can you write a note to say we were sick, or had unexpected visitors, or something, pl-l-ee-ze?"

"I don't think so," said Isabel. "You'd better have a quick shower and get into bed. You've got an early morning ahead of you. What time do you want to be woken up?"

"I'd better be going too," Dom said. "See you tomorrow night. Goodnight everyone." He whistled tunelessly, all the way to his old ute.

In their room, Josh told his brother, "The old codger did that on purpose because we carried on a bit too long about him stinking after he fell in all that slime. Now Mum knows about our homework. I was going to do mine on the bus in the morning."

"Me too; better get to bed, there's no way Mum is going to let us sleep in."

Alone, Isabel and Jock were having a bit of a chuckle. "Dom doesn't always get much of a chance to get one up on those two. He really enjoys it when a barb hits its mark," said Jock. "Are you really going to refuse to write a note for each of them?"

"No. They rarely forget their homework, but I'll let them sweat a bit in the morning. I won't wake them up too early and they jolly well can do a bit of work before I tell them the good news."

"That's fair enough, I guess."

"They were nice fish you caught. That was a pretty successful trip wasn't it?"

"Yep, better than we expected and, if we catch some mud crabs tonight, that'll be a bonus. Good night, Love. I'm just going to have a quick shower, and then it's off to bed for me too. I've got a busy day at work tomorrow. You'll probably be asleep before I get back, probably sounding like an old freight train on an uphill run."

He almost reached the door before the pillow hit him.

CHAPTER 16

"Wake up, you two," called Isabel, "It's 6.15am. You've got an hour and a quarter to eat your breakfast, do some homework and get dressed for school." The boys flew out of their rooms, grabbed some cereal and orange juice and sat at the dining room table with their books. They had been working steadily for twenty minutes when Isabel came in, handed them a note each and said, don't expect this to happen all the time, but here's a message to show your teachers. "I've said we had a special visitor around last night, so you weren't able to finish your work. Go and get changed into your school clothes. If you're quick enough, you might have time to make a small detour down to Boaties Bay to see what Dom has found in the pots."

"Gee thanks Mum," said Josh.

"Yeah, same here," said Jeremy. "I will get a bit more done on the bus this morning. I might even get it finished yet." The two of them flew into their rooms and ten minutes later they were racing out the door. "See you this arvo, Mum."

When they reached the end of the track into Boaties, the old ute was in the car park, so they checked the gap in the mangroves to see if they could locate Dom. A few minutes later, the old fisherman appeared with a hessian bag hanging over his shoulder. "He must have caught some," said Josh "Otherwise, the bag would be rolled up and stuck under his smelly armpit."

"Hey Dom," yelled Jeremy, "How many did we get?"

"G'day young fellas; we got really lucky. There are five. I've left the pots in but moved one of them to another spot. The bait has almost had it, but there's probably enough left. I didn't bother to renew it because this lot we trapped last night will feed us for a couple of days. No need to be greedy. I'll take the pots out after the next tide."

"Great; Dad's gone to work already, but he'll be happy with the result when he finds out," said Josh. "How many were in his pots?"

"One, and one each for both Josh and me," said Dom. "That new pot you made, Jeremy, did the best. It had two in it. It's been a long time since we've had such a good result. The tourists mustn't be coming around to this bay as often, these days. I told that bloody old Blue, to keep his mouth shut about the best spots. Maybe the old bastard is finally listening."

Whether the holidaying mobs made much of a difference or not, Dom always blamed them. When he didn't get a good catch of fish, it was the tourists' fault as well. He tolerated their presence though, because he enjoyed a good chat with them if he was in the mood. However, that wasn't very often, because Dom was a solitary man.

"Got the homework all done, eh?"

"Not all of it," said Jeremy.

"No," said Josh, "But we should get most of it finished in the bus. What we can't do then, we'll finish at lunchtime. The morning's session stuff is done so we'll be all right. I haven't got geography until this afternoon and, at a pinch, I can go up to the library and do the rest of it during my lunch break. No matter how, I'll get that work done, otherwise old Jessamy will rant and rave and carry on for ages. He wastes more than half the lesson these days rattling on about stupid stuff. The silly old codger should retire. He's getting way past his 'use by' date."

"Come on, hop in the ute. I'll give you a lift to the corner," Dom said, and lifted the twins' bikes into the back of the ute. He shoved the old girl into gear, drove off in his usual sedate manner and pulled into a park beside the bus shelter.

"The bus isn't in sight yet," said Josh after they leaned the bikes against a tree. Sitting in the cab of the old ute, they listened to music on the ancient radio as they waited.

Dom kept craning his neck to keep watching along the road. Waiting for school bus always made him nervous. Suddenly he elbowed Josh, "You pair had better hop it. Quick, here comes the bus now."

The boys slid out slowly and looked down the road at the speck on the horizon. While they waited, they said, "When you check the pots this arvo, Dom, we'll meet you down there. Will five o'clock be okay?"

"Yeah…Yeah…Hurry up." The old man was becoming agitated. "The bus will leave without you. Quick; you haven't got time for all this social chit-chat, move it, will ya."

They looked at the still distant vehicle and rolled their eyes. Ned, the driver, finally slowed to a stop and the twins made a beeline towards their favourite bench-seat at the very back. Josh said, "One thing's certain, Dom's never going to be picked up for speeding is he? Wonder if he ever blew the cobwebs out of the motor when he and the old girl were both younger."

Can't imagine it," said Jeremy, "But who knows? One thing is a dead-cert, though. If he ever has to catch a bus, he won't miss it, will he?"

*****

A few weeks later, Dom came up with a 'great idea,' to liven up those smuggler mongrels and slow their operation down a bit. He reckoned he needed the boys' opinions. As a result, the twins and Dom were rummaging around in a battered old tin trunk in which. his parents kept mementos of the trip out from Italy when Giovanni and his new bride were returning home. There was no way Dom would part with this treasured keepsake because the chest contained some of his mother's old clothes, especially the pink lace dress, and trousers and shirts of his father's from the 1920s and 1930s.

"C'mon Dom," encouraged Jeremy, "Put your gear on and we'll have a look at you." Dom tugged the old pin-striped trousers well up above his waist and clipped them in place with his father's old braces. To complete the ensemble, he tied a thin piece of rope around his middle. His father had been a much bigger person than Dom, so the clothes were a bit baggy but this all added to the authentic look.

"What's this grey scratchy, woolly shirt, Dom" asked Josh as he held a garment up so that the elderly man could see it.

"It's a grey flannel work-shirt. They were the height of fashion in the cane paddocks during those early years. Wool was the best material for the heat and for soaking up our perspiration."

"Well, how come it's in there?" asked Josh. "That wouldn't have gone to Italy with your father."

"No," replied Dom, "You're right. I found it after the old man died and put it in there myself. It reminded me of my Pop and also my brothers. Actually, I wore those types of shirts as well. I'm not really sure who it belonged to. Bloody hell, you blokes are messing me up. I haven't got my shirt on yet. After he tucked his father's white cotton shirt into the trousers, reclasped the braces and retied the rope, he carefully rolled the sleeves up to just below elbow level. Next, Dom put on a pair of his father's tortoiseshell-rimmed reading glasses and, as a final touch, he jammed a black beret on his head. He really did look the like an old Italian fisherman now.

Josh was amazed. "Cool," he said. "No one will ever know you in that get-up. What do you think, Jeremy?"

"If we can hardly recognise you, Dom, then no one else will be able to either."

The disguise was necessary in case Basil had seen Dom the day they had all gone yabbying after putting the crab pots in. When Basil, Dylan and Harry arrived in the next few days, Dom would be kitted up, ready to get out on the water. His boat was standing by. His fishing gear stowed in the front under the anchor well. His only last minute task was to grab the bait from the freezer. Once he was out on the water, it was just a matter of waiting patiently for the dinghy to row away from its mother ship.

The twins saw the boat arrive a few afternoons later. "It's definitely them." The twenty-four foot white half-cabin cruiser with a red stripe and towing a dinghy was recognisable now that they knew what to look for. Nothing ever happened until after dark, so they waited until Isabel was out in the garden before Jeremy called Dom.

"Tonight will be a good time for a spot of fishing. Dad, Josh and I are going down to Boaties. You said you couldn't come because you were taking your aluminium runabout out. Is that still happening or do you want to come with us?"

"So they are back again, are they?" Dom asked. "Jock was right about the full moon."

Dom motored out, sat in a spot behind Oyster Island where he couldn't be seen from Boaties Bay and threw a line out.

Jock said that they would ring Dom the moment Harry arrived and met Basil and Dylan at the top of the beach. They'd found a few spots in the underground room where they could get reception for the mobile phone. Now the plan was in place and it was just a matter of patience. "Be just my luck to be playing a 24kg cod when they ring. I don't fancy having to cut the line and forget about landing the fish," Dom muttered to himself.

Jock and the boys parked in the usual spot at the rear of the dump and walked down into the gully via the quarry. Because they had made this journey before, their confidence was high. It was too early for Harry to arrive, and the other two were still on board the cruiser.

"C'mon Dad, let's go. We can all go down together can't we," asked Josh.

"No," said Jock. "If we act too cocky about any of the safety things, such as getting into the gully, it could be our downfall. We're reasonably sure there's no one around, but we can't be absolutely certain. When we get close to the cement slab, we need to check that there is no one in the car park first."

"Okay, we get the picture. The rule is, don't change the routine. We go slowly down, one-by-one. If we have to hide in a hurry, it's easier if there's only one of us."

"Yes," said their father, "There's no way that we can afford to be careless."

The three of them made it safely into the tunnel with no dramas this time. "I'll take the first shift at the spy hole," said Jock. "You two boys open the door and have a rest on the bunks."

"I might go and listen from the back tunnel," said Jeremy. "We should be able to hear Harry coming from a fair distance away."

"I'll come and help you open the vents and wait back there with you," said Josh. "That's okay, Dad, isn't it?"

"It's more than okay. I'll feel better if you're both there together in case anything happens. Be careful about that tunnel too. We're reasonably certain it's still as strong as the day it was built, but we shouldn't be too complacent."

About half an hour later they heard a car in the distance. It stopped for about five minutes and then started again.

"That's Harry. He stopped to let Spot out, did you hear him?"

Their night vision was slowly improving in the gloom. They could just make out Jock's frantic signalling to be quiet. They signalled back that the car was coming. When they were standing beside Jock in the tunnel, their father whispered, "I thought so, because the other two are hiding up in the rocks again. The curlews will be out in full force again soon."

"What do you mean?" whispered Josh.

"Don't you remember the other times? There were two distinct curlew cries before they spoke to Harry."

"That's right, I had forgotten that. You think that's a signal?" asked Jeremy.

"I think so. If it happens again tonight, we'll be absolutely sure."

"Sssh! Listen… What's that noise? asked a voice on the beach. Jock and his sons froze. They didn't think their whispering had been very loud. "Hell, surely they weren't going to be found out."

"Y-y-yes I c-c-can h-h-hear it," said Dylan. I-i-it's a c-c-car. I h-h-ope it's H-h-harry. I-I-I'm g-g-getting bl-bloody un-un-comfort-t-t-table beh-h-hind th-th-this st-st-stupid r-r-rock.

The three watchers in the tunnel collectives heaved sighs of relief and thanked their lucky stars. They chuckled nervously as they remembered a similar incident on the night when this saga began. It was a Déjà Vu moment, almost word-for-word. It was as if Dylan had been programmed on a loop. The light, now-familiar rumble echoed from the direction of the underground room. Soon, there was a curlew cry, closely followed by another.

Josh waved his mobile phone at his father and brother, and took off quickly for the room.

On the other side of the island, while Dom waited, he was catching a nice supply of fish. That's a real bonus, and we need them for Isabel, he thought. No big cod yet, though. The mobile phone rang and Dom fiddled with all the buttons. It rang out and he was just about to put it down, when it rang again. This time he figured where the TALK switch was and had his finger hovering over it.

"Bloody Hell, Dom, are you ever going to learn to use the bloody thing properly?" a frustrated, whispering voice hissed from the earpiece.

"Ah! Hello Josh, and how are you?"

"Not too bad now that you have answered. What's so hard about it, Dom? We show you where the switches are, all the time."

"I was just testing you. I didn't want you to think I was just sitting with the phone in my hands, waiting for you to call. I'm busy you know. I've been catching some good-sized fish."

"Right, whatever you say, but Harry has just arrived. The three of them should be loading the boat soon."

"I hope you're not talking too loudly. We don't want them to hear you, do we?"

"I am in the room, Dom. How the hell can they hear me when I'm whispering?"

"Well, hang up the phone. Don't keep prattling on, Young Fellow. You're holding me up. See ya," and it was Dom who hung up in Josh's ear.

Bloody old coot; he's not the only one who feels like boxing someone's ears at times. I'd just love to be in the dinghy with him right now. I'd soon see how well the old blighter can swim. Josh checked that the mobile was in vibrating mode before heading back through the light-trap into the front tunnel. He didn't move too quickly though because he needed to calm down. "What a bloody old mongrel Dom is," he muttered.

Dom motored around to the front of the island, trailing his mackerel line. He'd been fishing for several hours, but he reckoned that they would still get a surprise when he started the outboard. He didn't have very far to go before he reached the larger vessel. Obviously Basil and crew would have heard him when he first arrived earlier in the evening but, as the time passed, they would have forgotten Dom was there, tucked out of sight, behind the island. When he was only a couple of boat lengths from the anchored half-cabin cruiser, he cut the engine and wound in his mackerel line as he slid smoothly to a stop.

The three blokes on the beach spotted him before he cut his engine. Carrying two small wooden cases each, they had walked down the cutting and just stepped onto the beach. "What the hell?" growled Basil. "There's a tinny out there."

"Quick; we'll have to put the travellers back in the Toyota. Stop, Dylan, settle down, you dip-stick, just turn around quietly and walk slowly back up the cutting. Don't make it look suspicious. The tinny is too far away. The fisherman can't see what we're doing."

"They aren't worried about being heard, by the sounds of it," Jeremy whispered.

There was a loud slam from the car-park as Dylan – undoubtedly – let the canopy door slip from his grip. Poor Dylan was in trouble again. "That's it Dylan, let everyone within a ten kilometre radius know we're here. Slam the door why don't you?"

"S-s-sorry b-b-boss, it sli-ip-ipped. It w-w-wasn't m-m-my faul-l-lt.

"Nothing's ever your fault is it? But you're right. I'm forever telling you that it was your mother's bloody fault for having you." Basil sounded as if Dylan was someone he could easily do without. By now they were halfway down the narrow sandy beach.

"Can you see who it is?" asked Harry.

"Do you reckon I've got super powers? My night vision is okay, but not that good. Can you see who it is yourself, you moron?" Basil was still uptight after his altercation with Dylan.

"No!" replied Harry in a frosty tone which was lost on the agitated Basil.

"That's exactly my point, you moron. If you can't see him how the hell do you expect that I can?"

"Listen mate, take care. You're over-stepping the mark," snarled Harry in a tight, cold voice.

"Sorry, Harry, I wasn't thinking straight. My mind is on the dinghy out there, more than on what I am saying."

Harry seemed to be ignoring the apology. "Don't you ever call me a moron or an idiot again, or you'll live to regret it. I can bloody well tell you that with certainty."

"Get over it. We've got more to worry about," was Basil's angry reply.

"A-a-anyway," stammered Dylan, "D-d-don't you think w-w-we sh-should go and g-g-get the f-f-fishing rods?"

"Well, well, well. He can think for himself," said Basil in a sneering tone.

"Leave him alone. I think what Dylan has said, makes more sense than anything you've contributed so far," said Harry, obviously enjoying himself now. "At least he's using his intelligence a lot more damned effectively than you have been in the last couple of minutes."

"Watch it mate. Now it's your turn to be a bit careful with what you say. One more remark like that and you'll miss the rest of the action. You're not the only one who knows how to use his fists." Basil was becoming very aggressive again.

"H- hurry up," said Dylan. "G- et over it, you two. He'll b-be here soon and we'll need to have the l-lines cast out before he n-notices that we've only just started fishing."

"Dylan must be worried about those two fighting," said Jock. "He seems to have picked up his act a bit and has taken on a degree of authority. Amazing what happens to the underlings when the bosses lose control. Even the stuttering has almost disappeared."

It seemed Basil reluctantly walked away from the brewing conflict. The three crooks gave the impression they were fishing by the time Dom was preparing to toss his anchor overboard.

"Dom must be a genius," said Jeremy. "They're doing exactly what he said they would do."

"I wonder what they expect to catch without bait" commented Josh.

By then, Dom's dinghy was only a few metres from the cabin cruiser. "Ciao," he yelled, greeting the deckhand with a friendly wave. "You catch many fishes? I got plenty Sweet Lip and Grunter. You not catch any, maybe you buy some off a me, eh?"

"Nah, we'll be right, mate," said the deckhand. "We're doing okay. Are you going to do some fishing here?"

"I bin in here before. Not much bloody fish in dis bay," said Dom, looking at the trio on shore. "Dat your mates fishing? I go tell dem, dat's all mud unda here. Ciao, see youse later, eh? You sure you no wanna buy some fishes?"

"No thanks mate, we're all right. See ya."

Dom heaved in his anchor and started the outboard. He motored in closer to the boat ramp, and idling the motor back, pulled up close to the three fishermen.

"Ciao," he said again. "You catch some fishes?"

"No," snarled Basil. Just what we don't need tonight, he thought, some crazy old coot hanging around. "Buzz off, why don't you? We're busy." He was watching Dom closely and gave him a nasty grin.

Ignoring the threat, Dom said, "You not catch anysing in here. Is a too muddy. You wanna buy some fish off a me?"

"No," Basil barked at Dom. "We are all right, thank you very much."

"Hoe-kay, I go back where I come from. See youse later," said Dom.

"Okay mate. Have a good night," said Harry.

"You too," said Dom shaking his head doubtfully.

"Hah, I nearly forget. I just stop to tell you somesing. Don't keepa many little fishes, eh? Da fishing inspector, he ees around."

"What?" said Basil, who now suddenly became extremely interested in the old fisherman. "When…? Tonight, you mean?"

That's a turnaround for the books, thought Dom, suddenly I'm not such a nuisance after all. Then he continued in his broken accent. "Yeah, he talk to me bout half hour before. Hees out at da islands. He been sneaky, I theenk. Everyone expeck him be at home now," said Dom, laying on as much drama as he could, waving his arms about and rocking his dinghy more than was necessary. "You watch da sizes of da catch. No excusi for breaka da rules." Dom gave them a thoughtful look. "Well eef youse no wanna buy da fish, I go."

Dom hit the throttle and headed for home. Josh and Jeremy knew, just by his body language, he was whistling tunelessly. From firsthand experience, they knew he always did that when he had thrown a spanner in the works or got 'one-up' on someone. Even though they hadn't been able to hear what he said, they knew Dom was pleased. His posture and the erratic zigzagging manoeuvre as he took the boat through its paces spoke volumes.

Jock said, "I wonder what he told them. He's happy whatever it was. Look at him out there. It's a wonder he doesn't pop a rivet or two. He's an excellent driver and he wouldn't put on that performance without good reason."

The trio gave one another a silent high five and could hardly contain their amusement, or their curiosity, for that matter. They watched Dom until his dinghy was out of sight.

"Whoa; back to your posts everyone. The rods are back in the dinghy,"warned Jock. "Here they come."

From halfway up the beach, the trio stared at the wake of Dom's boat. "How about that stupid old git? Did you see the way he was handling that boat?" said Basil. "Couldn't control it very well, could he?"

"No," laughed Harry. "That's probably the first boat he's owned. He'd be a bloody retired fruiterer, I'll bet," continued Harry with a sneer, as he watched the last of Dom's wake. "Most likely, he hasn't got a clue about the difference between reef and rubbish fish. Bet he hasn't done much fishing in his life, but he's still got to try to sell you something. I tell you, it's in their blood; once a salesman, always a salesman."

"Yeah, bl-bloody s-s-salesm-m-man," echoed Dylan.

"Basil, do you reckon he's right about the fishing inspector?" asked Harry.

"I wouldn't be surprised. If that crazy old bloke was talking to him in the last half-hour, I'd say the inspector would still be around. In fact, didn't the bloody old fruit loop say he was out around the islands? Well, there are three islands around here and one of them is sitting a few hundred yards away over there. That's where that old bloke was fishing. That could be a bit of a worry."

"What do you reckon we should do?" Harry wasn't too happy about taking any risks. "Our operation is too valuable to risk throwing it away on a dodgy gamble."

"Abandon tonight's plans," said Basil, "But be aware, once my contact leaves, he won't be back. His New Zealand run doesn't include a return journey. It's tonight, or next month, take your pick."

"Cancel tonight's operation then," Harry decided immediately. "I'm not prepared to take the risk. I've got too much to lose in this community."

Basil was already making his way down to the dinghy. He'd anticipated Harry's final decision. "So we won't be seeing ya, until next month. I'm off then. Gotta radio the contact and advise him of the change of plans. Don't want him within a couple of hundred kilometres of this area if there's a Government inspector hanging around."

Dylan was standing, staring out to sea, in the direction Dom had gone.

149

"C'mon you bloody stupid little twerp, get a move on or I'll give you a swift kick in the rear."

Dylan jumped to attention and ran after his boss, while Harry's footsteps could be heard crunching through the shell-grit and pebbles, in the other direction.

Josh cautiously strolled into the back tunnel, trying not to let his footsteps echo. It's handy to be able to listen to Harry drive off, rather than have to sit for ages, wondering when it's safe for us to leave, he thought. Ten minutes later, he reported back. "He's gone, and I'm sure I heard him stop to pick up the Spotter."

"We'll give it another ten minutes and then we'll head off too," said Jock.

Half an hour later, they were at Dom's front gate. He was out the back, hosing the salt water off his boat and tractor.

"Hey Dom, you got a rockmelon, or some lychees, we can buy?" asked Jeremy.

"Yeah," added Josh, "And don't try to sell us any fish, either. You've got to know what you're doing, when it comes to seafood. We don't want to end up with any rubbish."

"Huh?" was the puzzled reply. "What the hell are you pair raving on about?"

The boys couldn't keep a straight face any longer. They laughed until their sides ached. The whole charade at Boaties had been worth watching, but Dom's reaction, just now, was priceless.

"C'mon Dom, give me the hose. I'll finish this for you while the boys give you all the details. We're laughing at those gullible blokes, we've just been watching, not at you. Do me a favour, though, wait until I finish here before you tell your side of the story. I can't wait to hear what you have to say."

When they were all together, Dom began. "Well, I was having a great time. I can describe the deckhand, and learned the cabin cruiser's name and registration number. I like the name: *Red Watermark.*" He continued with his story, describing the actions the other three had witnessed. "The deckhand couldn't wait to get rid of me. I bet he nearly had a fit when I said that I was going to cruise in towards shore, to talk to the others. Old Basil was cranky as all hell, when I kept chatting to him. He didn't want to buy my fish. He was rude and kept yelling at me; told me to go away, in no uncertain terms. Now I ask you, is that any way to treat a fisherman trying to make a living? Talk about feeling like an uninvited guest. I was mortally wounded."

"Yeah, Dom, I would have felt the same," said Josh, "But you aren't a fisherman. You're a retired fruiterer, remember, and a fruit loop, into the bargain. You are the world's worst skipper who can't handle your new boat. According to them, you're a novice when it comes to fish or fishing."

"You were just brilliant out there, Dom. With the act you put on, they'll never suspect you're a professional fisherman." Jock was curious about Harry, Basil and Dylan's abrupt departure. "They've gone without transferring the goods. You frightened the life out of them. What did you say?"

"I just mentioned the fishing inspector I'd been speaking to half an hour before. That's the only time they gave me any respect. They sat up and listened very closely. It does an old Fruiterer's heart good to know that his advice is still valuable. We've got another month up our sleeves now."

"I can't believe it's been so easy this far" said Jock. "But, it's thanks to your parents and their kids. Catarina's Room and the tunnels are necessary, for our safety."

"Mama would be laughing like mad; taking great pleasure in those blokes' uneasiness," said Dom. "She had such a wicked sense of humour. You would have liked her. Come on, Josh, go and grab those fresh fish I couldn't sell. I want to give them to Isabel."

CHAPTER 17

Jock and the boys were down on their beach, collecting driftwood to top up the barbecue's fuel supply. "That was a great idea Dom came up with. He sent that mob scurrying, with their tails between their legs. It's given us another month before they're back. He wants to try to find the boat's permanent mooring, now that we have a name," said Jock, "And keep an eye out for Harry's 4WD."

"School's out for two weeks at the end of next week. We're on holidays," said Josh. "Dad, do you reckon Mum would let us stay in the Whitsundays for a week? A lot of our mates are going up there. It would make a good cover to see what else we can find out."

"I know your holidays aren't due yet, Dad," said Jeremy, "but Dom could drive over each day so we could do some detective work together, and you'd have at least two days off, to come with him."

"If we could convince him his house will be okay left to its own devices for a few days, he could stay up there as well. The kids think Dom's cool."

"When did you say? Monday week…?" Jock started to run his work schedule through his mind. "I think I've got four free days in a row. I'll check it out when we get home. C'mon we'd better get on with this. Don't make any more decisions until I have a think about it."

While they'd been down on the front beach, Isabel had made herself a cuppa and sat in front of the TV as a means of immersing herself in a daydream or two.

"Hello Mum, what's that you're watching?"

"Nothing much; just channel surfing. There doesn't seem to be much on TV these days. Well, nothing that interests me anyway," replied Isabel.

"What no assignment or craft work to catch up on, Love?" asked her husband.

"There is, but I wanted a break."

"Isabel, have you seen my work timetable anywhere?"

"Yes, it's on the desk beside the computer."

Jock grabbed his schedule and looked through the roster. "That's what I thought," he murmured. "I start night shift again soon. Come Monday week, I've got four days off during the crossover period."

"You weren't planning on us going away somewhere were you?" asked Isabel. "It's the start of the school holidays. I hadn't realised you had time off at the same time. I've been feeling guilty about what I wanted to discuss with you, and now, I feel absolutely wretched."

"Why what's the matter?"

"That literature workshop at the Uni; there's been a last minute cancellation and the spare place has been offered to me. They rang me today."

"That's a fabulous opportunity," said Josh. "We'll miss you, but you must go."

"Yes, Isabel, the chance is too good to miss," said Jock. "Of course you will go."

"But what about you lot? The three of you will be on holidays."

"We'll find something to do. Tell you what, you go to that workshop and Dom and the three of us will head off to the Whitsunday's for a fishing holiday. There were vacancies still being advertised for on-site vans at that new Caravan Park near Shute Harbour. I'll go and ring them now."

"No, wait! Don't do that. I'm not going to go. I'm being selfish and you're just offering to go fishing so I won't feel guilty. We'd already decided months ago to drive out to Middlemount to catch up with your best mate Len and his wife. We practically promised them we would when we found that your next four days off coincided with the school recess. I'd completely forgotten. We don't get much of a chance to do that, and you were excited about the plan."

"Don't be silly," said her husband. "You are going to accept the Uni's offer."

"No, I am not, and that is final. Come on, it's getting late. Let's all go to bed. I've got an early start tomorrow. I'm going into town to get groceries and pay some bills, so please forget all this rot about workshops."

The next morning promised to be the curtain raiser to a perfect day. Sitting on the front steps eating their Weetbix, the twins looked out over the bay. The water was glassed out again. It was a pure, clear aquamarine blue, the predictable colour of the Whitsundays.

Jock was at work, and Josh and Jeremy were drumming up the courage to go and speak to their mother.

"C'mon, it's no use putting it off. We've got to get her to go on her workshop," said Jeremy.

"Hey Mum, you know last night, when we were talking about the holidays, Josh and I were just about to ask you something, but you and Dad got in first."

"Yeah," said Josh, "We don't want to offend you, but Jeremy and I had wanted to ask if we could go into town and spend the first week of the holidays hanging about with some of the other kids from school."

"We thought that we'd take a couple of day trips to the islands, maybe even go right out to the reef, spend a day or two at the Airlie Beach Lagoon, take in a movie or two and generally chill out," added Jeremy.

"It's not that we don't want to go back out west with you and Dad. We will, if you want us to," said Josh.

"But, the first week is the only time the gang from school can get together," Jeremy added.

"Because most of us live in different directions and a fair distance out of town, we only get to socialise during school lunch breaks. It's a problem getting together on the weekends. We all thought this would be a cool thing to do." Josh was starting to feel bad about all the fibbing, but his mother's short course offer was just as important as their own plans.

"Yes," agreed Jeremy, "And the Uni thing, Mum, that's just too good an opportunity for you to miss, so grab it. You were feeling guilty about asking if it would be okay to go away and we were doing the same. The workshop actually solves a few problems."

"Dom and Dad can still go fishing too," suggested Josh. "They don't need much of an excuse to do that. What if we stay with them at the caravan park and meet up with the gang during the day," Josh asked his mother. "It will be easier for us to get to Shute Harbour from Airlie. Dom and Dad can drive us over. That'll save us all a bit of money too."

Jeremy chuckled as he said, "Some of the kids might even want to spend the day fishing. We can baby sit Dom for a change."

"Yes," agreed Isabel laughing. "I guess that would work out perfectly. I keep forgetting that you guys are growing up. I'm sorry. I never even considered that you might want to do something other than the family thing."

"Don't be sorry, Mum," said Josh, "We still love going places as a family. It's not that at all. To be honest, it's a couple of the other kids, who are really pushing the issue on this. They're a bit housebound during the holidays because of the distance they live from town. Their parents are so busy on the property just now that they have time management problems with ferrying the guys around each day. Jeremy and I just thought that this gives us all a chance to take part in what each of us wants to do without any of us going on a guilt trip."

"Especially you, Mum; you don't often get the chance to get away from the house and just be 'Isabel'."

Although the twins were trying to get Isabel safely out of the way so the four of them could continue their investigation, they really did feel strongly about what they were saying. The workshop would really help with their Mum's Uni Degree. She'd be absolutely mad not to go. Actually, they were secretly proud that she was doing this education thing. They'd tell her that when they were older, not just yet. It wasn't cool for teenage boys to admit to being emotional about their parents' achievements. It made them look a bit soppy.

After work, Jock sat down on the front landing to take off his work shoes and socks. He felt Isabel burrow in beside him. With a mug of coffee in each hand, she said quietly, "Hello Love, did you have a good day? I just made myself a cup of coffee and I made you one, as well, when I heard the car arrive." Looking out across the lawn to the beach and then over the water, she said "Isn't it beautiful here? I'm so glad you landed that job and we moved to the area."

"You got that right, in one, Isabel. I hope we stay here for a long time."

"Jock, the boys talked to me this morning. I keep forgetting that they are growing up and need to make their own decisions. How do you feel about them spending the holidays on their own, wandering around with their mates?"

"Terrified," said her husband, "But it had to come. I just keep thinking of them as our children who depend on us. I tend to forget that they are developing into young men with minds of their own."

"Yes, I do too. I guess I need to go and get my scissors."

"Why?" asked her puzzled husband.

"So you can help me cut the apron strings," she said, in a wobbly voice. "I'm going to go to that workshop, if that is all right with you," and then she burst into tears.

Putting his arms around her and giving her the biggest hug, he said, "Sweetheart, I'm really very pleased." And he was too.

Isabel booked a bus fare to go north for her workshop and Dom, Jock and the twins organised to spend the first four days of the boys' holidays at Airlie, in the Caravan Park. Rather than catch the passenger coach at the local servo, 11km away on the main highway, Isabel decided instead, to travel into town with her husband, her sons and the family's best friend, Dom, to start her journey from there. Her bus left at 4.00pm and Jock, the boys and Dom, stood in the main street to wave Isabel off before getting into the car and heading off to the beach. They still had a 25 minute drive ahead of them with Dom comfortably sitting in the front beside Jock.

"It's a bit less crowded in the back seat now," said Josh.

"Yep," kidded Jeremy, "And the smell of garlic isn't as strong."

"Just be thankful we didn't come in the ute," said Dom. "Your mother and father could have squeezed into the cab, but you pair would have to sit in the open air. That would have messed your lovely hairdos a bit."

After they checked in at the tourist park and put their luggage into the on-site van, they were rearing to get started.

"It's too late to do much, but we'll go for a walk along the front beach and then grab some fish and chips for tea," said Jock.

The next day they were up bright and early, ready for the ten-minute drive to the harbour where they checked out the boats, but found none recognisable. Later, back in Airlie, they sat on the edge of the old stone jetty to settle down for a few hours fishing and watching as vessels came and went.

"None of them even look remotely like *Red Watermark*," said Dom. "It's almost lunchtime so we'll wander back to the park, have a bite to eat and then see what's around the rest of the place." An hour later they were sauntering around the marina, looking at what was moored in there.

"Nothing here looks very promising either" said Dom.

Back on the old stone jetty at Airlie, they'd been fishing for about an hour, when a bloke wandered along with a little black dog trotting beside him. It was a nice little animal with bright eyes and an intelligent face. Sniffing the air as it scurried along; it wandered over to every nook and cranny it passed and checked everything out.

"G'day mates. Catching anything?"

"Not even so much as a bite," said Dom. "You a local?"

"Sort of; My old mate, Shandy and I, live on my old bond-wood over there," he said, bending to pat the small terrier.

156

"That'd be a good sort of a life, eh?" said Jock. "Do you take the boat out often?"

"A few times a week," said the old man. "I do a bit of fishing here and there. It doesn't hurt to give the motor a run every few days. I don't want it to seize up on me."

"I suppose there are quite a few local boaties living around here," said Jock. "Do you know many of them?"

"A few," said the old bloke. "By the way, I'm Jim Carruthers." After introductions all round, they settled back for a good yarn.

"Mingleton...," said Jim, "I haven't been down that way for years. The poor old bus I drive would probably shake itself to pieces if I drove it too far. What's the place like nowadays? Is Bob Woodbury still there?"

"Haven't met him," said Dom. "But then I've only been back about seven years. Maybe he came and went during the twenty years I was away."

"Could have done," said Jim. "He used to have a beaut old wooden boat called *Seeker*. From memory, it was a twenty-eight footer. We jokingly referred to it as the Sea Car."

"Actually, it's still there, but the current owner's name isn't Woodbury. Bob must have sold her."

"That's probably the case. He used to say it was becoming difficult for him to manage; getting a bit heavy to drag up on the trailer as he was getting older."

"Talking about boats, we had a new boat moored down their overnight just recently. Nice vessel. It would go close to being a twenty-four footer too, I reckon. A sleek fibreglass unit; *Red Watermark*, I think it was called. It was white with a red painted line just above the waterline," said Dom.

"Yes," said Jock. "I really liked the shape of it. I wouldn't mind getting to know the owner. I'm thinking of buying a new boat and I'd like to know where he got *Red Watermark* from. I didn't get close enough to check out who the boat builder was."

"Can't say that it sounds familiar at all," said Jim, "but then I don't know everyone with a boat around here. There are a lot of short-term mariners who pull in here for a few days and then move on."

"That's okay," said Jock. "I just thought it was a nice looking craft. It's not really that important."

Just then, with a series of high-pitched yelps, the little dog took off after one of the cats it had sniffed out amongst a heap of plastic fish crates. "Cripes, that was a bit of a wakeup for the poor feline," said Dom. "He's a good little hunter by the look of it."

"Too Bloody good at times... blasted feral cats," said Jim. "Shandy," he yelled, "Bloody well get back here." He whistled and yelled at the little dog. With ears twitching back and forth and obviously hearing his owner's shout, Shandy completely ignored it. He had much better things to do and was halfway along the bitumen road in hot pursuit of a half-grown ginger cat. "Better go I suppose, before he gets himself run over. That bloody little mongrel won't come back. He'll have the cat up the nearest pole and sit there all night waiting for it to come down." He started to walk off, hesitating long enough to ask, "Are you staying around here?"

"Yes," said Jock, "At the caravan park just around the corner."

"Nice place that; might see you around tomorrow, eh? I'd enjoy another chat with you all. Not everyone wants to stop and talk around here. See you later then."

After Jim and Shandy left, they fished for another quarter of an hour before packing up their gear. By then, Jim's dinghy was almost halfway out to his boat. Shandy was standing on the bow, looking back towards shore and still barking furiously at the distant cat. They gave Jim a wave, and then headed off for a well-deserved drink. After that, they reckoned that they'd find the pizza shop. They didn't eat junk food very often, so there was a lot of lost time to catch up on. They washed the Double-Decadence Pizza Supreme down with large glasses of Coke and checked out the TV programs, after which the twins settled down to watch some music shows for a couple of hours.

"C'mon Jock," said Dom, "Let's have a couple of stubbies, then we'll go for a walk along the esplanade. There's nothing but rubbish on the box these days." The two men walked halfway along the footpath, eventually perching on one of the park benches, to look out over the million-dollar beachfront view.

"Tomorrow, we'll do the rounds to check out some of the non-tourist areas where the locals dock their boats. It stands to reason that these jetties and Marinas around here are not going to be used as frequently by permanents," said Jock.

The next few days saw the four of them checking as many anchorages as they could find. In the end, they felt like they had run up against a brick wall. Then, on the day they were due to pick Isabel up from the bus, they admitted defeat. While sitting having breakfast beside the van park pool, they went through their activities over the last four days.

"One good thing was running into Mark, Hayden, Ben and Scott. Hanging out with them for a few hours every day was fun. Shame we didn't get out to Daydream or Hamilton though," said Jeremy.

"Dom and I were glad we met Jim, especially when he took us out for a half-day fishing trip.

"That bombie in the middle of the Whitsunday Passage is amazing. It's been years since I fished in that depth of water," Dom said.

"Those tourist-boat skippers are something else though," complained Jock. "I think they have competitions to see who's best at scaring the hell out of the fishing parties who anchor out there, especially the new chums in smaller boats."

"Their wake is a bit fierce," agreed Dom "I practically had to hang on by my toenails every time one of those big mongrels nearly tangled our fishing lines. They motored too close, the bludgers."

"I'm going to add Jim to my to-do list for grocery days. There are some good supermarkets down here. We've set it up already," Dom grinned, "And on your next shift changeover, you and Isabel can come too."

"What time does Mum's bus arrive?"

"Four o'clock this arvo. We have to check-out of our accommodation by10.00am so let's go back to town," said Jock.

"How about calling into Conway and checking the mooring situation there. We have to drive right past the turnoff."

They settled their bill and were ready to hit the road by around 9.30am.

"I wish we could stay a few more days," said Jeremy.

"We would have done, if I didn't have to work. It would have been good for your mother to wind down for a few days after her workshop. By all accounts, the content can be very full-on." Jock hit the blinker to signal a right turn at the corner into the main street of Airlie.

Dom quietly interrupted the conversation. "Parked up there on the right; quick, have a look and see if you agree with me."

"Yep, I wouldn't be surprised if it is. It looks like the vehicle you described to us." Josh seemed quite excited about it.

"There's a park. Pull in so we can have a look."

"The number plates are different."

"Don't let that throw you," Dom advised. "Remember what I said about that?"

"Well, it is Harry's vehicle. Isn't that him sitting over there, about three-quarters of the way down the block, talking to that blonde guy?" Josh said. "He's got his back to us, but I'm almost sure it's him."

They kept walking and, when they'd gone a couple of hundred yards past the fellow in question, they looked in a Dive Shop window before turning to retrace their steps. This time there was no question about it. He was their man. He'd never set eyes on any of them, so they felt relatively safe giving him a quick glance.

A couple of shops further along, they stopped and looked into the newsagency's window.

"Tell you what, young Josh. You walk ahead of me and when we get beside Harry's car, stop and let me accidentally run into you."

"Okay, but why?"

Dom had fished a fifty cent piece out of his pocket. "I want to drop this beside the back of his car. I want to check for my 'H/y' engraving."

"Oh that… Yeah; right you are, but you don't really need to because we all recognise Harry."

"Yes, but is this Harry's car? This make is a dime-a-dozen. He could be parked around the corner. No good recording the incorrect registration.

Jeremy shot ahead and, turning round, started to walk backwards, as teenagers do. "Bummer," he said quietly. "We better shelve that plan."

"Why?"

"Because Harry and his mate have both stood up and are shaking hands. Uh-oh, they've just parted company and our quarry is heading this way."

"Right, let's get back to our car, pronto," answered Dom.

Jock was watching the on-coming traffic and waiting for a break in the flow so they could cross the highway. As they stood at the kerbside, the boys and Dom chanced a quick look back at Harry.

"He's unlocking the car," said Jeremy, "So that's one less detail we have to check."

"Watch which way he goes. With a lot of luck, he'll drive around the block, and head back to town."

This is another lucky break, thought Jeremy, and the best we've had in the whole five days.

It was Josh's job to watch the rear of Harry's car as he drove off in the opposite direction. "He's turned left."

"Good; he's going to drive around the block. Unless he parks somewhere along the front esplanade, he should stop at the Give-Way sign just ahead on our right.

"Yep, there he is, at the intersection," said Jeremy.

The road's clear behind me, so I'll get going before he drives onto the main thoroughfare. We'll mosey along ahead of him and keep him in view in the rear vision mirror for a while. I don't want to give the game away." As he spoke, Jock adjusted his mirror so he could get the best possible view of the traffic behind him.

"So far so good" said Dom.

They drove for about 20 kilometres until Jock saw a couple of signs advertising a new housing estate. Still about six kilometres from town, he slowed and pretended interest in the new development. As he hoped, Harry became fed-up with the slower pace and passed them. They maintained a steady pace, keeping a reasonable distance from the white 4WD; far enough away to keep him in sight, but not close enough to attract Harry's attention.

"Bloody hell, he's indicating to turn down White's Lane. We can't follow him there, he'll get suspicious."

"What a bummer," said Josh. "Why can't we?"

Dom knew the street. One day a month, he spent the entire day in town. Grocery shopping was a necessity but also an excuse. The day in town, was his hobby day. With no specific agenda in mind, he went with the flow each month. Sometimes he looked at the different styles of houses and took note of the progress on any new buildings. Other times he went to the movies or went fishing at Cannon Vale, Airlie or Shute Harbour, and occasionally he even drove to Bowen for something different to do.

This new sub-division was on the outskirts of town. "It's quite new. White's Lane is a dead-end street with only about twelve houses built along it so far. If we turn down there now, he'll be very curious, seeing as how he's been following us since Airlie."

"Maybe he won't be. We were showing interest in the billboard advertising."

"I wouldn't like to test the theory out. We might need to stay unknown, in case we need to follow him around on another day."

"Well, what's the go now?" asked Josh.

"Conway, I think. What do you reckon, Dom? By the time we spend a few hours down there, it will almost be time to pick up Isabel."

"Yeah, let's grab lunch there. I know a great little take-away on the beachfront. They do a mean works' burger." Dom's grocery outings obviously encompassed a few more hidden extras besides basic Sunday driving.

"You wrote Harry's legitimate number down didn't you?" Jock asked the boys as they retraced their tracks back to the T-junction leading to Conway.

CHAPTER 18

The four of them, were of similar opinion. On that final day of their four days at Airlie, the chance of seeing Harry must have been a million to one. What was the likelihood of their target standing in the street just as Jock drove past? Think of the logistics. Even if the odds aren't quite as high as suggested, they mustn't be far off the mark.

"Bloody fluke that was," said Jock. "When he turned into White's Lane, it's a pity we couldn't follow him to see whether he lived there, or was just visiting." They discussed this at length.

When they finally had enough information to convince the authorities they weren't crackpots making up a fantastic story, surely the *Red Watermark's* name and registration number would be enough for the Government Department to make a start on its own search, and they had Harry's correct vehicle registration now.

Handing over those details would be a bit more of a problem. They had to decide how they were going to mention the newest number plate seen on the street at Airlie, and how they were able to connect it with their suspected crime when - supposedly - they had no idea what Harry, Basil or Dylan looked like. The four-wheel-drive parked at Boaties Bay that night wouldn't possibly have had two different number plates attached.

The next step in their report was going to be very dicey. They had no idea how they were going to go about it to avoid risking a verbal trouncing. They worried about not being able to convince Government Officials that the episode had happened recently; as recently as the previous week. If they were careless with their words, there could be accusations and suspicions tossed their way, not to mention their story being completely dismissed as being a misinterpreted fishing jaunt. There was nothing for it. They would have to conduct a more thorough search around White's Lane to see what story they could come up with, and do it sometime soon.

*****

It was almost 4.30pm. The school bus had delivered them to their stop, over half an hour ago, and the twins had just finished their smoko. Tonight was the next scheduled full moon, so the pick-up was about to happen. When the boys left this morning at 7:30am, the bay had been empty, and up to now, nothing had changed. The *Red Watermark* should have arrived by now, but where was it? There weren't any cabin cruisers, or boats of any type out in the bay.

"Maybe they've changed their anchorage. If so, hopefully, the new spot will still be in one of our bays," Josh said anxiously. The boys didn't necessarily want to wish the scam on the community, but they were so close to giving the authorities enough information to get an official investigation under way, it would be a tragedy for Harry, Basil and Dylan to escape the net so late in the piece.

Josh and Jeremy began to wonder if Dom's little episode when he scuttled the previous liaison had frightened the crooks away completely. They hoped they hadn't taken things a step too far. Dom had been really convincing. No doubt, the illegal business enterprise would still function, but last month's debacle may have influenced the suspected smugglers to move the rendezvous place. The chances the crooks suspected the Fishing Inspector was around because the Department had been tipped-off was a possibility.

"Perhaps we should have reported the thing earlier after all. What if they've found a new place for the transfer, somewhere closer to Airlie? I'd hate to think they might slip through the cracks," Jeremy moaned.

"C'mon, cheer up; I've just had a thought. Let's go and check the next bay south of Boaties." Josh grabbed his bike, urging his brother into action.

"We won't go down onto Boaties Beach though," Jeremy said when they were peddling along the open road. "We can't have them seeing us turn up, every time they're here."

The twins left the bikes at the quarry and wandered off, down their usual track. At the waterfall rocks, they sneaked down into the scrub and headed in the opposite direction, ignoring the path to the tunnel. They were trying to find the vehicle track which Dom had told them his family had used regularly, during the 1940s and 50s. When they came across it, the wallabies had created an animal track through the bladey grass. They followed the trail up to the top of the headland. From this distance, anyone standing on the deck of a boat out on the bay would just see a couple of bushwalkers. It was a popular spot for that activity. The view over Repulse Bay was breathtaking.

"Yep, there she is, thank God. They have changed their mooring spot; that's why we couldn't see them from home. They've anchored *Red Watermark* near the spot Dom used, last time he went night-fishing and frightened them away. They chuckled at the memory. Let's go home and call him."

*****

From the view through the spy-holes, the scene and the activities during this visit mirrored their previous visits'. The only change this time was that young Dylan threw his new pick anchor out the back as well as chucking the sand anchor out the front of the dinghy. "Not that he needed it tonight," whispered Josh. "It's a bit of overkill. The sea's like a millpond."

The entire operation was all over pretty quickly. "You're home early," said Isabel.

"Yeah," Dom said grumpily, "The ocean was so glassed out the big ones weren't biting at all. We caught lots of little nit-pickers but nothing worth keeping. We couldn't see the point in wasting good bait on the bludgers. Sorry Isabel, nothing for tomorrow night's supper."

"Yeah, fancy Dom not catching any fish," said Josh with the hint of a grin, "That must be a one-in-one-hundred years event."

Isabel sent her son a warning look. "Well, you'll come over anyway, won't you? I've got a nice piece of corned silverside. The vegies will be cooked in the corned-meat water and there'll be cheesy white sauce to go with it."

The elderly Italian's eyes lit up as Isabel knew they would. "Too bloody right I will; thanks. Will the sauce have onions in it?"

Isabel chuckled and nodded at Dom. She knew he loved corned meat and white sauce with onions almost better than his beloved fish.

The following week, Dom called in after they'd finished smoko. "Do you blokes want an early lift into school tomorrow morning? I'm going to do my grocery shop for this month."

"Will that be OK, Mum?" Isabel smiled and nodded. "Is it alright to get home a bit late, too?" Josh spun around to face Dom. "You've been promising to take us to look at the dam for ages now. Can we do that after school tomorrow?" The twins waited anxiously for both replies.

"Remember, I always leave here early. If I don't get in first, I miss the best of the baker's goodies. It's first in, best dressed, with that curly-headed Pommie bastard."

"Yes Dom; a six o'clock start, isn't it?" they grimaced.

As they drove along the main highway, Dom suddenly said, "I was serious about the baker's stuff, but I know exactly what I want. It will only take me ten minutes and then we'll go sight-seeing."

At a few minutes after six-thirty, Dom put his bread and selection of cakes in the esky before they set off across the main highway in the direction of White's Lane.

"Have you got that diary to write stuff in? Now don't make it obvious we're looking for anything. If he lives down here, I hope we're not too early for him. It depends on what type of job he has. If he's made an early start, we could have missed him." Dom drove along at a moderate speed. We won't miss anything happening in this street this morning, thought Jeremy. Dom's medium speed was equal to walking pace. It's a wonder he doesn't stall the old Holden.

They passed an early morning jogger, a couple of cars waiting in driveways and one which was reversing out, but no Harry anywhere. By the time they'd made a U-turn at the top end of the lane, the jogger was sprinting back towards his home, and Harry still hadn't appeared. Back on the main highway, they noticed a few empty parking bays up against the rear wall of the service station. This petrol station was immediately opposite the T-junction into White's Lane.

"As good a place as any to sit and watch the end of that lane," said Dom as he drove in, stopped at the bowsers and filled his tank. "Here Jeremy," Dom said as he handed him a $50 note, "You race in and pay for the petrol while I move the car over into a parking space. "Buy me a paper too, please. We need to sit and watch the traffic on the highway to see if our mate drives past."

They sat for another 20 minutes listening to Dom's tinny old radio while Dom read the daily news. "I suppose we can't have everything our own way, can we?" said Dom as he looked at his watch. "Seven-forty-five; you pair have to be at school at eight-thirty don't you?"

"Eight-forty-five at a pinch," said Josh.

Jeremy had angled the rear vision mirror so the twins could watch the highway while Dom relied on his side mirror. "We've been lucky, here he comes."

"He's waiting at the junction for the highway to clear," said Dom as he reversed out of his park. He too, stopped at the edge of the highway to allow a refrigerated truck to speed past. "Holy smoke," he muttered as the wind shadow of the passing vehicle slapped the front of his old ute with a thud. "Mongrels," he said as he savagely slammed the poor old girl into first gear and drove off.

…As slow as the proverbial turtle, thought Josh.

"You blokes keep your eyes glued. Jeremy, you watch the side streets on the right. Josh you look to the left," said Dom.

All other thoughts were sidelined when Jeremy spotted the rear of Harry's 4WD. "There he goes. Quick Dom, turn left, into Florence Street.

"Bloody hell, give me some warning why don't you," Dom was too far along to turn into the nominated street, so he took the next left and then left again, to come back into Florence Street. Which way do I turn now?"

"I'm not sure. I can't see the car anymore. Turn right and we'll go down to the end of the street and then chuck a U-turn."

"There he is, walking across the yard next to that red-brick building. Drive past Dom and we'll see what type of shop it is."

"I already know," Dom replied. "He's heading towards the Real Estate Office." They drove past unnoticed by Harry who inserting a key into the lock."

"He must work there, at that HT Realty place," commented Jeremy.

"Park just here please, Dom." Josh almost had the door open before the ute stopped. He raced up the street, grabbed a Real Estate newspaper out of the wire basket hanging from the wall and was back in the car before anyone had time to blink. Flicking through the pages, he came to what he wanted: HT Realty, proprietor Harry Tremayne, 43 Florence Street. "He doesn't just work here; it looks like he owns the place."

"Another lucky fluke discovering that information, I reckon," said Jeremy.

"No," said Dom. "It's a small town so it's not hard to find things out, in a hurry. The population isn't big enough to hide information for very long when you persevere." Dom watched the boy's faces, as he added, "Or when you get blackmailed by a stubborn pair of young hoons."

"I'm not sorry, Dom. Think of all those animals, or birds, that will be saved."

Josh added, "And hopefully we've kept some poor unsuspecting bloke from being hurt by being in the wrong place at the wrong time. Someone like old Blue, who thinks he's just going fishing, could become an innocent witness to Basil and crew's activities, when he should have been home in bed."

"Yes, I suppose my mother's room was always meant to be used for shielding someone from danger. I hate to say it, but I think you young whippersnappers might have been right. But just you wait until your mother gets hold of me and your father. I only hope you will have the common decency to feel guilty when that happens. It won't be pretty, I can tell you."

CHAPTER 19

"Well, that's it. There's sufficient information for the powers that be to have a look at the complaint." The four of them were in Dom's lounge room having a last minute discussion about the specifics of the alleged crime. Now they were within a few heartbeats of phoning the authorities, everyone's nerves were screwed up tight as springs.

"Before I make the call, remember that there is one small detail, we need to get right," said Jock, "That deliberate, but necessary, white lie we discussed earlier. Let's go over it again so we don't stuff up."

"Fair go, Dad, we won't get it wrong," Josh said irritably. "We're not likely to mess up."

"No, our tall tale sounds convincing enough to me. We won't feel the least bit guilty about telling it," added Jeremy. "We're hardly likely to stumble over a story which feels true enough."

Josh was as determined on that fact, as his brother was. "Those blokes have to be stopped. All we're doing is giving the authorities a pointer or two. Time frames don't come into it. If the experts can get straight to the nitty-gritty and catch Harry, Basil and Dylan, it will be a win-win situation."

His father frowned, "Yeah, I know, but bear with me, mate. We can't afford to uhm and ahh when we talk to that anonymous voice. The bottom line is, the bloke who we now know as Basil, referred to Harry mainly by his first name but did, just once, use his surname. We have to convince them that, when we recognised a local man's name, we didn't report our suspicions until we checked the real Harry Tremayne's car. We felt it wouldn't be right to drop an innocent bloke into the thick of it, only to find later his name was just being borrowed." Jock looked down at his scribbled notes beside Dom's phone once again, settled his nerves, and then made the call.

"Hello," Jock said. "Can you tell me if I have the correct department? I'd like to report some suspicious behaviour in our local area. I suspect it could be an illegal smuggling activity."

"Sure, I'll put you through. Do you mind if I place you on hold for just a minute?"

Jock covered the receiver with the palm of his hand and said "Well, here we go. We're on hold; no backing out now unless I hang up before the receptionist puts me through."

After a short delay, a new voice took over. "Hello, I believe you have something you want to report?"

The nature of the call and Jock's contact details were dealt with, before Jock went on to outline what he suspected and why. The bullet-like comeback from the other end began in earnest. Every new statement Jock gave repeatedly was rehashed and questioned. He shook his head and thought, I was expecting this reaction, but I didn't realise that I'd become annoyed with the bloke on the other end of the line. "What do you mean 'what makes me suspect the activity is illegal?' What I overheard a week ago while I was fishing, was interesting and I reckon it's worth investigating," said Jock, a touch of ice creeping into his tone.

"Why's that?" answered the annoying voice. And so it went on, one question after the other in response to Jock's allegations. The bloke was beginning to really irritate him.

"Because what I heard was damned incriminating, and not really the type of dialogue anyone would use on an average fishing jaunt." Jock rolled his eyes at the boys as he continued replying to the formal grilling he was receiving. The idea that, perhaps the overheard conversation was an innocent one was suggested repeatedly. Jock retaliated, saying he was reporting the conversation because he believed what he heard was genuine. He repeated that the blokes in the dinghy talked about Harry, the supplier, being late because the Police may have caught him. It all sounded authentic to Jock. That was what he intended to convey when he commented that what he overheard wasn't the usual fishing chit-chat. The conversation moved on to how many times the visits occurred, why that particular bay was targeted and what the timeframe of these blokes' return was likely to be.

"They didn't mention a date but I'd suggest that you try a few days each side of the next full moon."

"That seems like a bit of happy guesswork. Why the full moon idea? That seems a bit fanciful."

"No, I think it's a realistic supposition. It was full moon last week when they were here and I believe that they need enough natural light to conduct their business safely. Moonlight is much more benign than torchlight."

"Why?"

"There are no streetlights down there, Mate, and unlike fixed lighting, torch lights are mobile."

The conversation about the possibility of Jock's conclusion being the fabric of imaginative thinking to which he agreed continued. The query about the blokes just being innocent fishermen was raised yet again.

"But why are you so positive there was something illegal going on? It's a very small community; a harmless sort of rural place. Why would you suspect something like this?"

By then, Jock was beginning to get a bit snarky with the bloke on the other end of the phone. He had held his temper back quite well so far, but he was starting to feel the temperature rising. "Of course I realise that this area is a quiet seaside community. I bloody well should know, I live here, but I also heard the conversation that was suspicious in my opinion. Take what I say at face value or leave it. It's your choice, Mate. I'll consider that, with this phone call, my civic duty has been done and I'll get on with other things." Jock took a deep gulp of air to calm down. He did understand that the bloke on the other end of the line had to ask those questions in order to do his job. His duty was to his employer as he attempted to weed-out the crank calls. Even so, Jock was finding the whole process, somewhat galling.

The professional voice confirmed that the intention wasn't to doubt Jock's judgment, but to establish the level of urgency of the complaint. Jock's statement needed to have a strong base of believ-ability to warrant sending a crew to investigate.

At this point, Jock grinned wryly at his sons as he recognized his own speech becoming more formal the longer he went on talking. "We weren't supposed to be there, but..." Jock began, with every intention of creating 'a why would we make this up' scenario. The more the voice on the other end of the phone interrupted and revisited his allegations, over and over again, the closer Jock was coming to hanging up in the bloke's ear. It was all very well, he thought, for the fisheries department, or what other fancy name they wanted to call themselves, to advertise any suspicious activity should be reported, but when a concerned citizen did as asked and the report was treated with such suspicion, why would anyone bother?

"We...?" the voice on the other end interrupted. "Who else was with you?"

"My sixteen year-old twin sons, Josh and Jeremy."

It started again; the repeat questioning about whether the lads agreed with the father, why the suspected wrong-doers weren't aware of Jock and the boys' presence, why they hadn't been seen arriving, et cetera et cetera. "Mind you the look-out; the bloke back at the gully hadn't arrived at that stage or he might have heard us. Anyway, all in all, it seems that they slipped up big-time that night," Jock suggested.

"What's this? A lookout on land, you say. How do you know they had a lookout posted?

"Because Harry told them to be ready in case his mate rang from the washout to say someone was coming."

Jock was glad they'd reached this point in the conversation because it had added an element of variety: where was the so-called washout and why did Jock think these new arrivals had local knowledge. He explained about narrow roads, thick tree cover, theirs being the only house in close proximity and the area rarely being used after the sun had set. These were the reasons he believed would encourage anyone participating in illegal activities to take a risk on the place. The conversation moved onto the boat they saw on the bay.

"Wouldn't you wonder about a boat anchored out there all night?"

"You've got to be joking, haven't you, Mate? This is the Whitsunday's, an international tourist hot-spot. There are always visiting boats and yachts around here which sometimes stay overnight or even for a few days' – sometimes even weeks. Only last month, around at Mingleton, a trimaran was beached for a month while the owner visited relatives. It's certainly not unusual.

His phone-friend encouraged Jock to think back to why he thought the beach he and the boys used wasn't more thoroughly checked by the so-called crooks at the time. They moved onto the frequency of use Jock made of the fishing trail and why, on this particular night, they had covered the distance without being seen. Jock explained they were checking for new places to put the crab pots, so they wandered in and out of the mangroves. Maybe, they had been out of sight at the same time a pair of binoculars was sweeping the area, if that type of surveillance happened.

"Look Mate, this is all conjecture on our part. Let's move on, you're making me feel drowsy," Jock said.

The tone of voice on the other end of the line changed its timbre. The man's speech morphed into that of an interested tourist. "Was the new spot worth the walk?"

"Yeah, it looks promising, especially on a better tide. We got one keeper and tossed an undersized buck and a large female back into its habitat. A bit of a nuisance though; the old spot was much easier to reach. It was a quick walk from the car park so we don't have to carry the pots as far. They can be a bit awkward to handle."

"You're lucky to be able to walk out your front door and put your crab pots in."

"Yep, you're right there. We wouldn't live anywhere else now. People pay big bucks just to visit for a week or two."

"Well, half your luck. I envy you. Now I'd better drag my mind away from thinking about holidays and get back to what you rang me about."

Jock sighed quietly. It seemed they were back into repetitive question mode. The break of routine had been welcome, even if only for a few minutes. It reminded Jock that the person on the other line was no different from him. He wasn't trying to bully Jock, just making sure the claim was legitimate.

"Yes I suppose we'd better get on with it. The blokes from the dinghy were having a bit of a yike, because Harry was late."

"So Harry was the driver?"

"Yes. And that reminds me, Harry mentioned driving in behind old Emil Carrington's place on the Mingleton Road."

"Emil Carrington. Do you happen to have an address or a phone number for him?"

"Yes, I can give both to you, if you can wait a minute for me to check the phone book. You won't contact him personally though. The poor old bloke died a few months back and the place is deserted at present. Harry knew those details. That's why I think he could be a local."

"Right, I'll hang on until you get the contact details, thanks."

Jock hung the earpiece over his shoulder and turned around to pick up Dom's phone directory. He found the number and address and resumed his conversation. "You can check a boat registration number. I'll give it to you as well."

"I thought you said that you couldn't see anything from where you were."

"Yes, you're right, I did say that and that statement is correct."

"That seems to be contradictory. How could you not see anything yet have a plate number to give us?"

"I thought you'd find that a bit inconsistent. The fact is, we were expecting a mate to come fishing with us later that night. He expected to be an hour or more late." The invented saga of Dom's involvement began. Jock told the voice he allegedly had rung his elderly friend to prevent him arriving and immediately yelling out at them. The reasons for this were explained. They discussed the danger from incoming mobile phone calls in such a situation.

"When you rang your friend? Why didn't he just stay home?"

"Dom… Stay at home? You'll see what I mean when you meet him. We told him to do exactly that, but he told us he was coming to the top of the beach anyway to see what he could find out. He was worried about us. He's particularly close to my family, especially both my sons." Jock gave Dom a wink and sent him a thumbs-up gesture.

"It was a dangerous thing to do, especially if these blokes were doing something illegal."

"Yes, of course it was. We realise that, but we knew that you wouldn't have anything to go by if we couldn't at least get a rego number to give you. As I said, good luck with trying to stop Dom when he has decided on his own agenda."

Jock took a deep breath. He knew what was coming and wasn't disappointed. The lecture about citizens not acting as vigilante groups, etc., etc. The Department clearly advertises that fact Jock was told quite firmly as he expected he would be. He allowed his eyes to glaze over, held the handset a bit further away and mimicked the facial expressions of a nagging fish-wife to Dom and the twins.

"Anyway, what made your friend think he would be safe?"

"We were banking on them having some sort of contingency plan in place for if someone arrived unexpectedly. They wouldn't do anything stupid to alert the public to their presence, not if this is an ongoing scam, and especially if they intended using the same, convenient pick-up point again. They could hardly leave wounded or dead bodies everywhere could they?"

"Are you into detective stories or something?"

Jock had a chuckle over that before he continued. "It sounds like it doesn't it? Yes, we probably have been watching too much TV."

"You do realise, don't you, that you should have convinced your mate to stay home?"

"Not that again," Jock said. "You're beginning to get on my nerves, you know. Perhaps we'll finish our conversation at this point, eh?" Jock sighed, wait a second before continuing. "Yes, we're not stupid you know. We did in fact tell him exactly that…but, as I said before, good luck with that."

"You do acknowledge however, that it would have been the safe and correct option?"

"Mate…! If it makes you happy and stops you from going on and on about it…YES. There, are you happy now?"

"Indeed, and thanks. Don't be so defensive. I'm expected to do my job properly. Our department has a responsibility to the general public. We clearly state on our pamphlets and verbal advertising that any investigation of illegal operations must be left to the professionals."

Jock agreed and made a back-handed sort of an apology about Dom's interaction and congratulated the voice for being so well trained in his single-minded approach. At this stage of the call, Jock grinned at Dom and gave him the thumbs up sign.

"In future, you should abide by that advice," the voice continued.

"Yes, I totally agree, next time Dom probably won't take things into his own hands, but believe me, Mate, there isn't going to be a next time. We won't be going night fishing again until you catch those bastards."

After discussion on what Dom should have done if he came face-to-face with the alleged criminals and how they'd discussed the issue before Dom left home, Jock was able to quote the car's plate number and the boat's ID. The Department bloke expressed surprise that there hadn't been a bag draped over the boat ID. Jock continued Dom's invented itinerary of the beach jaunt. It was keeping this story believable, which stopped him from slamming the phone down. He was enjoying himself despite his frustration.

"Dom walked over to a log on the high tide mark where he could see the side of their dinghy and yelled out to them, asking if they'd found a really expensive fishing knife which he'd lost on the beach that morning.

"Did anyone answer him?"

"Yes, the short, older bloke did. He told Dom that they hadn't seen it. We could hear Dom carrying on something chronic about 'the bloody knife being pinched by some useless bludger'. He was fairly convincing."

"Once they answered him, did he go closer to them then?"

"No. Would you, if your mate rang and said he thought there were smugglers on the beach and in the middle of a job? I bloody wouldn't.

In fact, Dom was pretty gutsy to come anyway. He's a very valuable friend."

"So what happened then?"

"Dom asked them if they were catching anything, told them he'd caught nothing much today either and said 'see ya'."

"They seem to have made a couple of fundamental errors that you wouldn't expect from professionals, wouldn't you say?"

"Well, maybe they've been using the beach for so long, they've become a bit complacent by now. Who knows? Or maybe they aren't as professional as they'd like to think they are. I don't imagine every crook in this world is endowed with a high level IQ. Surely that's not a necessary job requirement."

"Once again, I take your point, Mr Somerville. I'll have someone call on you to go over this again face-to-face. Will you be home tomorrow afternoon?"

"Yep, no worries, we'll be home. You took my address before. There is one other thing though, and it's the reason we delayed a week in ringing you. That surname I mentioned which was dropped that night out on the beach when Harry arrived."

"Why did that stop you?"

"It was a name I recognised. I wanted to double check the owner's vehicle before I reported his involvement. Harry Tremayne is a local Real Estate Agent. I am a bit concerned about his so-called involvement because he is a community minded bloke. I think maybe his name is being used as an alias by someone else. When I told Dom, he was as cautious as I was because the Harry we know of drives a similar 4WD. We felt we owed it to him to drive into town to check his vehicle, but I had to wait until my day-off."

"How did you do that without raising his suspicion?"

Jock explained about the business car park where Harry's car sits all day because he drives a Real Estate vehicle during business hours. They discovered that the car looks very similar to the one Dom saw that night but the number plates differ. "We don't want to be involved in any more of this than necessary. You can do your surveillances and get your proof without our further involvement I hope. We can only add that the name is familiar, the vehicle is familiar but the number plates don't tally up. I hope we are wrong on that one. I rather like Harry Tremayne."

"Thanks, Jock. Can I call you that? Mr Somerville seems a bit too formal now we'll be coming to visit you. If there is a problem, we'll get onto it."

After school hours, wasn't a problem because the Department boys don't work normal office hours when conducting this type of work he was told. A cuppa, including refreshments, was offered and accepted.

Well this is it, thought Jock. I've got to go home, confess to Isabel and face the music. He had no doubt that he was in for one hell of a roasting. "Isabel, Sweetheart, we're having visitors tomorrow afternoon. Is there any possibility of knocking out a batch of pumpkin scones?"

*****

Twelve months later, the papers carried the news of the arrest of an illegal fauna trafficking organization operating locally. During the investigation a disused property in the Conway foothills as the location where two large aviaries were set up as holding coops for native cockatoos and galahs.

The Customs blokes had kept their promise. Jock, Josh, Jeremy and Dom weren't mentioned and wouldn't have to testify in court when the time came because the surveillance unit followed up on the information received, and gathered all the evidence they needed.

The agent who initially interviewed them, was pleased. "You blokes saved us from a very long investigation. We were able to keep the Real Estate guy under observation, and ultimately he led us to the others. Bit of luck for you though, getting all that information in one night. Someone must have been on your side. If Dom hadn't been as late as he was and walked onto that beach before you got a chance to ring him, then you would have been in serious trouble. All told, everything seems to have worked out to suit you lot very nicely doesn't it?"

The agent looked at them, long and hard, his glance a tad more than speculative than they would have preferred. His gaze suggested he thought they had quite a lot more to tell him. After waiting hopefully for a response for a couple of minutes, he sighed and continued his story. "The car registration was false, as you probably gathered. We were able to follow Harry in his Toyota around the place for a couple of months and we paid a great deal of attention to your full moon idea. That saved us wasting a lot of unnecessary time. The Department Unit created a hidden observation post at Boaties Beach, at that phase every month and watched the action. Unfortunately, Harry, the Real Estate bloke was involved. A watchman observed him drive out of his garage on those particular nights, in his usual vehicle sporting different plates. Other surveillance led them to the mother ship with which the *Red Watermark* networked. After watching for several months, when the time was right, the operatives were caught red-handed loading a consignment into the dinghy at Boaties Beach."

With a chuckle, the agent, knowing he could let his guard down somewhat, added. "Could you really believe Basil's unprofessionalism? He used his own registered cabin cruiser and dinghy. The young lad was supposed to shield the numbers with a sugar bag when the dinghy was anchored, but his nervousness caused him to be rather inefficient. When his uncle bullied him, he either forgot the hessian cover or it fell into the water halfway through the operation." The chuckles turned into a frown.

"When I think about the older bloke – his name is Basil – mentally abusing his young nephew, I'm afraid I see red. Dylan, that's the nephew's name. I remember that in your first phone call you said you didn't imagine every crook in this world is endowed with a high IQ. I become quite amused every time I recall the comment because, in my opinion, it's not young Dylan who is the stupid idiot, but his Uncle Basil."

Harry Tremayne had inherited his parents' property up in the hills outside town. A couple of large aviaries containing a collection of birds were found in a secluded clearing. "Sadly," reflected the Agent, "Harry really does seem to be a likeable bloke but, unfortunately, he is amoral. He was doing very nicely, financially wise, with his business. Why the hell wasn't he satisfied with that?"

Harry Tremayne broke down and admitted his involvement. There were a couple of unauthorised avian trappers in hinterland areas who were tracked down as well. Once the game was up, Harry hadn't been prepared to take the rap alone. "These people are a menace. They are scavengers who prey on our native wildlife and often take endangered species for their high-end market. There's quite a profit to be made. The buyers are as bad as the suppliers though, and we'll have to walk down a lengthy road before we put a stop to it."

"Will they all receive jail time, do you think?"

"Hopefully all but one will. We're recommending that young Dylan be given a community service penalty for his part. We're trying to arrange for Social Services to arrange some job training and accommodation for him. He has no money of his own and no skills to get him by. Poor little blighter is a victim of circumstance. It turns out he has been totally dependent on his uncle for survival years and has been used virtually as slave labour. He's been an orphan since he was nine years old. He had nowhere else to go. With nothing in the offing job-wise and with no cash flow to speak of, he was forced to do as he was told. It was either that or life on the streets living rough. He'd tried the street kid scene and found he wasn't tough enough. He actually ran away when his parents were killed rather than live with his father's brother Basil. He was frightened of him from the outset, but the young lad got really ill one winter and his uncle caught up with him."

*****

Down on the front beach Isabel, Jock, the twins and Dom sat and looked at another fishing boat out off the Point. "Those craft that keep coming and going may not be as fine-looking as the Red Watermark, but they were acquired honestly. Hard work to achieve what you want does no harm to anyone," said Dom.

Isabel was still a bit cranky with them but she was slowly coming around.

For the last ten minutes, Dom had been locked in his past. Suddenly, emerging from his reverie, he said contentedly, "We went fishing for feathers this time. It made a bit of a change, eh?"

Jock smiled at his old friend with affection. Dom's lifelong occupation hadn't been just a job. It had never been just a means to an end for him, he thought. Fishing was his whole life.

Jeremy laughed with pleasure at the elderly man's remark about fishing for feathers. "You're coming over a bit starry-eyed, aren't you, Dom?"

Josh drawled, "Nah, Dom's just playing the clever wordsmith angle, as usual."

"Laugh all you want, Little Mates," said Dom. "My family's secret is still safe and we didn't get sprung for sailing too close to the wind with those smuggler drongos. Those Authority blokes can't prove that we did the wrong thing and carried out our own investigation, though they definitely suspect it. They're not stupid. We got away with it by the skin of our teeth."

Jock thought back over the official stake-out period while they had all waited impatiently to hear what the outcome had been. "You realise that, if the powers-that-be hadn't been able to uncover enough evidence themselves, we would have had to feed them a bit more info. I've been on tenterhooks throughout their undercover operation. We would have been in for a bit of a roasting for sure, if they hadn't been able to prove that two and two, really did add up to four. We were going to be interrogated heaps more. Don't ever doubt that. We were more than lucky."

"Well," said Dom laughing, "We got away with it and I feel on top of the world."

Jock nodded, and laughed with his old mate. "Me too, Dom, me too."

"I would never have told them about Mama's hideout though," said Dom. He sighed as he said. "Harry and his mates would have been better off going mackerel fishing. They mightn't be anywhere near as financially well-off, but they would still be free. Could you imagine being locked up, and not being able to take your boat out on a lovely day like this?"

"Does that mean you are coming fishing with us after all, Dom?"

"No, not today, Mate. I've got a date. I'm taking a lovely lady on a tour of my underground hideout. Coming Isabel? I brought a bottle of chilled Chianti, some party food and six pink candles for Catarina's room." The old man crooked his arm and Isabel tucked hers through his waiting elbow. He winked at Jock, before the pair of them began walking across the yard, towards the old Holden ute.

"Why didn't he ask us to the party?"

"Because he knows, as I know with absolute certainty, that Isabel needs to see, and experience the room with Giovanni and Catarina's son – and with him alone. She needs to feel the magic of Caterina's Room for herself. Then she'll understand that we were never really in danger. Domenico Bellini would never have allowed that to happen."

The End

ABOUT THE AUTHOR

Annie K Urquhart: wife, mother, grandmother and older sister. It is that cohesive experience that underpins this book, her first work of fiction.

Her mixed-media art practice and love of writing both fiction and poetry, are bolstered by the stimulus generated her passion for digging into ancestral history.

The inspirational Northern Queensland cyclone belt has provided the perfect coastal existence for four generations of Annie's family. She remains forever grateful to her great-grandparents for having the foresight to see the potential of the place.